FOR FIRST NOVEL WRITERS,
THE WINDSORS ARE UNFORGETABLE

THE WINDSOR'S STRIKES AGAIN....
WITH A BLOW THAT IS DEVASTATING!

Mary and Rudolph Windsor Take You From One
Subplot to Another. Just when you think that you have reached
the climax of satisfaction, another subplot takes you on a roller coaster
ride of twists and turns with suspense, surprises, and humor. ALL
OF THIS IS INTERWOVEN SKILLFULLY
INTO THE FABRIC OF THESE PAGES.

WE

DARE YOU TO

READ THIS BOOK!

Deborah and Barak

Published by: Windsor Golden Series
P.O. Box 310393
Atlanta, GA 31131-0393

Distributed by:

Lushena Books
1804-06 West Irving Park Road
Chicago, IL 60613
Tel: 773-975-9945
Fax: 773-975-0045
E-mail: Lushena@aol.com
www.Lushena.com

In regards to the bombing of the World Trade Center; Billy Graham Sr. said this: **"Our nation needs to turn to God."**

... Washington, DC, September , 2001

In this book are spiritual principles and insights, which will help lead us to God and point the way to a greater morality and justice in our world.

A Few Interesting Passages
from This Book

He pushed the necklace toward her. "Take it! It's yours. "Take it!" he urged her.

She took hold of it. "It is so thoughtful of you Barak," she said smiling. Then, her countenance changed quickly and her facial expression became serious. "Oh Barak, I can't accept this."

———————————————

"Please Deborah, don't do this to me. When I am away from you...I think of you...morning...noon... and night."

"There are plenty of beautiful women in Galilee. Discover them Barak...and they will help you to forget about me."

"I told you that I want only you! Can't you understand? Even if you had a twin sister, I would want only you."

———————————————

"I am pass child-bearing age," Marah said, "What can I do?"

"There are orphans among our people who don't have mothers or fathers," said Deborah. "Adopt a son and a daughter ...and be a mother to them...raise them as your own...and give them love and joy. Then, in return...they will give you love and joy."

America

This book is dedicated to this great nation, the United States of America, which has opened its gates to countless people from around the world.

This nation will rise from the destruction of New York and Washington and will meet the challenge, which it faces. It will fulfill the promise to its neglected minorities, and grow morally stronger. This country will ascend to greater heights and achieve its destiny because it represents justice and balance in the world.

For those who may criticize our nation, I don't see them leaving our shores—in great numbers—to go to Europe, Asia, Africa, or Latin America. However, the opposite is true—many people flood to our shores—from all over the world—in order to enjoy our freedom, opportunities, and prosperity. God bless America for "He shed His grace on thee."

Other Books by Rudolph Windsor :

From Babylon to Timbuktu
The Valley of the Dry Bones
Judea Trembles Under Rome
When Is the Next War?

Acknowledgments

Thanks to our many friends for the contribution they've made to this work. Without their thirst for information and their faith that we could quench this thirst, we wouldn't have been challenged to produce this book.

We also wish to express special gratitude to our editor, and to the illustrator, Trecisa P. Brown who labored hour after hour with the cover.

A special thanks to Lisa Walker whose picture appears on the cover of the book, and to Devetta Acklin who also gave her time and talent.

We would like to extend our gratitude to Luther Warner of, Lushena Books of Chicago, IL who willingly agreed to help publish and distribute this book.

Finally, but most importantly, we thank the Source: The Creator of the universe—Love, and Light—for the inspiration and guidance we received throughout the writing of this book.

Dedication

We dedicate this book to our families and friends, who have been very supportive and encouraging over the years.

To our mothers, Eva Robinson, and Leatta Jones.

To my brother, Cole H. Windsor, who has been a source of great knowledge and inspiration to me over the years.

A special dedication to all people who have come to the realization as to why they have come to this earth plain.

Deborah and Barak

****

The authors realize that there maybe some readers who are not familiar with certain facts and concepts in this book. This lack of knowledge may be attributed to ignorance. In view of this, this novel can be liberating; in the sense, that it can unchain our minds from our dark past, and point the way to universal truths, to the brotherhood of all men, to great hope, and to the light of the future.

****

Deborah and Barak

by

Mary L. Windsor
&
Rudolph R. Windsor

Windsor Golden Series Publishing Company
Atlanta, GA

This novel is taken from the Bible: The fourth and fifth chapters of the book of Judges and other historical sources of this time period. Many characters and events in this book are true; however, there are some that are the creation of the author's imagination. This was done so that we could give the readers an entertaining story that would come alive in that ancient time period. The authors consulted countless historical records of various nations in the ancient Near East, in order that we could bring you the flavor of that time. We hope that we have not disappointed you.

Other fine books by Windsor Golden Series Publishing Company are available from your local bookstore or direct from the publisher.

Publisher's Cataloging-in-Publication Data

Windsor, Mary L
        Deborah and Barak / by Mary L. Windsor & Rudolph R.
        Windsor.
            p. cm.
            LCCN 98-90509
            ISBN 0-9620881-4-5

        1. Deborah (Biblical judge) 2. Barak (Biblical
    judge) 3. Bible. O.T.--Biography   1. Windsor, Rudolph
    R., 1935- II. Title.

        BS580.D4W56 2001   222'.32092
                                    BI01 - 700925

CHAPTER ONE

Palestine (c.1316 B.C.)

The Prophetess—Deborah, a spiritual woman—rose early this morning with anxious anticipation of the arrival of an unusual visitor. She sat in her bedchamber thinking of how handsome he was with those gorgeous seductive dark brown eyes. She thought about her late husband who was killed by Canaanites over three years ago. His death had caused her much emotional pain. Now, she sat there waiting for the arrival of Barak, whose primary mission is to fight the Canaanites. "Would the same thing happen to him,"she wondered. She became troubled and chills ran down her spine.

Deborah, a woman in her late thirties, quickly got dressed in her pretty white silk dress, decorated with purple and gold borders around the neckline, bodice and sleeves. The dress was long and loose; however, because she had a wonderful figure, it emphasized her shape in all the right places.

At that moment, Deborah felt like she wanted some fresh air and company, therefore, she called for her handmaid, "Sarah, come here please!"

Yes, my Lady." Sarah was a woman past middle age, with gray hair, and in good health.

"I want you to walk with me outside to get some fresh air," she said as she brought the golden colored linen shawl over her braids and shoulders. The shawl contrasted well with her white dress and pretty chestnut brown skin.

"It's my pleasure. My Lady, are you expecting a visitor today?" she asked, as they walked out the door made of cedar wood.

Deborah then rubbed the prominent bridge of her nose and squeezed her nostrils, which stood out slightly.

"Yes, I am. Why do you ask?"

"Because you are dressed up so special today, like...like a princess."

"Well, after all, I am expecting a prince," commented Deborah as she passed through the gate of the courtyard.

Sarah turned around to her. "I believe you are serious. Could he be a prince from Moab, Syria, or from our southern neighbor, Egypt?"

"No Sarah...don't be funny! He's from the Hebrew tribe of Naphtali."

They walked out to the main road, which was about sixty cubits from her house. As they walked along the pebbled walkway, they passed by red and purple lilies that bloomed every spring.

"Have I ever met or seen this Prince?" asked Sarah.

"I don't think..." Deborah paused and then continued. "Yes...we met him at the city of Bethel last year. At that time, one of the elders introduced him to us. His name is Barak Ben Abinoam."

"Ah...do you mean General Barak, the commander of the Hebrew army in northern Israel?"

"Yes! That's the man."

"He was devilishly...handsome"

As they approached the road, Deborah could see people and caravans, no doubt, going to Jerusalem, Syria, Tyre, Egypt, and Ethiopia, but there was no Barak. This was the north-south main road that passed through the land of Canaan—later called Israel, and thereafter—renamed

Palestine. This road was not far from the Jordan River and ran parallel to it. People and caravans traveled this road to go from Egypt and Arabia to Jerusalem, Shechem, Bethel, Galilee, Syria, and to other northern cities. This is the road that Barak will use when he comes to visit Deborah.

Deborah expected his arrival because she received a letter from him a week ago, stating that he will arrive today, after his leaving Hebron.

Then she closed her eyes, and she saw an image of him. He was tall, had dark brown skin, a thick black beard, and a turban-like rap on his head. His shoulders were broad, and he had a strong square jaw. The bridge of his nose was long and broad, which gave him a commanding appearance.

"Deborah, are you all right?" asked Sarah, seeing her standing there with her eyes closed.

"Yes Sarah, all is well. I was just thinking."

Deborah stood there wondering whether he was still lean and muscular, or had he gotten fat around the belly, rump and thighs, like some other men.

After time passed, Deborah and Sarah looked up the road facing northward, towards Bethel, and saw a group of people approaching. They looked like little children in comparison to the high mountains on both sides of the road.

"Sarah, I have a suspicion that those people are coming to visit us," commented Deborah as she adjusted her purple sash around her thin waist.

"Perhaps. We receive visitors at least three or four time a week. Maybe they are from the town of Bethel."

Deborah and her handmaid began to walk slowly back to the house, because they wanted to be there whenever anyone would arrive. Deborah turned her head, and gazed at the fresh green grass growing beyond the walkway.

As Deborah walked back to her house, she thought, since the death of my husband over three years ago, I haven't been involved with any man.

She concluded that Barak could possibly be the beginning of a new relationship. But, she remembered that he expressed a disinterest in spiritual matters. Nevertheless, she was still attracted to him. In view of this dilemma, the situation left her uncertain about him.

Finally, the group of people who Deborah saw coming, turned off the road and came down her walkway. There were a few men, but most of the people were women. From the steps where Deborah stood, she could discern from the faces of the women, that their hearts were full of grief. As the ladies approached the gate, they saw baskets of food near the entrance. Then the spokeswoman of the group stepped forward and greeted Nachshon, the gatekeeper.

"Peace be unto you my brother. We came to meet with Deborah, the Prophetess."

Nachshon, was a very tall man of almost seven feet, and approximately 250 pounds, with a powerful appearance. He served as a warrior in the army of Shamgar, the last deliverer of Israel. "You...have a meeting with Deborah?" he asked hesitantly. "I have no knowledge of such a meeting between..."

"This matter is urgent!" Rebekah interrupted him raising her eyes glaringly.

"Let the ladies in Nachshon," Deborah advised her gatekeeper. "The ladies must be tired after a long journey. Let them rest their feet and give them some fresh water and fruit. I'll be out in a short while."

Then Nachshon escorted the ladies into the courtyard where they sat down under the three palm trees that stood in the center. The floor of the courtyard was made from stone slabs. Also, there was a large stone table situated to the side of the courtyard. This is where Deborah sat when she listened to the complaints of disputants and gave council. In addition, the tribal leaders, elders, priests and princes sat here with her, when they convened to discuss tribal affairs.

It became a custom for Deborah to receive visitors on a regular basis. They came to seek expert advice, to obtain spiritual counseling, and to hear her interpretation and judgment on civil and criminal matters.

On this particular morning, she was not expecting this group of ladies, however, Deborah was not surprised because she usually received unannounced visitors.

Besides taking care of communal matters, Deborah operated a wick factory that she inherited over three years ago, from her late husband. She gave last minute instructions to Madreech, the supervisor of her workers, and turned to her handmaid.

"Oh Sarah, did I receive a letter from Caleb?"

"No, my Lady."

I wonder why it is taking my bother-in-law so long to write me, she thought as she went out to listen to the patient group of ladies.

As she walked with her handmaid into the courtyard, she greeted the ladies with a big smile and said, "*shalom,*" and the ladies responded. After Rebekah introduced everyone, Deborah asked, What tribe are you from?"

"We are from Zebulun, Manasseh, Naphtali, and Issachar, the northern tribes."

"The Northern regions? Interesting my sisters, and how can I be of service to you today?" inquired Deborah sympathetically as she raised her small dark brown eyes.

"This is our problem," answered Rebekah, as she turned slowly toward Deborah. "Most of us have lost husbands who have been captured by Sisera, the Canaanite. We don't know if they are living or dead. Our children are growing up without fathers; they cry and ask us about their fathers constantly. We don't know what to tell them. Also, we miss the companionship of our husbands. You understand, don't you?"

Deborah lowered her head in silence, and brought her hands together. She felt the pain and loneliness of the ladies because she could empathize with them. She thought about her own lack of companionship, due to the loss of her husband over three years ago.

She raised her head up slowly, looked at all of them and said: "Yes. I understand. I too lost a husband. After his death, all the responsibility fell on me; just as it has fallen on you right now."

"But...you can marry again," answered abruptly one of the younger ladies. "We can't. We don't know whether our husbands are dead or alive. What do we do Deborah? We feel trapped!"

The vehement, passionate request of the ladies struck Deborah like a thunderbolt. At that moment, she wanted to be still and meditate. Her face became very solemn; she closed her eyes and lowered her head. The courtyard became very quiet like the stillness of the night. The only sound that was heard was the chirping of a black bird in the distance. After about ten minutes of meditation, Deborah raised her head, opened her eyes, took a deep breath, and smiled at the ladies.

As Deborah turned her head slightly to the right, she saw a handsome rugged looking man, over six feet tall standing by the courtyard gate near her gatekeeper, Nachshon. When he caught Deborah's eyes, the stranger smiled and nodded his head at her. She knew who he was. He was Barak, the man for whom she was waiting.

"This is what the Lord said to me ladies, 'Be patient.' Maintain your integrity and loyalty to God, and to your husbands. Pray and meditate day and night. Go back to your tribes...and tell your people to pour out their souls in sincerity to the Lord your God...and He will hear your cry, just as He heard the cry of your ancestors in the land of Egypt."

"But, will we see our husbands again?" inquired another young lady.

"Yes! I am getting a strong feeling that most of you will be reunited with your husbands."

Deborah looked subtly at Barak. Then he smiled again and gave her a double nod of his head as if he was giving her his approval for something. She couldn't help noticing his well-trimmed black beard and mustache, which had gotten a little gray since the last time she saw him. His beard was the way she liked her man to wear it. Suddenly, she began to feel a little uneasy and became momentarily distracted. She quickly regained her composure and looked at the ladies.

"Some of us have been separated from our husbands for more than five years. Do you have any idea when we shall be reunited with them?" asked Rebekah.

Deborah said, "Your husbands will be free next year in the sabbatical year when we let the land rest and cancel all debts. Pertaining to this, I feel very strongly, and you can be assured of it."

Rebekah rose to her feet. "Deborah...when I first came through your gate earlier this morning, I saw baskets of various foods. What is this food for?"

Deborah looked up. "I thought you knew.... It is for the poor.

" For the poor?"

"Yes, Rebekah. It is our custom to give to the poor...to the widows...to the blind...to the orphans, and to the strangers. Have you forgotten this?"

"I guess...times are hard, and I haven't thought about it lately," said Rebekah, as she lowered her head.

At that moment, Deborah moved a few steps closer to the ladies and said, "I want all of you to give more to the poor. When you give, it will return to you many folds. This

21

is universal law. Remember, this is what Moses meant when he said, if you keep this law, 'all these blessings shall come unto thee....' "

"But Deborah, when I give, I feel that I am loosing something," said a middle-age man.

"You shouldn't feel that way. When you give today, remember," she said, "it will come back to you in the future. Do you have a barley or wheat field?"

"Yesss," answered the man slowly. What are you getting at Deborah?"

"When you plant a field of barley seeds, the barley will multiply unto you a thousand fold at harvest time. The same thing will happen for you, when you invest and give to mankind."

"Oh Deborah, how can I reap a thousand fold when the poor man is not able to repay me?"

Deborah smiled and continued. "The ways of the Lord are mysterious. Don't always expect your repayment to come from the poor. Your repayment may come from another source—or from another person. Remember this...when your blessings come from another source, they will, in most cases...be greater in value than if you had received it from the poor."

The man smiled. "You gave a very good explanation Deborah."

Finally, Rebekah asked, "How can I give what I don't have?"

At that moment, Deborah walked over to Rebekah, and took her by the hand. "You have good health."

"That's all I have."

"That's a lot..." Deborah assured her. "There are many ways you can give, Rebekah: if you have one slice of bread, then, divide it and give to the poor. Another way of giving is by giving of yourself: give your time, a helping hand, your interest, your conversation, and above all, give your sincere love. This is the greatest gift you can offer.

When you do this, you will bring great joy to the hearts of others. In giving joy to others, you will experience great joy for yourself."

After listening attentively, Rebekah leaned her head on Deborah's shoulder and remarked, "Your words have very deep meaning Deborah. Where did you get all of your knowledge?"

"I received it from our sacred books and traditions. Some of it, I received from my uncle Yoetz, who was a member of the council of the seventy elders, at the Tabernacle. Also, some of it I learned from the sages, who came with the caravans from India and the surrounding countries."

Rebekah stood back a little and said, "We admire you so much Deborah. You are truly God sent. "Thank you so much. You have been a great help to us. Now, we must be on our way."

Deborah then hugged all the ladies and kissed them on their cheeks. When Rebekah turned toward the gate, Deborah asked her softly and quietly. "Have you ever seen...that tall man near the entrance?"

Rebekah took one step forward and stopped. She placed her finger over her lower lip and chin as if she was in deep thought.

"He...looks familiar. Ohh...that's Barak, from the tribe of Naphtali."

"Yes, I thought you would recognize him. He is from up your way."

"Are you interested in him?" asked Rebekah nonchalantly.

"That's a big question. I'm not sure," said Deborah in a low tone. "I've met him once before."

"Put out the bait and the fly will come Deborah."

"The fly has come."

"Well, good luck," said Rebekah as she walked slowly away.

"Have a safe trip, and peace be with you," commented Deborah as she glanced at the entire guest.

As the ladies departed through the iron gate, they touched the mezuzah on the doorpost of the gate. This object was intended to evoke everyone passing through the gate to remember the commandments of the Lord.

CHAPTER TWO

The early afternoon came and Nachshon, the gatekeeper, introduced Barak to Deborah.

Barak wore a dark green turban-like wrap on his head. His body garment was the shape of a dashiki with bright red and green colors, which extended down to his knees. Around his waist, he wore a six-inch wide black girdle belt with a shief for his eighteen-inch long dagger.

"It is a great pleasure to see you again, Deborah," Barak said with an admiring smile. "And you look so wonderful...like a Cushite queen."

"Thank you...thank you Barak for your kind words."

"By the way, I have heard many good things about you."

"Oh...! Is that so," she responded, as she led the way to two stone Benches near the wall.

As Barak walked across a small rug, he noticed it had a picture of a green palm tree and a yellow sun set against a blue sky. "Oh! What a beautiful rug you have. Where did you get it?"

Deborah looked down at the rug, and said, "I purchased it from an Egyptian caravan several years ago. But, I'm thinking about buying another one."

Barak looked up at her with a smile on his face. "Deborah, did you know that a carpet is bought by the cubit yard, and is worn out by the foot?"

Deborah chuckled with delight. "Is this your manner...to make people laugh?" she asked feeling at ease.

"Yes! Sometimes...it depends upon my mood."

"Well, stay in that mood. It is pleasing in my eyesight. Barak...you were about to tell me what the people are saying about me."

"Oh yes...the words which I hear are that you are a good counselor, and a good listener."

"Well! It is surely nice to hear the good news," she said with delight. Then she looked up at him askantly. "Is there more, Barak?"

Barak raised his head and appeared to be in deep thought.

"Recently... when I was in the city of Beer Sheba, I heard a group of people say that you could become the next ruler in Israel, like uh...uh Ehud or Othniel."

"Well, that's interesting, we shall see what the Lord has in store for me. Tell me Prince Barak...may I call you just Barak?"

"Yes, I would like that, and I hope that this can be the beginning of a good friendship."

Deborah heard his words; however, she didn't want to give any comment at this time. Instead, she gave a slight smile. At that moment, one of the servants brought in a container of water and goblets. "I am curious...what brings you here to the territory of the Ephramite tribe?" Deborah asked starring straight into his eyes.

"Because we are at war with Sisera and the Canaanites, I have been trying to buy weapons from certain tribes in the south so that we can have some kind of defense against our enemies."

Then Deborah thought of the situation that produced the Canaanite threat: It was more than a hundred years after the death of Joshua—the son of Nun, that another, Jabin, the King of the Canaanites—attacked the Hebrew tribes in Galilee and the surrounding areas. Jabin was the king of Hazor, and the head of his army was Sisera. With his nine hundred chariots, Sisera took complete control of the Jezreel Valley; ravaged the countryside; taxed the Hebrews heavily; took away their blacksmiths so that they could not make any weapons; and put many of the Hebrews into hard labor. Since the regular roads were unsafe, the Hebrews had to take the longer routes around and over the mountains and hills. This is what Deborah remembered as she stood there in front of Barak.

"You seem to be deep in thought Deborah," he commented. "Is anything troubling you?"

"No...no, my mind was miles away for a little while. Oh...a moment ago, you said that you were trying to buy weapons for your soldiers. Have you had any success with your contacts?" Deborah asked softly.

"Unfortunately not." he replied as he looked dejected and lowered his head.

At that moment, she felt a strong magnetic attraction to him. She moved toward him and placed her hand on top of his, and said softly, "Everything will be all right."

"I thank you for the encouragement," he expressed as he placed his other hand on top of hers. "As a matter of fact, I like a kind and understanding lady like you."

As he touched and held her hand, she felt a vibration move up her arm. She pulled her hand away slowly, stood up, and walked over to the large vase that had a green plant in it. Then she squeezed one of the green leaves between her fingers, to hide her true feelings.

"Is there something wrong?" asked Barak, paying close attention to her reactions.

"No! There is nothing wrong," she assured him. "Do you have a family?" she inquired as she turned around in his direction.

At that moment, Barak took a sip of water from the goblet. "If you mean am I married, the answer is no. My wife died in childbirth along with my son."

"Oh! I'm sorry to hear this," she commented. "May peace be with their souls... Do you think that you will ever get married again?"

"I think about it sometime, but at other times, I'm fearful that the same thing could happen to my next wife, and this discourages me from wanting to get married again. If I get married again, it will have to wait until after the war."

"Does this mean that you have someone particular in mind?" she asked slowly and cautiously, hoping to hear an honest answer.

"No!" This means that I have only some admirers, but I am remaining unattached to commit more time to the training and organization of our mountain fighters. In addition, I hope there will be an end to this conflict soon, so that I and my people can live normal lives as other tribes."

"I've got a strong feeling that by this time next year, the Canaanite threat will be ended," Deborah intimated vigorously.

"This is really good news...better news than what I had anticipated. Thank you, Deborah. Thank you. By the way, I heard about the death of your husband by the hands of the Canaanites and I want to express my condolences to you."

"That is nice of you," she said as she sat down pulling her golden headpiece around the front of her neck. "How long have you been fighting the Canaanites?" she asked.

Barak answered, "About fifteen years."

"May I ask what caused you to fight the Canaanites?"

"What caused me...? I don't want to talk about that," he snapped turning his back to her. Then he lowered his face into the palm of his hands.

Because Deborah didn't want to be pushy, she waited a few moments then continued. "Perhaps, it must be painful, but I think that you should talk about it...it will help you feel better," she said touching him gently on the back of the shoulders.

He turned toward her slowly, placed his large hands on his hips and looked up into the sky. Finally, he took a deep breath. "It hurts too much."

Deborah could see that he wanted to shed a tear but the tear did not come. "You said that you like an understanding woman, and I'm trying to be just that...talk to me Barak! Tell me what's troubling you!"

"It's...it's about my mother," he muttered softly looking down.

"Your mother? Did she give up the ghost?"

"Yes…but it was not an ordinary death. Now, I find myself standing here…getting ready to reveal to you my inner most feelings."

"It's all right. You don't have to feel less than a man just because you are about to pour out your heart to me. Remember, you are still a human being…and you have feelings just like other people."

Barak glanced at her with a thoughtful look on his face. "Perhaps…you are right Deborah."

"Go on. I'm listening," she said as she gently touched the strong arm of his six-foot three-inch muscular frame.

"Sisera, the General of the Canaanite army…murdered…" Barak paused then, he took another deep breath and gritted his teeth with anger. He choked for words, and labored to speak. "He…murdered my dear mother…a kind and gentle woman," he informed her as he pounded his fist against the wall.

Deborah looked at him with sympathy. "Barak…I'm very sorry to hear this. Now, I can understand how your loss has left you with so much grief."

"Grief…is not the word!" he snapped, raising his voice.

"Well…a lot of anger, then."

"I want Sisera to pay for the murder of my mother and I'll get him…even if it takes me ten more years."

"I can understand how you feel. The Canaanites killed my husband; also, but vengeance belongs to the Lord."

Turning to her, he roared again, like thunder. "I hope heaven will grant me the chance to be the hand of God's vengeance."

"And that might very well be. Tell me Barak, what was the situation that led up to the murder of your mother?"

Barak began to tell her what happened to his family nineteen years ago when he had just turned twenty-five.

They had just completed the preparation for the feast of booths and had set out on their pilgrimage to the Tabernacle in Shiloh. They were traveling on the main road going south passed the Sea of Galilee. Also, there were many people on that road going to the Tabernacle. Moreover, his father and mother were traveling with him. Suddenly, they heard the hooves of camels and horses coming toward them. The people knew that it was the Canaanite soldiers and some tried to escape to the caves in the nearby hills. The Canaanites rushed down on them and rounded them up.

General Sisera gave orders to his lieutenant to line up the people. "Form one line over here!" commanded the lieutenant. The people moved slowly with resentment, and with hatred in their eyes against the Canaanites. Next, the lieutenant pointed to one man. "You...over there! Step it up...get moving!" After the soldiers lined up the people, Sisera approached ten cubits out in front of his soldiers with two of his officers on both sides of him. They held their spears in their hands. Sisera finally, spoke: "Now, I'll tell you why we stopped you. A group of Hebrew men have been raiding Canaanite merchant caravans and robbing their property. We have a good reason to believe that they might have come to your area. If you know of these men or have seen them, I want you to turn them over to us."

"Turn Hebrews over to you?" asked a young man with a shout in his voice. Why should we?"

"Because they are sons of belial and transgressors and I command you to..."

"Transgressors? Transgressors?" repeated Barak again louder. "You put a heavy burden of taxation around our necks, rape our women, and take our boys and girls to be burned in the fire as sacrifices to your god, Baal, and you have the nerve to call those Hebrews transgressors?"

"Yes! They are transgressors," Sisera then raised his head seething with indignation at the defiant young man.

31

"You...! come over here! Don't just stand there and stare at me like a fool. When I give you an order... you obey me!"

Barak moved forward slowly. "What do you want with me?"

All of a sudden, Sisera slapped Barak hard with the back of his hand.

"You have too much mouth boy...and if you are not careful, your mouth is going to get you in a lot of trouble!"

"Leave my son alone!" yelled his father.

Instantaneously, Barak's mother ran up to protect her son. "Don't you strike my son you brute!"

"Get back...! You wench," ordered Sisera as he jabbed her in the neck with his spear. As she fell to the ground, the crowd rushed forward to help the injured woman, but the mounted soldiers blocked their path.

Barak dropped down to the ground and held his mother in his arm, who was covered with blood. Then he cried. "Mother, mother, mother, don't leave me." At that moment, Barak looked up slowly at Sisera with tears in his eyes sobbing.

"I'll get you for this...I'll get you even if it takes me fifteen years," Barak cried bitterly.

"You'll get me... Huh...! Where is your army? You got your chance right now! Make your move. I want to see how stupid you are."

Barak just starred at him with anger.

"Either you are smarter than what I thought or you are just a low-down cowered. Let's go men and leave these wretched Hebrews to themselves."

After Barak finished telling Deborah how his mother had been killed, he stood there before her with tears in his eyes.

"It is good that you are getting it all out. It will help you feel better."

"Yes...I...suppose so."

For a while, there was a silence. Then Deborah spoke. "Would you like something else to drink Barak?"

"Yes, I think I'll have some tea."

"Do you like your tea dark?"

"Is there any other kind?"

Deborah smiled. "You do have a sense of humor, don't you?"

"Some people would agree with that."

"Oh Sarah, bring in some tea," called Deborah.

After a short while, Sarah brought in the tea and Deborah introduced Barak to Sarah.

"This is Barak, the General to whom I mentioned."

"It is a pleasure to meet you sire," she said as she bowed and walked away slowly.

"I want to tell you Barak...there will come a time in battle when you will become far more successful if you will rely on the Lord and become more spiritual," she said slowly.

"Spiritual? What do you mean by that?"

"I mean communing with your God by prayer, meditation, and tuning into the small subtle voice that speaks to you deep, down inside," she uttered.

"Oh, I don't believe in that stuff. I rely on the number of my soldiers, the chariots, which I don't have, and the number of my spears and swords. These are the things that can break the back of the enemy," he harangued as he stood on his feet and tightened his fists to express his emotions.

"If you trust God, He will work miracles in your life."

"I don't believe in miracles either."

"Why not...? Your birth is a miracle."

"Where was this God when Sisera stabbed my mother in the neck?"

"The works of God are mysterious. We cannot judge Him. If we patiently seek Him, He will reveal the hidden things to us in due time. Moreover, if you look at your loss in the right way, from your pain, will come a gain. Finally, in the process of time, you will receive a revelation so profound that it will change your entire life."

As Deborah sat on the bench, she wondered and was doubtful about a viable relationship with Prince Barak. He was a man of high social standards in his tribe; a commander of the militia in his area, a man of considerable means, he projected a strong handsome masculine appearance, and he had a nice smile that was magnetic. On the other hand, she had at least three reasons why not to become emotionally involved. There was her wick business and judicial duties; her husband was killed by the Canaanites; and if the same thing happened to Barak, this would only increase the emotional pain. In view of the fact that Deborah was a spiritual woman, Barak's rejection of her spiritual advice did not set well with her. Therefore, she concluded that she would not get her hopes up. In spite of this, she reminded him about their great teachers.

She explained to him: "It was by the power of God that our ancestors were saved from the Egyptians and not by the number of their soldiers and swords. This is what Moses, Joshua, and the elders taught."

"Well, if God has all this power, why does He cause us to suffer under the oppression of the Canaanites?" he asked, moistening his lips.

"God does not cause..." she paused and moved under the shady part of the palm tree.

When Barak followed her, she smiled with unconscious satisfaction, because she relished the attention.

She continued. "God does not cause mankind to suffer. Men and women cause their own suffering. Hence, they reap what they sew. This is universal law. If a person commits a crime and is punished by the court, is that person suffering for nothing?" asked Deborah.

"No...! He deserved it," he answered.

34

"So likewise with the heavenly Judge. He gave to our people His laws and word and our people rejected them and committed abominations. As a result, God delivered them into the hands of the Canaanites who oppressed them. God used the Canaanites as an instrument to punish our people for their misdeeds. This is what the priests, the seventy elders, and the scribes report to us from the Tabernacle in the city of Shiloh: *'The people served the Lord all the days of Joshua, and all the days of the Elders that outlived Joshua, who had seen all the great works of the Lord, that He had wrought for Israel...And also all that generation were gathered unto their fathers; and there arose another generation after them that knew not the Lord; nor yet the works which He had wrought for Israel...'* "

"Deborah, are we a part of this new generation?"

"Yes, we are, and you will understand this after I finish." Then Deborah continued to quote the elders in the city of Shiloh. "The elders taught: *'And they forsook the Lord and served Baal and Ashtaroth...And the anger of the Lord was kindled against Israel, and He delivered them into the hands of the spoilers that spoiled them and He gave them over into the hands of their enemies round about so that they could not any longer stand before their enemies...And the Lord gave them over into the hand of Jabin, king of Canaan, that reigned in Hazor; the captain of whose host was Sisera, who dwelt in Harosheth-Hagoiim.*

"Ahhh," Barak gushed as he yawned and drew both fists toward the direction of his dark brown ears. "Very interesting," he remarked as he smiled at her with admiration. After that, he fixed his eyes upon her with a long silent stare.

"Why are you staring at me like that?" she asked.

"It is because...you are so...beautiful!" Barak answered in a mesmerized low tone.

"Well, thank you Barak!" she smiled, looking at him with a surprised glance.

At that moment, he asked her softly and slowly: "Did anyone ever tell you...that you are beautiful?"

She became flattered and lowered her head. "Yes...but that was a long time ago...my late husband use to tell me this when he was alive," she assured him. "I don't think about beauty anymore," she uttered nonchalantly. Nevertheless, she enjoyed those words coming from Barak.

"Deborah, you are not just beautiful in your facial expression, but also, your beauty from within shines."

"Beauty is just the outward appearance," she said gently as she turned her head away with delight and feeling aroused.

"When I speak of beauty Deborah.... I mean also your inward beauty...I can feel your tenderness and the warmth of your feminine presence."

"You can?" she asked with an eager smile on her face, "but, let's not talk about me."

He became silent again. "Well then can we talk about your...deceased husband?"

She hesitated, and said slowly, "Yesss."

"What was he like?"

"He was gentle and compassionate."

"In what ways?"

She answered without hesitation, "He recognized my abilities, and he encouraged me to develop and use them in spite of the fact that, I am a woman in a role that has been always held by men."

"Are you referring to your ability to explain the laws to our people, and to advise and speak to groups of people?" he inquired while touching the frond of a small palm tree.

"Yes.... I am!"

"But, how did the people get to know that you had these abilities?"

""Oh! That's a long story...at first, men...but mostly women, would come to our farm to buy fruits, vegetables and other products. When the ladies came, we would talk about women's problems and the family. Slowly, the word got around that I was very helpful to many. Then, more and more ladies came to seek my advice and some skeptical men came as well."

"Deborah, it is strange to have a woman take a major role in public matters."

"Yes, but as I said, the women came to me first, and later, the men, because they were not getting satisfaction from some of the elders of the tribes. You must understand that the judges of the various tribes were handing down decisions according to what they thought was right in their own eyes, and not according to the interpretations handed down by Moses and Joshua. Moreover, some judges corrupted themselves by favoring the rich and powerful, and by the taking of bribes."

"Deborah, I can understand what you mean, because there are some judges in my tribe who are guilty of the very same thing."

"Barak, I want your honesty. What do you think of my work?"

Barak thought a moment: "Well, I'll be honest with you Deborah. In our times, it is not the custom to have a woman doing the work of men. However, at this time, there is no king in Israel, no unity, and few learned men. Furthermore, our people are suffering under the oppression of the Canaanites, and most men do what they think is right in their own eyes. In view of this, your work is very helpful, and I welcome it as the need of the times."

"Thank you Barak for being very truthful with me. I needed to know this."

"Well, honesty is my policy."

"Barak, I want you to understand that you will never completely remove Sisera's army from the northern territories until our people remove the abominations from our communities, which are distasteful before God. I believe that when we make right our society, the Lord will remove the enemy right out of our midst. This means that we shall be victorious in battle. Now, to achieve this, I need you to help catch lawbreakers who run and hide among the other tribes, and then bring them to justice. Can I get your support in this matter?"

Barak lowered his head in a thoughtful way, then looked up. "Yes! You have my complete support. Also, I am in favor of maintaining a peaceful and orderly society. I am against any robbers or murderers, whether they be Canaanites or Hebrews," Barak explained.

"Oh Barak, I think that it would be a good idea if you would stop by the Tabernacle in Shiloh and get a Certificate of Authority from the high court. Ask for Elder Ariel. He was a close associate of my uncle. This certificate would make you a bonafide officer of the court. With your position as prince, commander of the northern army, and my recommendation, I don't think you will have any problem obtaining it."

Then Barak asked her a question about the war. "When do you feel that the final battle will take place between us and Jabin, King of Canaan?"

"I..." she paused, "believe, it will be about a year from now."

"Can you give me a definite month?"

"No!" she replied, "but, I can tell you this, as that time approaches, it will become clearer and it will be revealed to me. When this happens, I'll send for you."

"Good! If I had half the number of chariots that Sisera has, I would attack tomorrow."

"To defeat Sisera, you'll need more than chariots.

"We'll see," he said softly. "Well, it is time for me to leave. May I call on you again...?" Barak waited for an answer. "Deborah, may I call upon you again...?" he asked louder. She remained silent. "Deborah, are you going to make a beggar out of a prince?"

She swallowed his words hard, and attempted to speak. "You...you can call on me again as long as it is important business," she said, as she looked at him askantly with longing, and inviting eyes.

"Important business!" he repeated. Hearing her comment, Barak seemed confused. However, he continued to speak. "I know what I like, and I know what I want, and I want you."

"As a widow living outside of my father's house, I think that I would have something to say about this. Barak, are you going to try to force me to submit to you?"

He turned towards her and answered: "No...! I am not that low.... In my desire for you, I will not violate you, not at the point of possessing you. But, I must inform you I intend to pursue, and pursue, and pursue until I have you. Peace be with you Deborah," he said as he departed.

Although Barak was handsome and charming, Deborah was leery of him because of his lack of spiritual interest. In addition to that, there was a letter that she was expecting from her brother-in- law, Caleb, which could change her marital situation. While she stood at the gate, she waived good-by to him with mixed emotions.

Now, Barak was on his way to the city of Shiloh to obtain the Certificate of Authority, which Deborah had requested.

CHAPTER THREE

The town of Shiloh was about ten miles north of Bethel and was situated off to the right side of the same road that passed through the city of Bethel. Shiloh became the national Capitol of the Israelites. It was at Shiloh that Joshua cast lots for the division of the land and sent out spies to describe the land. Here, Joshua and Eleazar, the High Priest, gave orders to the Levites and the priest to set up the Tabernacle.

Barak could see the hills and valley as he traveled that road. He was riding through the territory of the tribe of Ephraim. He passed by some of the people and caravans going to Megido, Tyre, Damascus and other places. At that moment, Barak met a man who just passed by Shiloh.

"Are you going to Shiloh?" inquired the man, anxiously.

" Yes, why do you ask?"

"Criminals and robbers were fighting at the Tabernacle when I passed by there," informed the stranger. "It was a terrible situation. Somebody needs to help them."

"Who were they fighting?" asked Barak looking worried.

"They were fighting the priest and the Levites," he said.

"Did you help them?"

"No... No... I couldn't get involved. I have a family to support."

Barak asked with great concern. "How many were there?"

"Twenty, thirty. I really don't know for sure. Shameful! Robbers fighting in the house of God," he said, shaking his head as he turned and continued on his way.

Barak knew that he had to do something and do it fast. There was no time to waste. He was about ten or fifteen minutes fast ride from the city. Then Barak lifted up his eyes and from a distance, he could see the town of Shiloh.

Barak was alone and he knew that there was not much he could do by himself, and there were very few people in this small town, at this time of the year. Therefore, he thought up a strategy to scare off the robbers. Not too far from him was a dry hill. He rode his horse up one side of it, racing back and forth kicking up dust with the hooves of his horse. With his ram's horn, he blew the sound of an attacking army. Barak hoped that his trick would work. At last, Barak rode towards the town of Shiloh with great speed to see what damage the robbers had done. As he rode, he passed by many houses and inns constructed from the many available beige stones found in the land of Israel. The owners of the inns would earn extra money from the thousands of pilgrims who would visit the Tabernacle on the Hebrew holidays of Passover, Feast of Weeks and the Festival of Booths.

As Barak approached the Tabernacle area, he could see the rectangular enclosure, which surrounded the entire Tabernacle. Approaching closer with great urgency, his mind reflected on its description. The courtyard extending from east to west measured one hundred fifty feet by

41

seventy-five feet. The Tabernacle itself was a hugh tent with two compartments: the holy place and the inner section called the Holy of Holies separated by a veil. The holy place contains the following furniture: the table of shew-bread on the right or north side, the golden candlestick on the left or south side, and the altar of incense in the center. These objects are considered as being placed before the presence of Yaweh who dwelt in the holiest of all places.

When Barak approached within fifty cubits of the sanctuary, he could see some of the bandits riding off frantically. He decided not to pursue them because he was alone. No doubt his strategy of stirring up the dust and blowing the ram's horn had worked. He wondered had they desecrated the Holy of Holies within the veil. The place shrouded in darkness, where there was but one object, the Ark of the Covenant, containing the two tablets of stone inscribed with the Ten Commandments and on top of the Ark stood the Cherubims. In order for Barak to talk to the guards at the entrance, he had to press his way slowly throughout the crowd. As he pressed forward, he remembered from his previous visits that the tent of the Tabernacle was located in the western half of the court, and the largest court area was situated in front of the tent of the Tabernacle.

In the court stood the altar of burnt offerings and the brazen laver. With the water of this laver, the priest would wash his hands and feet before he entered the Tabernacle. Barak also remembered that the furniture of the court was connected with sacrifice, but the sanctuary itself dealt with the deeper mysteries of meditation, prayer, and communication with the Creator. Near the entrance of the enclosure was where the seventy elders met. These elders represented the Supreme Court of the Hebrews. During the time of Moses and Joshua, they were the chief justices of this court, but in later years, the high priests became the heads of this tribunal. When Barak approached the guards at the entrance to the Tabernacle, the crowd demanded to know the details of what happened.

"Some bandits forcibly took some gold shekels from the treasury of the sanctuary, and two of them were killed in the foolish act of robbery. The rest of the robbers were scared off by the sound of the ram's horn, which came from beyond the hills," explained one of the guards.

Then Barak stepped up to the guard.

"My name is Barak and I came to see the Elder Priest, Ariel."

"That name sounds familiar. You wouldn't know who blew that ram's horn would you?"

"Yes. It was I."

"You...? You know if you hadn't blown that horn, many more lives would have been lost. Follow me and I'll take you to the Elder."

The guard led him to one of the private chambers. There, he introduced Barak to the ninety-year-old Priest named Ariel. Barak bowed to him and said, "Peace be unto you oh honorable one."

"Peace," replied the Elder. "You wouldn't happen to be General Barak from the tribe of Naphtali, would you?"

Barak nodded his head in agreement and said, "I am he."

While he spoke, the Elder cast his eyes down at the ram's horn Barak had stuck in his waist.

"No doubt, you must be the same man that blew the horn and scared off the robbers."

"I am," answered Barak modestly.

"Then it is a blessing that you came to our town. Because, when the bandits heard the sound of the ram's horn, they stopped fighting and robbing and made haste out of town. Our people are very grateful to you."

"It was just a small thing what I did."

"Small thing! If it hadn't been for you perhaps some Levites would have died in the fighting. As it stands now, we only have a few flesh wounds."

"Did anyone recognize any of them?"

"No. They all had their faces covered with their kaffiyehs, however, one of them referred to the other, who seemed to have been the leader, as Reuben and he walked with a slight limp." The Elder paused for a moment and then, continued. "Oh! What brings you to our town, General Barak?" he asked while stroking his long white wooly beard.

"Deborah sent me to you. Here is her letter. Do you know her?"

"Do I know her? Yes," he answered pointing to a cushion for Barak to take a seat. "She has a very good reputation," he continued. After he had read the letter, he said, "There shouldn't be any problem to get the Certificate of Authority."

"Good," Barak smiled.

"You come highly recommended. She said that you would catch a thief, even if, he crawls in a foxhole near a cave. Do you agree with her?"

"Your Excellency, I am the youngest son in my father's house...Who am I...to question the Prophetess, and the most beautiful woman in Canaan."

"I understand. Now, all I need is the signature of two more judges. Wait here!"

While Barak waited for Ariel to return, he could smell the aroma of sweet meat roasting on the altar of the inner court. Then, he took a deep breath and leaned back with delight. His appetite was stirred up, and he wished he could saver its delights.

Within a short while, Ariel returned with two judges and a scribe. The Elder told the other judges about the strategy that Barak used to scare off the bandits and they thanked him for his ingenuity. Then, Ariel dictated the provisions of the certificate and the scribe wrote them down on papyrus. Ariel placed the seal of the court on the document, and all the judges signed it. The two judges departed, and Ariel remained with Barak.

"Well, it looks like everything is all set," said Ariel as he rolled up the papyrus and gave it to Barak.

"Thank you sire," he nodded. "I am just sorry that I waited to the last moment to obtain this certificate."

"That's all right Barak. Sometimes, if it wasn't for the last moment...nothing would get done. Moreover, this work that you are undertaking will be a great service to our people. As you probably know, the enemy among us is worse than the one without."

Finally, Barak understood more fully why Deborah asked him to undertake this task.

"I agree Elder Ariel," said Barak, "That our people can be their own worse enemy."

"Tell me Barak, is the war situation with the troublesome Canaanites getting better or worse?"

"It is worsening, Sisera has increased his patrols throughout the Jezreel Valley and other areas. Our people are afraid to use the open roads and fear to travel through the plains. Because of this, I have stepped up our patrols. This situation keeps me very busy and I believe all out war will come."

"I see"...Ariel commented slowly as he placed his thumb and index finger of his right hand on each side of his mouth. "Then if"...Ariel paused, "If this is true, how are you going to find time to apprehend fugitives and bring them to justice?"

"I'll make the time. I promised Deborah that I would bring them to stand trial."

"Ummm, I see...." Ariel groaned suspiciously. "To stand trial? It seems that you might have other interest in her. Is this not so?"

"Well...yes, She has many good qualities. Is there anything wrong with that?"

"No! Of course not. But, I would hate to see you overload yourself. You see it is our custom for a man to perform everything that proceeds out of his mouth. Here lately, the law and other customs of our people have been disregarded and that's why there is so much distrust among the tribes of Israel."

"I understand," he said as he looked up to the two brown cherubim embroidered on the purple curtain. "When Deborah asked for my help, I promised that I would give it; and I meant it, even if it kills me," Barak answered him firmly.

"Very well, I believe you! But, remember Deborah is no ordinary woman! She has her own business; she is a spiritual advisor, judge, prophetess and a mother in Israel to many. Now, there is something which I must warn you: Some people complain that Deborah takes a man's role, but in these terrible days, good men are hard to find, and it was the need of the hour that pushed her into this position."

"Can you explain to me how she was pushed into this...this need of the hour, as you call it?"

"Yes Barak, but first let us go over to my house and have supper...then, we'll talk further," he offered as he lifted himself up slowly supporting himself with his staff.

CHAPTER FOUR

As the evening approached, they both walked down the path about fifty cubits north of the Tabernacle to the house of Ariel. They passed by the palm and fig trees, which lined up along the way. Then Barak picked up a small branch of a fig tree that had fallen to the ground. The branch was comparatively soft and light brown. The leaves were dark green and resemble the shape of a pear. Barak smelled the leaves, which emitted the fragrance of the sweet skin of a ripe orange. The pleasant fragrance reminded him of whatever Deborah was wearing when he was with her and he held the branch close to his heart.

They entered into the gate of the four-cubit high stone wall, and walked to the courtyard in the back. Beautiful pink and purple flowers were growing along the side of the wall. They sat down on soft cushions placed along the side of a low stone round table. This table was only about one half cubit from the floor. Then, Ariel called his housekeeper and instructed him to prepare an extra dish for Barak. After the introductions, the housekeeper asked Barak.

"Would you like something to drink?"

"Just water, thank you."

"Where were we last?" asked Ariel.

"You were getting ready to explain to me how Deborah was pushed...."

"Oh yes, How Deborah was pushed into her situation. The answer to your question is in two parts. First, what qualified her for her work? And second, what was the social conditions that pushed her into her public role," he explained as the big orange-red sun was setting in the west.

"Yes, this is what I want to know."

"You see Barak, Deborah's father died when she was four years old and her uncle Yoetz helped to raise her. Her uncle taught her about our laws, customs and history. He was, also, one of the leaders of his tribe. On many occasions when he had to go to discuss tribal matters, he would take her with him."

"It sounds like they were very close," said Barak, as the housekeeper placed the water on the table.

"Yes, they were. By the way, Deborah had a great memory and as her uncle grew older his memory waned and he would rely on her to help him to remember things he had forgotten. When she went with him, she preferred to sit in an adjacent room and listen to the discussions rather than to go play with the other children. She preferred to be around older people and her uncle intimated that Deborah said that she could not learn anything from children her own age. Deborah listened to her uncle's instructions on the law month after month, and year after year until she became proficient in legal matters."

"Wonderful," said Barak, as he stood up holding his hands behind him, and gazing at the setting sun reflecting its red rays on the white clouds.

Now Ariel, the Elder, began to tell Barak about a special event that Deborah had experienced several years ago, while she had visited her brother, Asher, in the town of Beer Sheba. She could not talk to him long because he was the recorder for the local court, and a trial was about to begin. In view of this, Deborah decided to stay around and listen to the proceedings. Deborah's brother introduced her to Shallum, the head judge. After a short talk, the Judge was so impressed with her demeanor and her knowledge of legal matters, that he invited her to participate in the discussions if she so desired.

"Who taught you about law Deborah?"

"My uncle Yoetz."

"Hmmm, that name sound familiar. It will be interesting to see how you perform in this trial."

Usually, the trials were held in a small brick building at the entrance of this town, but the crowd was too large so they held the court outside under three large palm trees.

After the preliminary formalities were finished, the head judge among the seven on the panel asked, "Is everyone ready?"

"We are present your honor," answered one of the judges for the prosecution.

"Then, the court of Beer Sheba will now commence its proceedings," said Shallum, the head judge.

"Are all witnesses and the defendant present?"

"Yes, Elder Shallum," answered the officer of the court.

Zedekiyah, the wife of Abraham, the merchant, is charged with adultery.

"Zedekiyah, what is your answer to these charges?"

"I am innocent. Absolutely innocent. I be...."

"Hold your peace, interrupted the head judge, You will get your chance to speak."

Rising to his feet, the prosecuting judge said, "I call the first witness, Dan Ben Shafat. Dan, do you swear the holy oath to speak the truth?"

"I do."

"Dan, please tell the court what you know about this case."

"Well, it isn't very much. But, on the late morning of the twenty-seventh of last month, I saw Zedekiyah holding the hand of a man as I walked by her house looking through her gate."

"Have you ever seen that man before that time?" asked the prosecuting judge."

"No."

"Are you sure?"

"Yes," I know every one in this town and that man, I never saw before."

"Thank you Dan." The prosecuting judge then turned to Zedekiyah and asked: "Do you swear our holy oath to tell the truth?"

"Yes, I do."

"Was your husband at home on the day stated by the last witness?"

"No. He went out of town on business and he hasn't returned yet."

"Did any man come to your house on that day?"

"Yes," as she answered the crowd looked at one another with surprise.

"What is his name, and how long have you known him?"

"His name is Benjamin...Benjamin Ben Hur, and I have known him for three years." she answered as the crowd roared in surprise, gossiping.

"Zedekiyah, what was the business of this man at your house?"

"He delivered to me some jewelry, which I loaned to my sister."

The prosecuting judge walked away from her, stopped, then turned around toward her. "Zedekiyah, why didn't your sister bring the jewelry to you instead of Benjamin?"

"Because she gave up the ghost, but before she died, she told her husband, Benjamin to bring the jewelry to me."

"Are you claiming that this man Benjamin is your brother-in-law?"

"Yes."

"What time a day was it when he arrived at your house?"

"Before noon."

"Where is this brother-in-law now?"

"I don't know. I sent for him to testify in my behalf, but he hasn't showed up yet."

"You don't expect your lover to show up, do you?"

She answered, "He is not my lover!"

"Do you have any maid servants?"

"Yes, I have two."

"Where were your maid servants when your brother-in-law came to your house?"

Zedekiyah looked down and remained silent

"Answer the question," ordered the head judge.

Zedekiyah raised her head slowly. "I sent them to the market," she said reluctantly.

"How convenient this was for you. Isn't it true that you sent your handmaid away so that you could be alone with your lover?"

"No...! It is not true!" she yelled crying.

"Then why was a married woman like you seen holding the hand of another man?"

"I don't know," she answered, looking very confused. "It happened so quickly..." she paused. "Furthermore...he was my brother-in-law."

Deborah rose to her feet, raised her head slowly, and spoke softly: "It is clear to me...that this woman is innocent. If we put to death (on false charges) every young innocent woman, there wouldn't be any women left to marry your sons," responded Deborah as the crowd smiled and chuckled.

The prosecuting judge turned to the audience and spoke. "Deborah calls her an innocent woman, who would be put to death on false charges. Now, we shall see...!" He walked three steps towards Zedekiyah and looked at her. You admitted that your husband was out of town. You admitted that you sent your maid away. You admitted that you held the hand of another man on that day. Moreover, everything was made more convenient for you and your lover. Why don't you confess your guilt and save the court money and time!"

"No! No! No! I'm innocent," she sobbed dropping her head into the palms of her hands.

As Deborah watched and heard the interrogations, she said to Sarah, her handmaid, "This sister is going to need lots of help. Oh Lord, I beseech Thee, please help her."

The prosecuting judge continued, "Were you once a very close friend of the man, Benjamin?"

"Yes," answered Zedekiyah as the audience roared in surprise.

"Isn't it true that you were once betroth to marry him?"

She remained silent for a moment, "Yes," she answered hesitantly as fear enveloped her.

"Isn't it also true...that you had sex with that man, Benjamin?" Zedekiyah dropped her eyes in silence.

"Well...speak! Isn't it true?" he demanded.

Zedekiyah raised her eyes slowly and labored to speak. "Yes...!" she snapped reluctantly with pain in her voice. But, that was a long time ago."

The prosecuting judge pointed his finger at Zedekiyah and then looked at the audience and asked, "Is this who Deborah calls an innocent woman?"

Deborah lowered her head a little and remained silent.

Waving their fists high over their heads, the crowd roared, "Guilty, Guilty, Guilty!"

"Well Deborah! You have nothing to say?" asked the head judge.

Deborah walked slowly toward her seat with the appearance of deep thought on her face. She stopped and turned towards the head judge and the prosecution.

"Shallum, our chief elder, judges of the tribe of Simeon, and people of Beer Sheba; even if, she did have sex with Benjamin, that was before she got married to her present husband. She cannot be guilty of that. Furthermore, our law requires that a matter be established by two or more witnesses...as of now, I have heard from only one...."

The prosecuting judge looked at Deborah, and gave an insidious smile. "We have them.... The court now calls Ishmael and Katan." These two were well-respected businessmen of long standing in the community. The judges and most people in Beer Sheba knew them; and the word went out that many folks supported the accusations of the businessmen.

Then Deborah whispered to Sarah: "This prosecuting judge is very shrewd.

"Yes, and he blocks you at every turn."

"But, he can't block the Lord."

After the two witnesses came up to the front row, the prosecuting judge asked: "Do you swear our holy oath, to speak the truth?"

"We do."

"Please give to the court your complete names, and your occupations."

"I am Ishmael Ben Jacob."

"And I am Katan Ben Zeef. We are business partners of Joseph Ben Abraham, the husband of Zedekiyah."

"Now, Ishmael and Katan, will you please tell the court what you observed," asked one of the judges.

The older man, Ishmael, spoke up first. "We arrived at the house of our business partner, Joseph Ben Abraham, and looked through the opening of the gate and saw

Zedekiyah holding and kissing a stranger. The stranger fondled her all over her backside then, they went under a tree surrounded by some bushes," he reported as he looked at Zedekiyah.

"That's a lie...lies, lies," shouted Zedekiyah with anger.

"Order, order, order in this court. One more outburst like this and you'll be fined," warned the head judge.

Deborah turned to her handmaid and said, "I don't like the smell of this case...it has all the trimmings of a frame-up. This sister is going to need help," she said to Sarah in a low tone. At that moment, Deborah said a short prayer again. "Oh Lord, I beseech Thee. Touch this court to do the right thing."

"Have you ever seen that man before," asked the other judge with his right fist and index finger resting on his chin and jaw.

"No Ephraim...I mean, no your honor."   After that slip of the tongue, the head judge looked at Reuben and Ishmael suspiciously.

"Now, let's hear from the other witness," requested one of the judges.

"Katan, let's hear your side of the story," said one of the judges.

"I, I, I, agree with Ishmael," he stuttered.

"Speak up! Speak up! I can't hear you," the judge commanded.

"Everything that Ishmael told you is exactly what happened your honor. We both looked through the gate at the same time."

"Did any of you warn the so-called stranger that what he was doing was wrong?"

"No! We were afraid for our lives, because he was a hugh man"

"Lies, lies, lies," shouted Zedekiyah once more with tears running down her cheeks.

"Order, order, this is enough. You are fined five shekels," the head judge reprimanded her.

"Guilty, guilty, guilty," shouted many of the people in the courtroom.

"Our law says that we only need two witness to punish and we have them."

"Quiet or I'll clear this court. Officers, if there is another outburst like this, you have my permission to remove anyone from this court." Everyone was completely still and there was a dead silence, as if everyone was afraid to speak.

"Is there anything anyone would like to add before we recess to make our decision?"

Deborah stepped forward three paces graciously and slowly with a commanding appearance.

"Your honor, I have some information which I think will be valuable to this court. This information will cast light on this case and help bring out the truth."

"Oh...!" the head judge uttered. "Tell us about this information you have!"

"It is information about the procedure in interrogating witnesses. If it please you, your honor, may thy humble servant, Deborah suggest that each witness be interrogated separately and more in depth."

"This is highly irregular," exclaimed the prosecuting judge. "We know that she is guilty. Let's not waste the court's time...and pronounce sentence."

The head judge raised the palm of his hand at him indicating for him to hold his peace.

"Deborah, on what do you support your request," asked the head judge, sympathetically.

"In the book of Deuteronomy, it is written that '*the judges shall make diligent inquisition,*' in regards to legal matters and the questioning of witnesses."

"This is a waste of time," shouted an angry man from the audience. "She is guilty." Finally, two officers grabbed the man, and removed him from the court.

The head judge spoke to Deborah. "I assume you have training in this area of the law."

"Yes I do. My uncle Yoetz instructed me in these matters."

"I've heard of that name before. Did he not sit on the council of the seventy elders at the Tabernacle in Shiloh?"

"Yes, he was on the council for many years."

The prosecuting judge interjected once more: "Elder Shallum, I vehemently object to Deborah's suggestion. We never had procedures like this in our town before."

"And in this town, we never had a trial like this before. A woman's reputation and life is at stake.... The purpose of this court is to seek out the truth, so that justice can triumph. For these reasons, I shall permit her to proceed."

"You may begin Deborah," the head judge encouraged.

"Your honor, may we have Katan the second witness escorted from the courtroom so that I may question Ishmael alone?"

After the usual formalities were complete, Deborah asked Ishmael many questions in the categories of queries, inquiries and cross-examinations.

Deborah continued her battery of questions. "Ishmael, how many times would you say you had visited the house of Joseph, the husband of Zedekiyah?"

"About... uh...fifteen times."

"And when you went there, how many times did you see Zedekiyah?"

"I would say about eight times."

"Did you ever discuss with anyone about the fact that Zedekyah is a beautiful woman?"

"No…" answered Ishmael with a surprised look on his face.

"Do you think that she is beautiful?"

"No," he answered slowly.

Deborah turned to the judges on the panel and continued: "This is very strange. Ishmael, you a man, don't think that she is beautiful, and I a woman think she is very beautiful. Indeed, this is very strange"

The prosecuting judge then spoke up. "I don't see where Deborah is going with this line of questioning."

"I do," replied Shallum. "Deborah, you've made your point. Now, I must ask you to get to the specifics."

"Ishmael, you claim that Zedekiyah committed adultery. Tell the court where did this act take place?" asked Deborah.

"In her courtyard, under a tree surrounded by bushes."

Deborah lowered her head, paused and then, looked up.

"What kind of a tree was it?"

"Ah… ah…I believe, it was a fig tree." Ishmael stuttered.

"Now, in regards to his clothing, what was the color?"

"Red."

"Are you sure?"

"Yes."

"One more question, Ishmael. Did this act take place before sunset or after sunset?"

"It was before sunset."

Then she summoned the officer of the court to bring in Katan for interrogation.

"Katan, you said that the defendant was kissing in the courtyard. Exactly where at in the courtyard did this kissing take place?"

"Under a tree," he said wiping the sweat from his forehead, looking nervous.

"What kind of a tree?" she asked sternly.

"I don't know!"

"You don't know? I see..." said Deborah looking at him with discernment. "Did this alleged meeting between Zedekiyah and the stranger take place before sunset or after?"

Katan paused and then said, "After sunset. Yes! After sunset." Deborah turned around slowly and looked at Ishmael and paused. Ishmael lowered his head and rubbed the upper bridge of his nose.

"Are you finished Deborah?" inquired the head judge.

"No your honor. I have one more question for Katan. What was the color of the clothes the stranger was wearing?"

"Must I be questioned like some criminal?" he asked turning to the head judge.

"Answer the question!" ordered Elder Shallum.

There was a silence. Then the head judge reminded him. "If you want your testimony to be accepted, you must answer the questions truthfully."

For the second time, Deborah asked Katan: "What was the color of the clothes the stranger was wearing?"

"His clothes were...white," he said hesitantly.

"I am finished your honor," she said as she noticed the judge nodding his head in approval.

The prosecuting judge rose to his feet, and called for the defendant Zedekiyah. "Did you commit the crime as alleged by the two men?"

"No! Absolutely not! I love my husband and I would not do anything like that," she assured them.

"Where were you on that day and at the time stated by these two men?" asked one of the judges.

"I was at home."

"Was there anybody else in your house with you, male, female or both?"

"No. Just me your honor."

"Do you have anything to add to cast light on this case?"

There was a period of silence in which Zedekiyah didn't say anything and the judges starred at her waiting. "I shall repeat, do you have anything to add? We are waiting!" replied the judge.

"No. No," she murmured. "These evil men."

There was a deep silence and pause as the judges looked at her with wonder in their eyes.

"Are there any more statements anyone would like to make?" There was a long silence, but no answer.

"Now, we shall recess for an hour, then bring you our decision. Deborah, would you like to join us in our discussion?"

"I would consider that an honor sire."

CHAPTER FIVE

They went to a stone structure about thirty feet from where they were. There were beautiful green shrubbery planted around the sides and front. As they walked along the beige stone walkway toward the building, Deborah could see a replica of the Ten Commandments engraved over the front door. Then she read the ninth commandment in a low voice.

"Thou shall not bear false witness against thy neighbor." The rest of the judges heard her reading and looked at her with approval.

After they finished the serious deliberations and reached a decision, they agreed to let Deborah render the summation of the case and they returned to the court area outside.

The news about Deborah traveled rapidly, and as she looked around the court area, she noticed that the crowd increased in size.

"Attention please! The court of Beer Sheba is now back in session," proclaimed one of the officers.

"You may begin Deborah," the head judge urged.

Deborah walked up front and began to speak: "First of all, I call this case, *The Ghost Man.*" We do not have a complete description of the evil man who is supposed to have committed adultery with Zedekiyah, and nor do we know of his where-abouts. It is doubtful that he even exists at all.

"The facts and truth of this case," explained Deborah," hangs only on the testimony of the two witnesses. First of all, Ishmael testified that he saw the defendant kissing under a fig tree; and Katan said that he didn't know what kind of tree it was. This answer renders their testimonies void."

"Eh," gasped the entire crowd.

"Second of all, Ishmael testified that the clothes of the stranger was red; and Katan testified that they were white. This is a contradiction that renders their testimonies void." Again, the audience gasped with a deep breath.

"Point number three, Ishmael testified that the act took place before sunset; and Katan stated that it happened after sunset. This discrepancy renders their testimonies void, because everyone knows what the difference is between before sunset and after sunset."

"Judge Shallum," said Ishmael, "We are men of high standing in this town. Are you going to let this...this woman stand here and humiliate us?"

"Our law shows no respect to person," said the chief judge. "If you feel humiliated, then, it is your guilt that has seized you."

"What?" You mean that you are going against us?"

"Your lust and wickedness has blinded and condemned you. This court finds you and Katan guilty of being false witnesses. What you, and Katan sought to do to Zadekiyah, so shall it be done to you!"

Then, Ishmael starred at the judge with a hateful look. "Curse be the day you were born. You will pay for this."

"No!" Shallum snapped back. "You will pay for your transgressions. You have accused Zadekiyah falsely, and now you have reviled the judges of Israel. Officers of the court, seize the false witnesses!"

As the officers escorted the false witnesses away, the crowd stood in an uproar and shook their fists at the prisoners. Then Shallum rose to his feet and raised his hands above his head. The crowd became quiet and listened attentively.

"You have heard the evidence in this case and it is the decision of this court that the defendant, Zedekiyah Abraham, be set free. As for Ishmael and Katan, their wickedness and lust have condemned them. Furthermore, let it be proclaimed from here northward to the tribe of Dan, that these two men have been convicted for bearing false witnesses against a daughter of Israel. This we do in order to remove evil from the midst of the children of Israel. Also, we want to give thanks to our God for sending us our beloved sister Deborah whose knowledge, wisdom, and fortitude helped to exonerate the innocent and convict the guilty. This court is now dismissed," added the chief judge smiling slightly.

Later, Deborah went over to meet with Zedekiyah. As soon as she saw Deborah, she embraced her enthusiastically and warmly.

"Thank you! Thank you! Thank you so much Deborah, you are God sent. Without you, I don't know what I would have done. Oh! Would you like to come over to our house for dinner tonight?"

"Yes! I'd like that."

"During supper, we'll have plenty of time to talk," added Zedekiyah anxiously.

"There is more isn't it?" asked Deborah.

"Yes. I'll see you later."

After her visit with Zedekiyah, and her brother, Deborah returned to her home outside of the town of Bethel.

When Ariel, the senior Elder of the Supreme Court had finished telling this story, he looked at Barak and said, "That court case in Beer Sheba was the starting point that began to push Deborah to national fame among the tribes of Israel. After that, people from many tribes came to her for judgement, knowledge, counsel, spiritual advice and inspiration. Her audience included men and women, but many women came for special reasons because it was said that they could confide in her concerning intimate issues. In short, the people felt that, in Deborah, they had an understanding and receptive ear. She was open, accessible, and humble. These were her spiritual qualities as they are written in our sacred books."

Barak lowered his head, scratched his eyebrow, and looked with wonderment. "Let's back up a minute." There seems to be something missing about that court case in Beer Sheba. Was it ever revealed why those two wicked men brought false charges against Zedekiyah?"

"Yes. I'm glad you asked me about that. When Deborah went to Zedekiyah's house for dinner that night, Deborah asked her did she have any idea why those two men tried to frame her. This is what was revealed: You see these two men had been coming to her house to discuss business with her husband, and that's how they knew Zedekiyah. Zedekiyah was a beautiful woman not quite thirty years old. As time passed, their hearts were drawn to her with lust. So, one day when they knew her husband was not at the house, they came and pleaded with her to lie with them, but she refused. Finally, after she had turned them down many times, they said to her, 'if she don't lie with us, we shall tell the judges that we saw you commit adultery with a stranger.' "

"Those evil men," gushed Barak as he took a deep breath with disbelief, shaking his head.

At that moment, the servant brought out a water basin with a towel, bread, very warm beans, cut corn simmered in onions and olive oil, vegetable salad and hot roast juicy beef ribs and placed them in front of Barak.

"Wow!" he shouted as he breathed the aroma through his nose. After the recitation of the blessing of the bread, Barak took a spoon-full of fried fresh creamy corn and exclaimed, "This is delicious."

During the course of the meal, Barak reflected again on the two accusers of Zedekiyah, and his spirit was troubled. He started to take a bite from the juicy beef rib that was in his hand, but paused. "Why didn't Zedekiyah testify in court that her accusers wanted her to lie with them?"

"Good question," commented Ariel. "Zedekiyah knew that her husband had a very important business deal with two business men and she didn't want to say anything that would disrupt that arrangement. In view of this, Zedekiyah didn't even tell her own husband that the businessmen wanted to lie with her. Somehow she had hoped that the men would leave her alone. You see, Zedekiyah knew that the business deal meant a lot to her husband, and that's why she remained silent before and during the trial."

"Hmm. Well. Wasn't the business deal still in jeopardy during the trial?" asked Barak.

"Not really. The business deal that her husband had was not with her two accusers, but with two other men. But Zedekiyah didn't learn of this fact until after the trial."

"You mentioned earlier that there were other social conditions that contributed to the rise and fame of Deborah. What were they?" inquired Barak poignantly.

"It was the complete breakdown of the political, religious, and social structure of the Israelite nation. You must understand, that after the death of Moses, Joshua, and the elders that outlived Joshua, there was no central leadership or king in Israel that had witnessed the miracles and experiences that our ancestors had faced in Egypt and in the wilderness."

"During the time that Moses and Joshua led the Hebrews in the wilderness, all the Israelite tribes were encamped around the Tabernacle, the shrine of central leadership. All the tribes looked for leadership and guidance from the Tabernacle because Moses, Joshua, the high priest and the seventy elders were there. Furthermore, the Hebrews brought their offerings and tithes to the Tabernacle. These factors contributed to the Tabernacle's central leadership role."

"However, after Joshua had completed distributing the inheritances to each tribe in the land of Israel, everything changed. The tribes were no longer encamped around the Tabernacle, but were remote from it and many people for one reason or another refused or neglected to make pilgrimages to it on the three festival days or at other times. Many elders, heads of tribes, and judges stubbornly refused to go to the Tabernacle at Shiloh to seek advice, guidance, and instructions from the Lord, from the high priest, and the seventy elders. Many of these elders and leaders did what they thought was right in their own eyes. The thing they should have done was to ask those at the Tabernacle who knew more than them, but they didn't."

"Also, the leadership of the Hebrews became corrupt from top to bottom. They took bribes, committed idolatry, adultery, convicted the innocent, and let the guilty go free. In other words, the people corrupted themselves in every way possible.

"Our people did evil in the sight of the Lord. They saw no unity among themselves, no central leadership, no justice, no righteousness, no mercy, no harmony, and no peace. The children of Israel lived among the other races, the Philistines and the Canaanites. Their social structure based on the law, completely crumbled. Distrust, jealousy, despair and hopelessness were the norm of the day. They began to hate themselves and to despise their history, laws, and culture. They became like the Canaanites, the other nations and races around them. They accepted the evil culture and gods of the Moabites, Ammorites, and Canaanites who sacrificed their sons in the fire to their gods. You see Barak; it was all of these evil conditions that contributed to the rise and fame of Deborah. The time was ripe for her. She became the welcomed cool breeze that came after a long hot spell of hopelessness.

"Your Excellency, I could listen to you all day and night."

"I'm sorry to disappoint you Barak..." he said, "but the days are for you to listen...and the nights...are for me to sleep!"

Barak smiled and continued. "Why didn't more leaders of the various tribes come up to the Tabernacle for instructions?" Barak asked.

Ariel sighed with a deep breath and paused. "The heads of the individual tribes and the elders of the various towns became self-centered, they became infatuated and protective of their petty tribal authority and power. The tax or tithe they retained for themselves and refused to give it to the central leadership. If they had done this, they would have helped to make the government at the Tabernacle much stronger. Instead, it grew weaker, weaker and weaker. In short, the local tribal leadership became too haughty, proud and arrogant. They interpreted the sacred laws according to what they thought was right in their own eyes.

"The ultimate interpretation of our holy books was never intended to rest in the hands of the individual tribes; but to rest in the hands of the high priest and the Supreme Court of the seventy elders at the Tabernacle. They were the men of higher knowledge established by Moses. The book of Deuteronomy instructs us in this regard: '*If there arise a matter too hard for thee...then thou shall arise and get thee up into the place which the Lord thy God shall choose (that place is the Tabernacle)...*' " said Ariel.

"Now that you mentioned it, that makes sense," Barak admitted. "And, some of the leaders in my tribes also are guilty of not going up to the Tabernacle to seek guidance from the Supreme Court."

"Eh...I am going to put it very simple young man, and I say young man because I am almost twice as old as you. When the elders of the various tribes rejected the guidance of the learned men of the Tabernacle, they rejected knowledge; and when they rejected knowledge, they rejected God; and when they rejected God, God rejected them. Consequently, he delivered the Hebrews into the hands of their enemies, the Canaanites, to punish them for their transgression. Just like a parent punish their children when they do something wrong. In view of all of these evil conditions, many of our people were ready for a change...ready for something better...ready for righteous spiritual leadership and Deborah was there to give it."

"An extraordinary lady," remarked Barak as he yawned. "Elder Ariel, some of my soldiers asked me how could they get wealth. Can you give me any advice for them?"

"Yes...! But, the answer I give may not be the answer they want to hear...! The way to get wealth is to give first. Then it will return to you later. I'll use a parable to convey my complete answer: First, pursue the goddess of knowledge...and pursue the goddess of wisdom...and use that knowledge and wisdom to help mankind. Afterwards, the goddess of wealth will get jealous and pursue you," he said with a smile on his face.

"Umm!" Barak expressed surprise. "I like that answer."

"Oh, Barak your day time has passed, and the night has come. Now, it is my time to go to sleep."

After their discussion, Ariel asked Barak to sleep overnight at his house and the next morning Barak continued on his journey to the city of Kadesh in Naphtali.

Chapter SIX

A Month Later

On the fifth day of the week, two days before the beginning of the Hebrew Sabbath, Deborah received a letter from Barak. The letter was in the form of a rolled-up piece of parchment, which he had deposited in a pouch made from animal hide. As she laid on her bed, Sarah the handmaid handed her the pouch. Deborah opened it and read from right to left (as it was the custom of the Hebrews):

"Peace be unto you Deborah. I hope you are well. It seems like it has been a year since the last time I saw you. I stopped by the Tabernacle and had a long informative discussion with Ariel, the elder. He gave me the Certificate of Authority, which I requested, thanks to you. Also I would like to inform you that we had a skirmish with a Canaanite company of soldiers. We lost three men and I was slightly wounded on my right arm. But, I am much better now. So much for the unpleasant news.

I have been thinking about you every week. I wish I were there with you right now. I miss your presence, your smile, your beauty, and your tenderness. By the way, your name has become a household word and your fame has spread all over the northern tribes. People have nicknamed you Mother Deborah. In closing, I hope there is a place in your heart for me. I'll see you as soon as I can. Peace be with you. Your friend, Barak."

As Deborah lay on her bed, she reflected on Barak's letter with mixed feelings. After her morning prayer and meditation, she finished the breakfast that her handmaid served her.

"My Lady, is there anything that I can do for you before I leave for the market?" asked Sarah, as she held a pot in her hand.

"No...but wait for me. We'll go together."

Nachshon, the gatekeeper, prepared the donkeys for the market. He took several sacks from the storage room and placed them over the back of the donkeys. In these sacks, they usually put the food and other items they bought. The fifth day of the week was the most important shopping day because the next day was the beginning of the Sabbath. Among the Hebrews, the Sabbath began in the evening the day before the actual Sabbath day and most people had their cleaning and cooking completed by high noon on the sixth day of the week. Sarah and Deborah walked together and Nachshon remained behind five or ten paces to allow the women some privacy to talk women talk. They were on their way to the town of Bethel about a mile and a half down the road that connected Jerusalem with Shechem. It was at Bethel that this road intersected with the east west road that led from Jericho to the Mediterranean Sea. Bethel was a thriving town long before the arrival of the Hebrews. It had many houses, shops with pavements, and a sanctuary. There was an adjacent mound and several springs where the local inhabitants could get water. This particular day was cloudy and still Deborah was in a reflective mood, as she walked along the main road to Bethel. For the first half mile of the walk, there was no conversation between the women. Sarah looked at Deborah but held her peace for a while. Then, as they walked a little further, they could see the town of Bethel off into the distance. "Deborah, I don't want to appear prying, but is there something...troubling my Lady?" Sarah asked softly and cautiously.

Deborah held her peace and looked up at the gray clouds. "I have a lot on my mind today," she said guardedly not intending to reveal too much. She stepped up the pace of her walk leaving Sarah a few steps behind. They passed palm and sycamore trees as they walked. Sarah was a woman at least fifteen years passed childbearing age and she had worked many years for Deborah's late husband. Her hair was completely gray and she was about seventeen years older than Deborah.

"My Lady, I have worked for you and your late husband for many years and have tried to be a good servant. I have not seen you like this before. I beseech you...please tell thy humble servant what troubles thee?" It is about that letter you received this morning, isn't it?"

"Yes..."she said reluctantly.

"Would thy handmaid be wrong in saying that the letter is from the handsome man with the mustache that came to the house on the last full moon?"

"No...you are not wrong. The letter came from him," answered Deborah, as she looked at Sarah with amazement.

***

They began to enter into the central section of the town of Bethel. There were many shops, inns and houses. Some houses had stone steps on the outside that went up to the second floor. There were many men, women and children walking in the outside market area leading their donkeys and asses along the way. People were bumping into each

70

other not watching where they were going because they were gazing at the fresh produce, meat and other items on sale.

The market place, for many, was a good place to come for shopping, but it also served another purpose: People could meet old friends, talk about their personal concerns, discuss something new and watch the strangers going and returning from Egypt, Arabia, Moab, Syria, and Tyre near Lebanon. Moreover, there were Greeks from Europe, and Circassian, from southern Russia, who were shopping in the market place. These travelers were headed to Egypt.

Deborah sensed that Sarah wanted to talk more about the letter she received, but the congestion, the crowd conversations, and greetings of the people kept Deborah busy. She also had her shopping to do, so they didn't have much time to discuss personal matters. Nachshon, the gatekeeper, acted as a bodyguard especially when Deborah was away from the house. He was a very tall man weighing about two hundred pounds and moved closer to Deborah to be ready to protect her against any would-be assailants. Nachshon was an expert fighter and he had received his training in the army of Shamgar, the last Hebrew judge who fought the Philistines.

Many people who knew Deborah greeted her and smiled. Various people were saying to each other "that's Deborah, the Prophetess." As Deborah walked in the market, she gazed at the onion, beets, leeks, beans, grapes, nuts, melon and other produce. She bought a sack full of vegetables and Nachshon fastened them to the donkey.

"Can I pay you with these shekels and gerahs?" asked Deborah.

"Yes, " replied the shopkeeper.

After Deborah paid for her produce, she turned around and bumped into a shopper. "Oh! Is that you Ophrah?"

"Yes!" she said smiling.

"I haven't seen you since apples were ten gerahs (ten cents) a basket," said Deborah as she embraced Ophrah.

I've been hearing so many good things about you lately."

Ophrah was a sleep-in house servant for Deborah's brother-in-law whose name was Caleb.

"How is Caleb?" I haven't heard.... Oh Ophrah, what are those bruises on your neck, hands and arms?" she asked with deep compassion.

"Oh Deborah, you shouldn't ask me," she commented pitifully.

"Has Caleb been mistreating you?"

"He supports me and my children."

"But, has he been mistreating you?"

Ophrah lowered her head and remained silent. Then Deborah starred at her with empathy.

"I understand.... You can't talk about it because you are afraid that if Caleb finds out he will punish you."

She raised her head and eyes slightly and looked at Deborah. "Sometime you just have to bear things," she mumbled weakly.

Deborah took a deep breath and exhaled as she placed her arm around Ophrah's shoulders. Both of them slowly walked away from the crowd. Then Deborah spoke again. "I am sorry for your sake and mine that this has happened to you."

"You are sorry for your sake? I don't understand."

"It is a long story, but you will understand before the end of many days."

Ophrah turned toward her. "So be it, as you have spoken."

"I think that you will be free of this burden that you have."

"Did a voice of God tell you this?"

"No! It is just a strong feeling that I have and I am usually right...."

"Yes, you usually are."

"Ophrah, we must support one another. What I am saying is that if things become too unbearable with Caleb, you can always come and work for me."

"Thank you Deborah. You are so kind, and it is good to know that I have another way out."

Furthermore, before I go, I want you to pray daily and God will answer your prayers."

***

It was now midday and Deborah and her servants were on their way back home. After doing some reflection on the letter of Barak, which she received that morning, she was now in a better mood to discuss it.

"My Lady, before we arrived at the market you were telling me that the letter you received came from Barak. It seemed to disturb you. Did it not?"

"Yes, it did...Barak was wounded in battle."

"Oh no...! Was it serious?" asked Sarah as she walked turning her head toward Deborah.

"No. It was just an arm wound."

"My Lady...because your countenance fell, I thought it was something more serious than that. Could it be that your heart and eyes are drawn to him like a flower is drawn to the sun?"

"I don't know...I like him but my life is uncertain."

All of a sudden, Deborah, Sarah and Nachshon heard the sound of horses and a chariot coming rapidly behind them, so they moved to the side of the road to let them pass. As the horses passed, Nachshon noticed that the driver was an Egyptian and he had a whip in his dark brown hand, which he cracked at the team of horses. The whip swung around in Deborah's direction and could have struck her in the face, but she ducked down.

"That was close," she said, "bless it be the name of the Lord."

After that incident, Deborah and Sarah returned to their pervious conversation and continued down the road.

"What did you mean when you said that your life is uncertain?" inquired Sarah, as she looked puzzled.

"I'll reveal it to you when I know more about the problem that is heavy on my heart...I promise."

"All right.... But...on the other hand, Barak is a handsome man. Almost every woman would want him."

"True, he is handsome. He has a good position, he's a prince, he is a general and he has a beautiful and large estate. But, his spirituality is doubtful," she reminded Sarah. "Because I am spiritual and in tune with my Creator, my mate or husband must also be the same. If he is not, he will despise my spiritual interest and make fun of it."

"What did he say that indicated to you that he was not spiritual enough?"

"Barak told me that, 'if he had half the number of men and chariots that general Sisera had, he would attack tomorrow.' This was his boasting. Then I told Barak that he would 'need more than chariots to beat Sisera.' His reply to me was 'we will see.' You see, he left God completely out of the picture."

"Did he mention anything personal of how he feels about you?"

"Yes...he said that he thinks about me every week, he misses me, my smile and my tenderness and he wants me to hold a place in my heart for him."

"Will you?" asked Sarah.

"I am not sure. He has a lot of the qualities that I admire, but, then he congers up unpleasant feeling in me..."

"Feelings! Like what my Lady?"

"Feelings like...." Deborah paused, and then continued, "like sorrow and death."

"My Lady, where does those feelings come from?"

"They come from my late husband, Lapidoth, as you know, he was killed by Canaanites. Barak fights Canaanites and was recently wounded by them. If I hold a place in my heart for Barak and he falls dead in battle, the emotional pain will be too much. Can you understand the position I am in?" Deborah inquired as she stopped walking and starred at Sarah.

Sarah took a deep breath and continued to walk along side of Deborah. They passed other men, women, and children with their animals travelling north and south on the road. As they walked further down the road, Deborah saw a bush of beautiful red roses. She picked some to take home, but she pricked herself on a thorn and a little blood oozed out.

"You see Sarah, we cannot even enjoy the pretty roses without their thorns. Is this the nature of the men of the world?"

"It seems that way," commented Sarah.

"I would like to get married again to the right man, but right now, I can't commit myself to Barak or to any other man because of the problem that is vexing my soul."

"Problem? What are you...?"

"Sarah, I mentioned to you earlier that I have a problem that is troubling my soul and I promised to reveal it to you soon, but not now. This is one of the reasons why I can't commit myself to anyone"

***

They arrived home while the sun was still high in the afternoon. Sarah and Nachshon performed their usual duties. In the meantime, Deborah had made inspections of her flax and wick factory. Afterwards, her supervisor, Madreech, reported to her concerning the workers and the production output. By now, the sun had set but it was not yet dark. After supper, she lied down on the reclining couch to retire for the evening. Deborah heard a shot out at the front gate, but paid it no attention, thinking that it was one of the servants. Then, her gatekeeper Nachshon called her.

"Deborah, you have a visitor, it is your brother-in-law, Caleb. Where shall I bring him?"

"Caleb? Give him a seat in the dinning room, I'll be out in a minute and offer him something to eat."

"Finally, he shows up when I least expect," she thought. Deborah had been waiting for his decision for more than two years. He had kept her hanging. She wondered what would be his decision now. Did he have a selfish reason for coming now? This was the final moment she was waiting for. She had mixed feelings about Caleb; she was not sure about him. Her heart pounded in anticipation of his decision. A decision one way or the other would be uncomfortable for her, but she had to face it.

Sarah came to her room. "Can I be of service to you, my Lady? Oh! You are perspiring," said Sarah as she pulled out a handkerchief and wiped her forehead. Deborah sat down a minute, closed her eyes and thought: I must get control of myself. Whatever happens, it is God's will. He has His purpose in mind and it is not for me to understand all of His actions at once.

Then she got up with confidence and went into the dinning room to meet with Caleb. Caleb was about fifteen years older than Deborah, and about her height. He was bald on the front half of his head and was wearing a brown garment with yellow stripes. When she entered the dinning room, Caleb's back was to her and he was looking up at a painting on the wall. It was a painting of the beautiful Jezreel Valley with Mount. Tabor on the north.

"Peace be unto you Caleb," she said cautiously.

After they exchanged greetings, the cordial conversation continued. "I was just looking at the painting of the Jezreel Valley.... It seems so peaceful," explained Caleb as he stroked his full gray beard.

"And that seems so contradictory, in light of the fact that so many wars have been fought there. I was there when I was younger and at times I fee...feel like I shall return there for some special reason," Deborah explained.

"Deborah, I am sorry for not contacting you sooner to give you my decision on levirate marriage. I must fulfill my duty to my brother so he can have an heir. This is our law," he emphasized as he walked to the shelf and picked up a small scroll of the five books of Moses.

"Before we talk about marriage, I want to talk about another matter.... I was at the market in Bethel today and I met your maid servant, Ophrah."

"Oh!" He almost dropped the scroll and looked up at her. "I suppose she said bad things about me."

"No, she didn't. Are there any bad things to say about you?"

He gave a silly grin and looked away. "You know some women like to gossip and exaggerate."

"She had bruises on her neck, hands, and arms and no telling what other parts of her body. Is this an exaggeration? How did she get those bruises Caleb?"

He stuttered and searched for an answer. "Sh-sh-she fell. Yes, she fell down the stairs."

"Do you expect me to believe that? If Ophrah had fallen down the stairs, she would have told me."

"It is not my concern what you believe."

"But you came here expecting me to agree to levirate marriage. How can I do this knowing that you abuse your maidservants? If I marry you, should I expect you to abuse me also?"

"I don't intend to abuse you."

77

"You don't intend to.... By the way, it has been three years since your brother's death, you could have given your decision to me earlier," she pointed out as she walked to the large cedar table and took out three nuts from a clay bowl. "I wrote to you three times in the three years and all you could say was that you were busy and that you would let me know soon."

Caleb began to look guilty and bowed his head in shame.

"You could have given me your decision three years ago, or two years ago, or even one year ago," she said softly as she placed the three nuts on the table. "Why now Caleb, why now...?" she inquired as she looked at his potbelly and waited for an answer.

"I...I...I..." he stuttered, "neglected to give you my decision earlier, but I am here now ready to fulfill the law. You see our marriage also, can increase and combine our assets and I can get out..." remarked Caleb, making a slip of the tongue.

"Out of debt you mean, don't you? Hmm. I see, so you came here now to make a proposal of marriage to help you get out of debt," concluded Deborah staring at him with distrust.

"The fact remains that you do have a legal obligation to marry me; in spite of, what you say my motives is," he said with a soft smile on his face as he placed the scroll back on the shelf. "What will it be Deborah?"

"Give me a little time for meditation. I shall return shortly. Then, I'll give you my answer."

Deborah went into her room and sat on a soft mat, folded her legs with her back erect, took deep breaths and exhaled slowly. After she had relaxed, she evoked the Lord of Creation and the God of her ancestors. At last, there was a total silence in the dept of the darkness. At that moment, the voice uttered: "Do what you know is right and then let God work out his purpose."

After the meditation and prayer, Deborah returned to the dinning room. As soon as she walked in, Caleb stood up. He gazed at Deborah with a long stare as if he had seen a ghost. His hands trembled as Deborah spoke. "I agree to marriage to fulfill our customs, not because I trust or love you."

"Who said that levirate marriage had anything to do with love."

"I get your point, but with most women love is foremost. Do you have a date in mind?"

"Six months from now will be fine. I'll have to leave now and I'll contact you to discuss the plans. Peace be with you."

Deborah sat down and thought about the conversation she had with Caleb. It bothered her and she wanted to talk about it. Then she remembered that she had promised Sarah to reveal to her what was troubling her soul and there was no better time than now.

"Sarah, will you please come here," she called.
Sarah was a small thin energetic lady for her age.

As Sarah entered the dinning room, she bowed slightly and asked, "What can I bring you my Lady?"

"I don't want you to bring me anything. I want you to give me your ear."

"Oh my Lady, I am at your service to give you both of my ears," she said sincerely and humbly.

"Let's go outside into the back courtyard," Deborah suggested.

The night was clear, the stars were out and the moon was full. In addition, Deborah was full of things to say.

"Sarah, I told you that I would soon reveal to you the things that have been troubling my soul. Well, I am ready. My deceased husband's brother, Caleb, visited me earlier this evening and asked me to marry him. I agreed to do so, but I am *not* in love with him."

"Why did you agree then?" asked Sarah looking puzzled at her, with eyes stretched wide open.

"Because I am bound to do so under our law of levirate marriage."

"That's right! There is a law that stipulates that you must marry your deceased husband's brother."

"Yes! But it is conditional, this means that if a brother dies without a male heir, his brother must marry his wife and the first born male, which she births shall succeed in the name of the dead brother, so that his name will not be blotted out of Israel. You see, I don't have a male child, so it is my duty to marry Caleb."

"Is there any other way out of this marriage?" Sarah asked.

"Only if he refuse, and this he has not done. Finally, there is a Divine way out; but that is left up to God to work out His purpose on earth," she said as she looked up at the stars and moon reflecting on the universal power of the Creator.

This dilemma left Deborah confused and torn emotionally. Torn between disobeying the customs and laws of her people, or on the other hand, marrying a man she didn't love. She knew that if she refused, she would be denounced as a fraud and disgraced in the eyesight of her people. In view of this, Deborah poured out her soul unto the Lord: "Oh my Heavenly Father...! Why couldn't there have been another man that I could have love? Oh Lord, I beseech Thee...hear my cry and deliver me from this awful pain..." she murmured as tears ran down her cheeks.

CHAPTER SEVEN

As Barak led his mountain fighters through the hills of Zebulun, a personal conversation developed between him and his next in command.

"General, you seem deep in thought," observed Captain Enoch.

"Deep in thought?" repeated Barak.

"Yes! I've been watching you for the last three days...your body is here with us...but your mind has flown away like a bird to some distant land. Would you be willing to confide in your humble servant and reveal to me what weighs heavily on your heart?"

Barak hesitated; he looked at Captain Enoch with a serious glance then, smiled. "All right, I might as well bring my mind back from this distant land that you spoke of and, let you know about my secret thoughts."

"A little discussion," said the Captain, "will no doubt cast some light on a dark problem."

"Well Captain, it was some time ago that I wrote a letter to a friend of mine named, Deborah, and I haven't hard from her since."

"I had a hunch that your problem had something to do with a woman.... Women are strange creatures. They are difficult to understand. Do you think that she likes you?"

Barak remained quiet, and looked down at the ground. Captain Enoch grabbed his horse's reigns. He said to Barak, "Hold your thought!"

The General glanced at him suddenly: "But, I didn't think it yet."

The Captain looked at him and grinned.

"Do you need more time?"

"No... I believe she likes me, or should I say, she admires me."

"Give her a little more time," urged the Captain, you'll probably hear from her soon."

"You have a point. Riding around in these hills, day after day, has made me lonely. I truly miss her."

Barak, the general of the northern Hebrew militia, spent the rest of the summer pursuing and capturing Hebrew lawbreakers. The capturing of transgressors and criminals was a necessary step to bring about tribal and social tranquility, trust, hope and justice for Hebrew victims. On a higher spiritual level, if the Israelites expected God salvation and deliverance from the oppression of the Canaanites, it was their obligation to remove criminality and injustice from their society, first. As Barak hunted the robbers and thieves from Upper and Lower Galilee and from the east and west ends of the Jezreel Valley, he noticed the growth of the flowers, trees, grapes, barley, wheat and other vegetation.

Then the fall came, the season of repentance, atonement, and the harvest festival. Some people went to the Tabernacle at Shiloh and some didn't. The harvest season came to an end with the dwelling in the booths. This festival also commemorated the dwelling in the booths when the Israelites came out of Egypt. During this time, the leaves of the trees turned yellow, red and brown. The brown pine needles of the evergreen trees fell to the ground. The rainy season of the fall, which was so vital for this land, came in abundance. Many times, these rains became so unbearable in hunting down lawbreakers.

By the time of the approaching winter, Barak had put under his command one thousand men. He divided these men into four companies and appointed a captain over each one of them. This conscription of men was very essential because of the increased confrontation with the Canaanites and the hunting of lawbreakers. Up until now, Barak never commanded a thousand-man militia. He thought about how his army was increasing and that all out war with the Canaanite, General Sisera, was unavoidable. It was unavoidable because King Jabin and Sisera imposed heavier taxes on the Hebrews, their soldiers molested some of the Hebrew women, the Hebrews could not use the open roads for traveling, and the Canaanites put more Hebrews into hard labor camps. Barak knew that this situation could not remain the same for long. Because he wanted his men to be ready when war broke out, he increased the training of his men. But, there was a scarcity of spears and swords. This condition came about because the Canaanites feared that the blacksmiths among the Hebrews would make weapons. Because of this, they arrested them. In view of this, Barak relied on sling shots, stones, and spears without the iron tips on them.

One day as Barak was leading his men through the hills of Zebulun, just north of the Jezreel Valley, a messenger on horseback arrived.

"Where is General Barak?" the young man asked. "I have a letter for him."

"Who is it from?" inquired Captain Enoch, the commander under General Barak.

"The letter is from Deborah Lapidoth."

"I am he!" answered Barak anxiously as he nudged his horse Laban over to the young man to receive the letter.

Barak opened the pouch, unrolled the letter and began to read.

> *"Peace be to you Barak. I received your letter and you informed me that you were wounded. I hope that you have fully recovered. Your good health means so much*

*to our nation and us. I was grieved to hear
about the loss of three of your men. I realize
that war is so terrible but at certain times it is
necessary for the greater good that will
result. So much for that and I'll move on.*

*"Now, no doubt you have heard
about the Hebrew robbers in your area.
They have been stealing cattle, sheep and
goats and selling them to the Canaanites.
Our people need you to catch these
transgressors a s soon as possible and bring
them to justice. Keep your arm strong
against all transgressors. It is your mighty
arm of the law that makes the law legal.
Without the enforcement of the law, the law
has no power. Our people will not have
trust in one another until we get rid of crime
in our midst. I have confidence in you that
you will succeed. May God bless you and be
with you. Signed Deborah Lapaidoth."*

After Barak finished reading the letter, he rolled it
up and thought about what Deborah had said and what she
didn't say. He wanted to hear intimate things, pleasant
things of how she felt about him. He didn't get them and
his soul became heavy with disappointment. The weather
was chilly, cloudy, gloomy around him, and he felt gloom
overtaking him. Nevertheless, he pressed on trying to find
the thieves, which Deborah had mentioned and, which he
had heard about previously. Barak had been looking for
these robbers for more than a month without any success.

After searching all day for the men, Barak decided
to pitch camp for the night. His camp was not far from the
town of Shimron near the foot of one of the hills. He
stationed guards at strategic points, ate supper, and had a
briefing with his first officer, Captain Enoch. The Captain

was about forty-three years of age, and his hair was long and wooly. He had been with Barak about ten years and he had a wife and four sons.

"I think that we should get an early start in the morning," advised Barak as he placed his hand over his mouth and yawned.

"How early General?"

"Just before dawn. These robbers do their dirt just before the break of day when most people are asleep."

"I agree General.... By the way...before the messenger departed, he mentioned the name Deborah...was that Deborah the judge?"

"Yes that was her," answered Barak smiling.

"I bet she's beautiful!" asserted Captain Enoch waiting for a confirmation from Barak.

"What makes you think that?" asked Barak as he stood up and closed the curtain to the tent.

"Because you smiled when I mentioned her name. General, I am..." Captain Enoch paused.

"Speak up! Speak up! What's wrong with your tongue Captain?"

"General, I am confused, earlier today after you finished reading the letter from Deborah, you seemed sad, but now, after I made a reference to her name, you smiled..." the Captain paused.

"Yes? Get on with it," Barak encouraged wanting to hear more.

"Well, I am confused General. Would it be not in good taste for your humble servant to ask you to explain this difference in mannerism?" he asked softly.

"Hmmm," Barak drew back, remained silent, raised his head and thought: "Shall I let this man into my private world? After all, he is just a subordinate and I am the General. On the other hand, if I tell him about the letter and how I feel, maybe he can be helpful, as he has been in the past. Stop being too proud," he said to himself, "and open up as ladies do for one another. Could it be that I am too close to my problem to have all the answers?"

"Anything you tell me General, I'll keep it between me and you."

"You'd better or else you'll be demoted to a foot peddler."

"I understand," the Captain assured him.

"All right, this is the situation. I smiled because I was thinking of Deborah when I first met her. She was so beautiful inside and outside, so warm, tender and compassionate. And I was sad after I read her letter because she didn't mention anything that suggested that she liked me as a friend. What I am saying is that I was expecting her to have said more than what she did. Since she didn't, I was disappointed. Maybe...I am expecting too much."

"Perhaps, could I see...the letter?" he asked softly.

Barak hesitated, then gave him the letter and after he read it, the Captain said, "I see what you mean. There are a couple of subtle things I see about the letter."

"Oh...I should have known you would pick it to pieces like a shepherd shears the wool from the sheep," commented Barak.

The Captain smiled and continued. "The fact that she wrote to you, I think this indicates that she is interested in you. You see, she didn't have to write you," the Captain said looking very positive.

"Maybe, she wrote me because she wanted to tell me about the cattle robbers."

"Not really. We probably knew about them before she did. Most of these events take place in our territory and we know about them before the rest of the country."

"You really believe, wholeheartedly, what you are saying, don't you Captain?"

"Yes I do...secondly, in the letter, she mentioned that 'your good health means so much to our nation and us,' Deborah could have ended that sentence with 'our

nation,' but she chose to conclude with the words, 'and us.'
I truly believe that she wanted to say 'and me.' Other
words, the sentence should have read: your good health
means so much to our nation and me."

"Captain, you give a very convincing argument,"
Barak complimented as he held his head up high and
smiled.

"For some reason, I felt that Deborah was
uncomfortable to express her true feelings, and General,
when you see her again this is something you might want to
explore with her."

"I think I'll do just that...well, Captains this
discussion has been very interesting and it; at least, gives
me more insight. Now, let's go over and visit the men at the
campfire."

As Barak and the Captain walked closer to the fire,
they could feel its warmth because the wind blew the heat
in their direction. Then they stepped on a small branch,
which cracked, and the sound alerted the men that they
were approaching. When the men turned around and saw
Barak and the Captain, they started to stand up. But, the
Captain stopped them, "As you were, men. Continue to tell
your jokes and riddles."

"We just finished Captain. We would like to hear
one of your stories or one from the General," requested a
new recruit.

"Yes!"
"Yes!"
"Yes!" shouted some of the soldiers, who were new
recruits.

"Tell us General, about one of your most important
battles," another soldier shouted.

" All right, it was the battle that we had planned at a
meeting in the city of Kadesh, over two years ago," he told
them.

***

Barak and his officers had met to plan a surprise attach on a company of Canaanite soldiers. Barak had wanted this meeting because the Canaanites were taxing the Hebrews heavily and those who could not pay or refused to pay were forced into hard labor. The Canaanite soldiers executed this policy by the orders of General Sisera. In view of this, Barak wanted to put an end to their actions or if not totally, he wanted to reduce them by some great measure.

"Captain Enoch would you bring over that map?" asked Barak.

The Captain attached the map to the wall, which was made of cowhide. The map showed the area of the Jezreel Valley, the hills of Zebulun to the north, and the tribes of Asher and Naphtali, which included the Galilee area.

"My fellow officer of the Hebrew nation, I shall make myself brief. We are here to discuss ways how we can attack larger Canaanite patrols. In the past, we only attacked smaller patrols of thirty to fifty soldiers, however, this is going to change." Barak emphasized looking stern.

"How are we going to do this General Barak? We don't have any chariots, nor sufficient spears and swords," commented Captain Maher.

"Good question. We're going to deal with that in a few moments," he said as he took a sip of grape juice from a goblet. "I have spoken with the elders and I've asked for more men, gold shekels, and supplies, and they informed me that they will not consider any increase until we defeat a Canaanite force of more than four hundred men. They want us to destroy more of these Canaanites who are capturing our young men and women to be used in hard labor and to be sacrificed to their idol god, Baal."

88

"That's almost impossible General, considering our predicament," said Captain Enoch looking bewildered.

"I said the same thing also, when the elders mentioned it to me. But on the next day, as I was reading: *The Book of the Wars of the Lord*, and *The Book of the Wars of Joshua*, I realized that we could succeed if we set a trap for the enemy. Now, this is what we shall do." Barak then explained to his officers the strategy and all the details of the trap, which he prepared for the enemy.

A week later, Barak brought his soldiers to the place where he had planned to set the trap. The place was the mountains and hills of Zebulun near the city of Japhia. This city was located on the northern edge of the Jezreel Valley near the hills and only six miles west of Mount Tabor.

Barak led his men going southwest until he first reached the valley, north of Japhia, which is now called Nazareth. He rode past the steep cliffs and hills, which were covered with aromatic herbs and pink, purple, and yellow flowers. He continued south and arrived at the section of the valley where it became narrower on the southeast and ended in a winding pass leading to the big Jezreel Valley.

As he entered the winding path, he explained to Captain Enoch, "We shall hide men in the cliffs of the mountains. And when the enemy pursue after us into this pass, we shall rain down rocks and stones upon them like hailstones from heaven."

"But General, how are we going to get the enemy to pursue us?"

"That will be simple. We shall have one of our men to disguise himself as a Canaanite; and when he sees a Canaanite patrol coming, he'll tell them that the Hebrews stole his sheep. When that happens, we'll have five or six men not too far from him with some sheep and when the Canaanites see them, we hope they will pursue the Hebrews into the pass."

"Oh, I get it General. When the Canaanites pursue the Hebrews with the sheep, they will lead him into the winding pass where we will be waiting for them," commented Captain Enoch with a big smile on his face.

"I knew you would understand it, Captain."

Then Barak ordered Captain Enoch to select a special person to disguise himself as a Canaanite and to select six men to act as sheep thieves. Also, Barak told the Captain to select lookout men and post them on the high cliffs. These watchmen will let the rest of the Hebrews know when the Canaanites will arrive, by using the wailing howl of a jackal. The Captain informed all the men of their duties and all plans were prepared.

The first day passed without any observation of the Canaanites. By the arrival of the third day, the men began to get restless and bored. After a while, the Captain came and reported bad news to Barak.

"General, the men are getting tired of sleeping among the rocks of the cliffs, and in caves. They say that the Canaanites are not going to come."

"By the sound of your voice, it seems that you too are getting weary."

"Well...yes. I might as well admit the truth, I am."

"Listen Captain," Barak took two steps to the side looking down and then looked up and reminded him. "Tell the men to be patient. Victory is lost many times because men do not hold out to the end. This will be a good lesson in self-discipline for them."

Toward the late afternoon of the fourth day as the soldiers sat around talking, they heard the wailing howl of the lookout man. The Captain ran over to Barak and asked, "Isn't that our signal?"

The wailing howl sounded again.

"I believe it is. Tell your men to take up their positions quickly and don't attack until you hear the sound of the ram's horn."

After giving the men their instructions, Captain Enoch returned to Barak. "All the officers know their positions on the cliffs and know what is required of them, General."

"Good, the ram's horn will be blown after the last Canaanite soldier enters into the winding pass. We shall seal off their exit point so that none will escape."

"General, let me express my joy to you for your upcoming victory. Your fame will now spread all over the land of Canaan from Dan to Beer Sheba."

"I am not seeking after fame," snapped Barak suddenly, as he stomped his foot on the ground. "My task is to destroy the Canaanite threat...so that we can bring peace to our people."

"Yes General!"

At that moment, Barak heard the sound of the hooves of horses. He looked to his right and saw the six Hebrew riders leading the Canaanites unaware into the winding pass. The Canaanites rode into the pass with horsemen pursuing the Hebrews relentlessly. After the last Canaanite horseman rode into the pass, Barak gave the orders to blow the ram's horn and his five hundred men began the sustained barrage of stones and rocks. At the same time, they sealed off both ends of the pass with large boulders, and with barn fires. The Hebrews were able to subdue the Canaanites quickly, because they surprised them, and they held the high ground.

When the battle was over, Barak and his men went down into the narrow pass to count the dead and wounded and to recover the spoils.

"We have a great victory, General," commented the Captain as he passed by a hugh rock on the cliff.

"Yes, we do. Get me a complete count of the dead and wounded and collect all the booty," ordered Barak as he walked by the wounded Canaanites.

After a short while, Captain Enoch returned to Barak with the good news.

"General, we count 564 Canaanites. This number includes the dead and the wounded. We have more than exceeded our goal."

""Well done Captain. Is there anything else?"

"Yes there is. We have a double victory," said the Captain, with a smile on his face.

"Captain, my time is valuable. I have no time for playful words. Explain yourself."

"Not only have we defeated this Canaanite regiment, but we recovered eleven Hebrews who the Canaanites had chained to a cart. No doubt, the Canaanites were going to put these men in hard labor. We found the cart near the entrance of the pass, which lead to the Jezreel Valley."

"Well, this is good news. The elders will be pleased to hear this," said Barak with a sly smile on his face. Oh Captain, assemble the men. We are moving out."

Now, as Barak sat around the campfire, he finished telling his soldiers about that great battle and trap he had planned for the Canaanites. Moreover, this victory gave the soldiers more faith in their General.

CHAPTER EIGHT

Just before daybreak the following morning, Captain Enoch awakened General Barak and informed him of the approach of men and livestock. Barak immediately jumped to his feet and asked: "How many are they?"

"We don't know General."

"Put all standard orders into action, and treat them as the enemy until we know otherwise, and I'll be out in a few moments," Barak ordered as he put on his sandals and adjusted his kilt and girdle belt.

As he walked outside his tent, he fastened his sheath to his belt and went over to the five-foot high boulders where the Captain was standing with some of his men.

"General, I think we have found what we have been looking for...the robbers," said the Captain as he gazed over the boulder into the dimness of the dawn.

"Are you sure? There is one way we can find out. Get your men ready to move on a moment's notice and report back to me."

"Yes General!"

After the soldiers were assembled and ready for action, the Captain returned to the General.

"Captain, have your men blow the ram's horn. If the men remain with the livestock, this probably means that they are honest men. If they run and leave the livestock, this means that they are thieves. In that case, assign some of the men to gather up the flocks."

After the men blew the ram's horn three times, the suspected thieves ran away on their horses, donkeys, and camels toward the Jazreel Valley. Barak and his men pursued the thieves into the Jazreel plains, which separated Lower Galilee from central Israel called Samaria-Ephraim.

There were about ten men in the group of thieves and Barak's men caught up first with three men who were riding on the slow moving donkeys.

"Grab those men on the donkeys and tie them up," yelled the Captain as he veered his brown horse toward his men.

"Barak and his soldiers continued to pursue the men on the horses. They were running at top speed across the Valley in the direction of the Hill of Moreh.

"Hurry up Laban, we don't want to loose those men," he said to his horse, Laban as he leaned over his long white mane and urged him on.

Barak looked back and saw Captain Enoch coming up on his rear. The thieves were no longer in sight; they lost them somewhere around the Hill of Moreh and adjacent hills. He slowed down his horse a little to let him rest. All the horses were breathing hard. Then Captain Enoch and his men caught up with Barak.

"Captain, they can't be far away. They must be hiding in these hills," said Barak as he focused on the landscape.

"Or they might be hiding behind some of the boulders or bushes," suggested the Captain as Barak heard a noise off in the distance.

"Captain, take your men around to the right of the hills and I'll go to the left. Let's search every foot of these hills thoroughly. I don't want these villains to get away."

"Yes General!"

Both companies of Captain Enoch and Barak searched on and around the Hill of Moreh and the nearby area and met at the southeastern section of this group of hills.

"Captain did your men see anyone?"

"No General, we searched every hill and all through the bushes, and nothing. I don't understand where they could have disappeared," he said as he looked up at the orange sun overhead.

Momentarily, Barak looked defeated. He wanted these thieves caught to help bring more trust and hope among the Hebrews. Also, he had to admit to himself that he had another reason to bring these men to justice. If he apprehend these men, it would make him look good in the eyesight of Deborah.

As he sat on his horse, he wondered in his mind, which direction they could have gone. He remained calm and reflected. He knew he couldn't waste any more time. If he did, the thieves would get away. Realizing that he had to make a decision right away, he turned to his officers.

"General, you look like you have gotten a revelation," commented one of his junior officers.

"I have," Barak said. "I don't think that the men went to the southwest toward Megiddo. If they had, we would have seen them. I believe that they escaped toward Mount Gilboa to the southeast. We couldn't see them in their escape because the Hill of Moreh was blocking our eyesight. However, there are two reasons to back up my contention that they went to Gilboa. One, there is plenty of water at the Spring of Harod and second, they can easily hide among the multitude of trees."

"That makes sense," the Captain remarked.

"Captain, assemble the men and let's make a fast run to Gilboa."

"General, the men haven't eaten yet."

"Then they'll have to nibble on bread as they ride. We can't afford to loose these scoundrels," Barak said as he speeded away.

The mountain range of Gilboa was about six miles from where they were. They rode their horses at rapid speed in a two-column formation. As they approached the mountain range of Gilboa, they stopped about fifty cubits from the foot of the mountain, where the Spring of Harod was located. This Spring was situated near the northwest spur of the mountain range. Barak took a hard look at the Spring to ascertain if the thieves were drinking there or hiding among the nearby evergreen trees. He quickly concluded what he must do.

"Captain Enoch! Give orders to your soldiers to surround this entire mountain range and then report back to me. We want to cut off all escape routes of these bandits."

"Consider it done General."

After the Captain had cordoned off the entire mountain, he returned to General Barak. "All of the soldiers are in place General."

"Good, captain I..."

"Excuse me General, may I suggest that we give water to the men and water the horses?" said the Captain.

"I was going to get to that but first, I want you to send one of your officers to the tribe of Zebulun, and request reinforcements, because our lines are spread very thin. After that, you can see to it that water is given to the men and horses."

Barak goose-stepped his horses around the general area of the Spring of Harod and watched the deployment and watering of his soldiers.

As Captain Enoch was talking to one of his officers some distance away, Barak realized that he had not questioned the three captives who were riding on the slow moving donkeys. Then he got the Captain's attention and waived him to come over.

"Yes General."

"Do you have the three men who were riding the donkeys?"

"Yes General."

"Bring them to me!"

The Captain's soldiers brought up the three men and they seemed to have a guilty look on their faces. In addition, their hands were tied together behind their backs.

"What are your names," asked Barak looking at them sternly.

The men slowly raised their heads and one after the other muttered.

"Dan."

"Aharon."

"Benjamin"

"Where are you from?" asked the Captain.

"We are from the tribe of Asher," answered the older looking man.

"Where were you going before we stopped you?" Barak asked.

"To...to the valley," muttered one of them.

"Yes! That right, to graze the sheep in the valley," answered the second man.

At that moment, Barak sensed that they were just trying to make up lies as they talked.

"Why did you run off when you heard the sound of the ram's horn?" inquired Barak, watching their every reaction.

Each man looked at each other as if they were searching for an answer, and said. "We thought you were murderers, that's why we ran."

Checking them over carefully, Barak noticed something hanging on the neck of one of them. "You!...Step forwards two steps."

"You mean me?" asked one of them.

"No! I mean you...with the long beard. What's that hanging on your neck?

"It's nothing...just a charm," he casually replied.

Barak then leaned over the side of his horse and took a close look at his so-called neck charm. "What do you think I am...a fool? This is an image of the idol god,

Baal. Idol worshipers! Get them out of my sight," Barak commanded as the soldiers grabbed them.

"General, the reinforcement should be here shortly," assured the Captain.

"Good, now you can begin the all-out search of Gilboa. If possible, bring all of these scroundels back to me alive."

They blew the ram's horn and the search of the entire mountain range began at one time. Barak was convinced that he was going to catch these bandits this time. It was just a matter of hours. After an hour's search, the Captain reported to Barak.

"Have your men seen anything Captain?"

"Yes! One dead man. He looked like he was mangled by a wild beast."

"I wouldn't be surprised...bears and lions have been seen in these parts. Press on with the search and tell the men to be careful."

Yes General!"

"Oh! By the way, tell the men that if they happen upon a cave, don't go in, but set a fire at the opening of the cave and smoke out what ever is in there first."

"Yes General."

After an hour, the reinforcements of five hundred men arrived under the command of Captain Maher.

"I came as quickly as I could General. What is the situation here?" he asked.

"We have about seven bandits trapped in these hills. The entire area is surrounded by our soldiers and they are searching for them right now."

After Barak had finished briefing Captain Maher, he gave him his orders.

"Captain Maher, send half of your men into the mountains to help with the search and keep the other half here at the foot, as stand by units. Your stand by units can help protect and guard the rear of the searching units, which are in the mountain just in case any of Sisera's Canaanite patrols come."

As Barak watched the sweeping search operation on the mountain, he thought of what Deborah stressed in regards to capturing criminals. Their capture was necessary to bring more trust, love and unity among the Hebrew tribes. The army was needed to achieve this objective because the local law enforcement had broken down and the Canaanite and Philistine danger was evident everywhere.

Off in the distance, there was a horseman riding rapidly in Barak's direction. As he approached closer, Barak could see that it was Captain Enoch. The Captain came to a sudden halt and Barak knew that he was carrying evil tidings.

"A Canaanite regiment of soldiers has been spotted General," he reported as his horse panted for breath.

"What is their location?" he asked quickly.

"They are coming from the direction of the rising sun, but they are closer to the city of Beth Shean," the captain informed him anxiously.

"How many are there?" he asked so that he could make the right decision.

"We estimate that there are between seventy-five to a hundred charioteers," he summed up eagerly waiting for further instructions.

"Hmm...charioteers," he mumbled. Barak thought: 'This is too large a force for us to deal with.' "Give the orders to your men who are at the foot of the mountain to kneel down in the high grass, and it will be less likely that they will be seen by the enemy."

"Is there anything else General?"

"Pray that the enemy turn north or return to the east. If they continue to come in our direction, we'll have to give up the search and chances are, that the bandits will escape." Barak nudged his horse toward the mountain. "I am going to keep a close eye on this Canaanite regiment. If you need me, I shall be at the lookout post on top of the mountain."

Within a short time, one of the lookout posts spotted smoke going up from the middle position of the mountain range. Then, the soldiers knew that the bandits were in that area and they closed in on them from every side. They grabbed them and brought them to Barak with their hands and feet tied. Barak then gave an order to bring all the Hebrew soldiers around to the western side of the mountain so that the Canaanite regiment could not see them; he also left men at the three lookout posts.

Now, he was ready for the questioning of the six bandits, which they captured in the mountains. After Barak received their names and the name of their tribes, he continued to question them.

"Why did you run?"

"We ran because we thought you were robbers and violent men," one man said hastily.

"It is an old saying that 'a guilty man flee when no man pursueth him,' " said Barak. "And you fled before we pursued you."

As Barak was questioning the suspects, he was glad that he had good news to report to the Supreme Court in Shiloh and to Deborah. Then he continued his questioning.

"How many men were with you?"

"There were eleven of us," said Rueben," who acted as spokesman for the group. He was about forty years old and over six-feet tall.

"We captured three men before you reached Gilboa, and captured six of you after you reached the mountain. That's a total of nine. Where are the other two?"

"They probably escaped."

"Captain Enoch, have your men bring over the body!"

The soldiers brought over the body, which was covered with a large white mantel and then took off the covering. It was obvious that a wild beast mauled the man. His neck had teeth marks on it and his stomach was torn opened.

"Do you recognize this man?" asked Barak, as he petted the head of his horse.

"Yes! I do...cover him up...that's a nasty sight to look at," he snapped as he turned his head away with a horrified look.

"We'll need to notify his kin folks. What is his name?" inquired Captain Enoch.

"Nathan," answered the spokesman."

"Was he Hebrew?" inquired Barak.

"Yes! An Asherite."

"Well, that accounts for ten men, but you said there were eleven...what happened to him?"

"He reached Gilboa before the rest of us. When we arrived there, we never saw him. So he must have escaped. He had the fastest horse."

"Mmm...what was his nationality?" Barak probed searching for all the information he could get.

"It is surprising that you asked because that one was a Canaanite."

"Canaanite?" Barak asked with astonishment as he looked at Captain Enoch.

"I suppose you wouldn't know what city he was from would you?"

"Uh...uh some name that sounds like uh... Hazier or...uh Hazur," he said.

"Could it have been Hazor?" asked Barak.

"Yes! That's it. That's it...Hazor."

Barak became very perturbed when he learned that one of the escapees was a Canaanite and possibly from the city of Hazor, the city of Jabin, king of the Canaanites and his General, Sisera. It was a known fact that Jabin had his spies among the Hebrews. It was difficult to tell who was a spy and who wasn't because some of the Hebrews lived among the Canaanites, served their gods and even intermarried with them.

Hadn't Jabin prohibited the Hebrews from taking their armies into the Jezreel Valley? In spite of this prohibition, Barak had done just that. No doubt sooner or later this news would reach Jabin and Sisera.

"Rueben, I want to thank you for being forthright with the information you gave us, but this doesn't lessen the fact that you are most likely guilty of stealing livestock. You will be taken to the court in Shiloh and in my report I shall mention that you were cooperative in giving important facts to the military. This might be an advantage to you in some way, but I am not making any promises."

"Thank you general," Reuben said.

"By the way, Rueben, why did you make a fire on the mountain?" inquired Barak curiously.

"We thought by doing so, the Canaanite army would see it and thereby, see your soldiers also. Then you would have had to flee."

"I see, but the opposite happened...because of the fire, we were able to find you sooner."

Sensing that the situation was under control, Captain Maher asked, "General, is there any further orders for me?"

"Uh...yes, I would like you to deliver the dead body to its nearest kin so that it can be buried before sundown."

"Speaking of burials, General, why do we bury before sundown?" asked Captain Maher.

"I thought you knew," interrupted Captain Enoch. It is our law and custom.... However, I will add...our sages and elders teach that as long as the body is not buried, the soul is not at peace...because it yearns to get back into the body."

"Oh...! That's interesting," remarked the Captain. as he saluted and departed.

"Captain Enoch, I am going to take seven days leave of absence. I'll be two days at my farm and one day visiting Deborah."

On that same day, Barak sent a messenger with a letter to Deborah informing her that he would be arriving in a few days.

CHAPTER NINE

Deborah was walking along the path lined with palm trees when Barak arrived on the seventh day of his leave of absence. She had given instructions to Sarah her handmaid and another female worker to follow behind her twenty cubits so that no one would question her integrity and moral conduct. After all, she was engaged to marry Caleb, her dead husband's brother; even though, she didn't love him.

As she waited for Barak to arrive, she thought about the fact that she had to reveal to him about her engagement to Caleb. This weighted down heavily on her heart. "How do I tell a man who I like that I am engaged to a man that I don't like?" she asked herself. She knew that it wouldn't be easy and it drained her energy like a parasite that drains the vital fluids from it's' victim. After all, she was human.

It was the middle of the winter, the leaves had fallen from the trees, and the day was cloudy, chilly and dim. She prayed silently: "Oh Lord, I beseech Thee, give me the strength, the courage, and the wisdom to deal with this pain." She could feel the despair in the air all around her.

As Deborah raised her head, she could see Nachshon, her gatekeeper escorting Barak to her. When Barak approached three cubits from her, he held out his hands to hold hers; but she decided not to reciprocate. It wouldn't look right. It would send the wrong message, but she wanted to do it.

"Is all well Deborah?" he inquired with an expression of doubt on his face.

"I'm fine, we've had a very good harvest this year and the business is thriving," she said as her blue green cotton mantilla fell from her head and shoulders.

Barak, then, bent down to pick it up and his muscular thigh accidentally touched her soft hip. He placed the mantilla over her shoulders and smiled with pleasure. She enjoyed the attention; but she didn't want to encourage him.

"You've talked about your business but haven't said much about yourself...you know deep down within. I've missed you and I am glad to see you," he said waiting for a response.

There was a silence. "I've had...."

"You've had what?" Barak probed.

"Let's not talk about me right now, I see you are all healed from that wound you suffered on your arm. "Oh, that's an ugly looking scar," she thought.

Deborah didn't want to reveal any news of her marriage to Caleb right now. She wanted to move slowly.

"Have you had any success in catching any more law-beakers?" she asked as she turned her head and looked in his eyes.

He chuckled and Deborah knew that he had good news. "Come with it. Tell me about it," she urged.

"Well, we caught ten men, cattle and sheep thieves..."

Barak told Deborah all what happened about the story and capture of the sheep thieves. This included the details of the man that was killed by a wild beast; the details of the man who had the necklace of the idol god, Baal, and the details of the Canaanite who escaped to Hazor.

Deborah said, "you were wonderful just wonderful, the way you organized and executed that search at Mount

Gilboa." As she praised him, she looked at him with admiration, respect and gave him a big smile. "Moreover, I get the feeling that the escaped Canaanite is a spy for Sisera."

"He just might be.... By the way, Deborah, how and when did you first hear about Sisera?"

"Oh, that was many years ago when I was a young woman of nineteen years old. That's when I saw him for the first time in person."

"You saw him?" Barak turned around in great surprise. "When? Where?" he asked anxiously.

***

Deborah began to tell Barak of the time when she had been living with her uncle Yoetz in the town of Jezreel. She had been spending a lot of time with her uncle after her parents had died.

At that time, Sisera was approaching the town with his army. He said that his mission was to enforce the laws of Jabin, king of Canaan, and to collect taxes.

As soon as Deborah learned that the Canaanite army was coming, she ran and told her uncle who was reading a scroll in his stone house.

"Uncle Yoetz, I believe, the Canaanite army is approaching."

"Quickly my dear, go...! Gather the children and the young ladies and hide them in the barn."

"Yes, yes, yes!" she said eagerly.

"And don't forget to hide under the straw," he shouted as she hurried out the door holding her cute puppy in her arms.

After Deborah and her friend Malcah finished hiding the children under the straw, they peeped through a crack in the barn, because they wanted to see what the soldiers would do. Deborah watched the soldiers ride up and stopped about twenty cubits away from the barn. The man who was riding ahead of the soldiers appeared to be the leader. Deborah could see that he was dressed in a fancy uniform of red and gold with a black leather girdle around his waist. He took off his gold colored helmet, which was a symbol of his rank and held it in his left hand. There was no one outside to be seen.

"Lieutenant, announce to the people to come out," Sisera ordered, as he wiped the sweat from his baldhead.

"In the name of Jabin, King of Canaan and General Sisera, I command all of you to come out at once."

There was complete silence and no one moved. Again, the lieutenant spoke: "We know you are in there. If you aren't out by the count of ten, we shall break down your doors and drag you out. One, two, three, four, five, six, seven...."

At the count of seven, an old man appeared at the door of one of the cluster of houses. He stepped out three feet and stopped. Then the others opened their doors slowly and came out. Sisera put back on his gold colored helmet and nudged his horse forward a few feet.

"I am Sisera, the commander of the King's army. Who is the head elder of this place?"

As Deborah peeped through the crack in the barn, she watched her uncle turn to one side and answered.

"I am," he said softly.

"Speak up old man! What is your name?"

"Yoetz."

"Yoetz what?" Sisera snapped.

"Yoetz Ben Joshua," he said stroking his long white wooly beard.

"Uh Joshua!" Sisera sneered with scorn. "Do you have your back taxes for the past year?"

Elder Yoetz cleared his throat, hesitated, then spoke. "No, General Sisera" he said.

"Why not?" asked Sisera.

"We've had a famine for the last passed year and we are a very poor community."

"Excuses, excuses, that's all I hear. Now, the King has ordered that if you don't pay your taxes, two of your men will be taken to work in the stone quarries. Also, two of your boys will be taken to be sacrificed in the fire to our god, Baal, and two of your girls will be taken to be raised up in the service of the goddess, Ashtaroth. Now, what will it be?"

"Oh my Lord Sisera, I beg thee. Ask us not to make a choice because we have no choice in this matter," remarked the Elder walking up close to Sisera. "I beg you, give us another year my Lord."

"Another year? You've had an extra year already. Get out of my way old man," said Sisera as he pushed the Elder to one side.

As soon as Deborah saw this incident, she started to go out to help her uncle, but Malcah grabbed her arm.

"You can't go out there Deborah. If you do, you will be taken away and you will endanger all of us in here."

"You are right Malcah."

Looking through the crack, Deborah saw and heard Sisera again.

"Lieutenant, take a squad of men and search the houses. There must be some children, and some young ladies around somewhere."

After a thorough search of all the adjacent houses, the lieutenant returned to Sisera.

"General Sisera, we found only a cripple old man lying on the floor."

Then Deborah heard the lieutenant address Sisera: "Do you want me to search that barn over there?"

"That is a good idea, go right ahead."

As Deborah, peeped through the crack, Malcah said, "The soldiers are coming, let's go and hide."

They hid behind a large pile of straw on the opposite side of the barn. As they were kneeling down on the ground, they heard the door open. Deborah held her puppy close to her, rubbing his head gently. When the three soldiers passed through the door, they stopped and looked around cautiously. Everything was quiet and still. The lieutenant walked over slowly to an animal's stall and looked in. No one was there. Afterwards, he walked back to the other side and he stepped on a twig and broke it. The puppy that Deborah held in her arms then made a growling sound. The lieutenant looked at his men and asked.

"What was that?" He put his hand on his sword and began to walk in the direction of the sound.

Deborah could see everything that was happening. Her lips moved in silence and she let the puppy loose. It ran over to the lieutenant and began sniffing around his feet and legs.

"Oh, it's just a puppy. Hello little fellow. You are a cute little thing."

Suddenly Deborah heard a shout. It was the voice of Sisera

"Do you see anyone lieutenant?"

The lieutenant and his men went out of the barn. "No General, not a soul. Just this cute little puppy," he remarked as he rubbed the puppy on his back.

"Put that creature down. We have more important matters to attend to."

Finally, Sisera turned to Elder Yoetz. "Where are the young ladies? Did you send them off?"

"No...we married them off." He lied so that he wouldn't place them in a risky situation.

"Well! Since you don't have the taxes, two of your young men will be taken and placed in hard labor," said Sisera angrily. "Take them!" Sisera ordered his soldiers.

In the meantime, Deborah and Malcah returned to the front of the barn. Peeping through the crack, they could see and hear everything that was said.

When the Canaanite soldiers seized the young men, Malcah cried. "They are taking my boyfriend. What am I going to do?" When Malcah began to walk toward the door Deborah grabbed her.

"There is nothing you can do, Malcah. It is all in the hands of the Lord."

"But, I'll never see him again," she wept, looking at the door.

"You can't go out there. If you do, they will take you, and abuse you. And finally, they will burn you in the fire as a sacrifice to their god, Baal. Do you want this to happen?" asked Deborah.

"No," she replied crying on Deborah's shoulder.

Then, Deborah heard Sisera once more. "Now, this is the King's order: Next year, your taxes will be twice as much and if you cannot pay, your property will be confiscated...."

"Oh Lord Sisera," pleaded the Elder. "We cannot pay this year's taxes, how are we going to pay double taxes next year?"

"That's your problem," shouted Sisera as he grabbed the reins of his horse.

"You are milking us dry," cried the Elder looking helpless. "You are like a man who milks the goat of all its milk and then butcher it for its meat."

"I had enough of your whining. If you were as good at collecting your taxes as you are with your flowery words, you wouldn't be in this situation."

Sisera turned his horse around and said to the Elder, "Get out of my face old man," and then he kicked the elder in the chest. The Elder fell backward to the ground and the soldiers galloped away. After the soldiers had gone, Deborah told Malcah to bring out the children and young ladies. After that, Deborah ran out to see how her uncle was doing.

"Are you all right uncle?" she inquired.

"Yes, I'm fine. I just feel like I was hit in the chest with a thunderbolt. How are the children?"

"They are fine my dear uncle."

In the meantime, Malcah came out with the children. "That was a smart thing you did in the stable by letting the puppy loose," Malcah said. It prevented the lieutenant from finding us. If you had not let the puppy loose, the lieutenant would have walked over in our direction and found us. What made you do it?" asked Malcah.

"I was praying silently for God to help us, when suddenly I heard a silent voice in my mind say, 'Let the puppy loose, Deborah.' "

At that moment, Malcah walked away and Deborah remained there and listened to her uncle.

"Because you listened to the inner voice, which spoke to you in the stable," explained her uncle, "you saved yourself and everyone else that was with you from being taken captive. How did you feel when you heard the voice?" he asked, as both of them strolled over to a bench and sat down.

"At first, I hesitated because I didn't want to part with my dear puppy," she said as the puppy played at her feet. Then she picked him up and continued. "The voice was direct. It was as though God was inside me," she explained as she caressed the white hair on the back of her puppy.

Her uncle turned to her. "You know, as time pass, I believe that you will become even more spiritual, and possess a keener sense. You will become something like a prophetess."

"How do you know this uncle?"

He turned towards her: "The years teach my dear child...and I've watched you grow up. You have a sharp mind and an unexplained good inner sense to know things. Now, I think it is time for me to teach you the steps of how to fast, relax, and meditate. We'll start tomorrow...!"

Deborah turned around and looked down past several houses from where she was sitting. Several women were crying. Deborah knew they were crying because Sisera took their sons captive. She got up and went over to them to express her sympathy for their loss.

After the terrible event of this day, Deborah never forgot the cruelties of General Sisera. Moreover, she knew that this would not be the last time that the Canaanite soldiers would affect her life.

Now, here was Deborah almost nineteen years later sitting in her courtyard. She had just finished telling Barak she first saw Sisera and learned of his cruel ways.

Barak looked directly at her. "From your account of the story, I've learned a lot about you and Sisera. Deborah, I admire you...for the way you handled yourself."

CHAPTER TEN

It was in the late afternoon that Deborah escorted Barak to her factory, which she inherited from her late husband. The building was a fairly large one, and in it her workers made linen garments, fishnets, twine, shrouds, sails for small boats and wicks. All these products were made from the flax plant that grew in the land of Israel.

"Deborah, a while ago, I mentioned to you that you have not said much about yourself. I mean how you feel about me."

"Isn't it a little bit early for that," she reminded him gently.

"Did not Jacob fall in love with Rachel the first time they met...and he kissed her?" he stressed as he bent down to pick up a dried flax plant.

"Well, that was a different situation, Rachel was single living in her father's house. I've been married before...and now, I have the responsibility of my business and communal duties to perform."

"Are you saying this because you are independent and have communal duties...that you don't have time for me?"

She stopped walking, turned around and remarked: "Yes and No! Let's think about it Barak. You have your own farm; you are a prince of your tribe and a general of the northern militia. Do we have time for each other?" she asked as she passed by a worker peeling stalks from the fibers of the flax plants.

"Well, you do make a good argument, but it will not always be this way?"

"No, probably not. But there are other things."

"Other things?" he inquired looking at her confused.

"Yes, other things. For example, permanency and spirituality in a relationship."

"Please explain my sister," he asked gently and sincerely.

"You see, Barak, if two people are going to have harmony in a relationship, they must be one spiritually. My brother, you are a good man, but you believe in the might of your army and in your own strength... and I meditate, trust and pray to the Lord everyday. This is the difference between us. It is not by might nor by power, but by the spirit of the Lord. My brother, if you can learn this, you will be more successful in your everyday struggles."

Barak listened carefully and took in every word without interruption. "I see what you mean Deborah. You are truly a spiritual woman."

"Barak, there is another thing that keeps me from thinking about you in a serious way. It is your dedicated fight with the Canaanites. My late husband died by the hands of the Canaanites; and if I open my heart to you, I would have to live in constant fear thinking that the same thing might happen to you. Can you see the situation that I am in Barak?" she asked with trembling in her voice.

"Yes, I do," Barak answered.

"I am only trying to help you to understand that the greatest might and light come from heaven. If you can't understand and accept this...now... I am sure that you will in the near future."

Both of them walked by several stone buildings on which flax was laid on the roofs to dry in the open air and sun. Previously, they had been soaked in water. They saw and passed by another group of workers separating the fiber from the stalks. The last process was the hackling. Finally, they came to her supervisor, Madreech who was giving instructions to a worker on how to weave the fiber into wicks to be used for lamps and torches.

The name of Deborah's late husband was Lapidoth, which means torches. He first started his business by making wicks and torches. In the process of time, he became known as the man of torches and Deborah became known as the woman of torches.

As they were walking back to the house, they had about another hundred cubits to go. Then Barak decided that he would ask Deborah about the two ladies who were walking about twenty-five cubits behind them.

"Deborah, I am curious...those ladies behind us have been following us for sometime. Something is wrong! You sent me a letter a short while ago and you didn't mention anything about the fact that you find me pleasing in your eyesight or that you missed me. Something is wrong! When I first arrived to meet you today, I held out my hands to hold yours and you refused my offer of affection. Something is wrong! Now, tell me...I beg thee, what's troubling you?" he pleaded looking her directly in the eyes.

"All right Barak. I'll tell you. I was going to tell you anyway before you departed...so this is as good a time as any," she revealed, being somewhat relieved.

"Thank you," Barak remarked looking a little pacified.

"This is not going to be easy Barak and it has left me with a lot of emotional pain. You must understand Barak, I am not really single."

"Not single?" he asked with surprise and confusion. "Go on."

"You've heard of levirate marriage, haven't you?"

"Yesss...Oh no...!" exclaimed Barak, realizing the point she was making, and shaking his head from side to side. "Are you saying that you are committed to marry your deceased husband's brother?" he asked expressing complete shock, as he threw his hand down and looked away.

"I am saying that."

"What is his name...? and why did he wait so long to decide to fulfill his obligation?"

"His name is...Caleb. I...I don't know...I mean I am not sure why he waited so long. I wrote him three times and asked him to either marry me or subject himself to halitza. The only reply he sent me was that he was busy and he would contact me soon. But he never did until over a month ago."

"Deborah, what is halitza?"

"Halitza is a ceremony in which the husband's brother must perform when he refuses to marry his dead brother's wife. The elders and judges send for him and speak unto him concerning his obligation, and if he still refuses, the dead husband's wife can come unto him in the presence of the elders. Then she loose his shoe from off his foot, and spits before him and say so shall it be to the man who refuses to build up his brother's house. 'And his name hall be called in Israel, the house of him that has his shoe loose.' "

"Do you love...this man?"

"Not in an emotional sense...but it is not...a question of love, Barak...it is a question of loyalty to the law...and the love of family."

"Well, since you don't love him, why don't you ask him to refuse and let him subject himself to halitza?" he added.

"That would be contrary to everything I believe in, contrary to what I teach, and contrary to my position as a judge. It would be like asking me to disregard the law of God that I am duty bound to obey. I couldn't do that. If I did, I would become a mockery to my people.

Barak took a deep breath and shook his head in dismay and anger. "Why in the name of heaven did Caleb wait so long to give you a definite answer? Why now? ...Why now Deborah?" he cried out as he walked between the palm trees and gave gestures with his hands.

"This is what I asked, also. There was something that slipped out in my conversation with Caleb," Deborah remembered.

"And what was that?" Barak asked as he turned around to her.

"When Caleb admitted to me that he neglected earlier to give me his definite decision, he also said. 'But I am here now, ready to fulfill the law. You see, our marriage can also increase and combine our assets and I can get out...' he said. "I said to Caleb, 'out of debt, you mean, don't you?' Barak, I told Caleb: 'I see, so you came here to make a proposal of marriage to help you get out of debt' "

"What was his response to that?"

"He said to me: 'The fact remains that you do have a legal obligation to marry me in spite of what you say my motive is.' I want you to understand Barak that I agreed to marry him not because I love him...not because I respect him...not even because I trust him... but, only, because it is my duty according to our custom and laws."

"Has a date been set for this so-called wedding?"

Deborah shook her head up and down in confirmation, and said: "You don't have to be sarcastic...! The marriage will take place five months from now."

They approached close to the walkway that led to the back gate of the house. The stone walkway was lined with pretty green plants on both sides. The plants looked like the green cactus. Barak stopped on the walkway, he looked defeated, lowered his head, scratched his eyebrow and commented: "There must be something we can do...something," he growled as he balled up his fist and hit the palm of his left hand. "Oh, we can hand this matter over to the seventy elder judges in Shiloh," he added.

"Barak..., I want to thank you for giving your attention to my problems and wanting to help me, but there is nothing else you can do at this time. Even if I handed this matter over to the seventy judges, and they ruled in my favor by nullifying a marriage with Caleb, the turmoil from this action would cause an uproar among my enemies."

"Before any more hair on my head turns gray, please explain to me how this...action would cause an uproar," my sister.

"If the court ruled in my favor, sooner or later, bad news would leak out that I bribed the court in order to free myself from marrying my deceased husband's brother, whom I didn't love."

"Mmm," Barak gasped.

"If this happens, my critics and enemies would say, when God's law is beneficial to her—she upholds it, and when it is not, she gets around it—so that she won't have to perform it. If this occurs, the court and I will loose the trust of the people and there will be a further breakdown of justice. I can't let this happen... Barak. The importance and righteousness of our laws are greater than I am. I must do the Lord's will first, and then I believe He will work out His purpose. Even though, we may not understand his purpose at first. Let's be patient Barak. Be patient my brother and place your hope in the Lord. Can you understand what I am saying?" she asked gently with compassion.

"Yes, I can understand...but it is hard for me to accept defeat...and to accept the fact that you are engaged to a man you don't love."

"Barak, if this is hard for you, it is harder for me, because I have to think about living with this man.... At least, you don't have...to live with him."

"Barak, I think that you should just forget about me. Go find yourself another woman who is not anchored by levirate marriage.

He turned around and faced her. "I don't want another woman. I want you!" he pleaded gesturing with both hands.

"Well, I an spoken for...so just go, and leave me be!" she said turning her back to him with her arm folded.

He approached close behind her and grabbed her by her upper arm. She squirmed and shook herself loose from him. He pleaded: "Please, please, please Deborah, ask me to do some crazy thing like...like to jump off the pyramids of Egypt...but, ask me not...to stop from wanting you, or stop from pursuing after thee, because my heart cleaves to you."

"You may want to give me your heart, but I cannot give you mine."

"Please Deborah, don't do this to me. When I am away from you... I think of you morning...noon...and nights."

"There are plenty of beautiful women in Galilee, discover them Barak...and they will help you to forget about me."

Barak moved quickly in front of her and continued to press her. "I told you that I want only you...! Can't you understand this...? Even if you had a twin sister, I would still want only you."

She looked up at him with her arms still folded in front of her. "I understand Barak, but you are the one...that don't understand. You forget that by our law and customs, I am obligated to Caleb. This...I cannot change!"

Barak stood there frozen and speechless, as if he had been struck by a snowstorm.

Then Deborah approached him softly and touched him gently on the back. "What is the matter Barak?" she inquired.

"What is the matter? You know what is the matter," he snapped. "I haven't felt like this," he said, "since the death...and loss...of my dear mother!"

There was a silence then she struggled to speak. "I am sorry Barak, but there is nothing...nothing I can do. I am so sorry!"

Barak turned around with a little consolation on his face. He reached his hand into his inner garment, and pulled out a leather pouch. "I brought something for you." He untied the thin leather cord and took out the necklace made from pure gold and diamonds.

She opened her mouth and eyes wide with disbelief and surprise. "Ohhh...Barak...it is beautiful, so beautiful," she said as she looked down at the necklace.

He pushed the necklace toward her. "Take it...! It's yours. Take it...!" he urged her.

She took hold of it. "It is so thoughtful of you Barak," she said smiling. Then her countenance changed quickly and her facial expression became serious. "Oh Barak, I can't accept this." She shoved the necklace back into his hands, turned around and broke down in tears, dropping her face into the palms of her hands.

Barak took several steps toward her. "Why?" he asked? "Why can't you accept it? I had this made with deep love!"

"But...I can't give you my love. Give it to someone else who can return your love."

"How can you expect me to give this necklace to another woman, when I had it made especially for you...and only for you."

Deborah seemed confused and she felt fluttery inside. Then she squirmed and labored to speak. "Well..." she said hesitantly and slowly. "I'll accept it under one condition...that you expect nothing from me, understood?" Barak nodded his head in acquiescence. "I want you to understand that I promise you nothing: no intimacy, no marriage, and no special favors."

Barak relaxed a little and explained. "I went through great sacrifice and effort to get this for you...and I want you to have something of mine."

"I understand," she said.

"Well...the day is getting late..." he said showing exhaustion in his voice.

She became silent again, and after a few moments, she spoke: " Oh, Barak, you mentioned earlier that one of the thieves you were searching for was a Canaanite who escaped to the city of Hazor. I just want to warn you that when Jabin and Sisera hear that you took your soldiers into the Jezreel, expect some reprisals."

"You are right Deborah, I had thought about that also. Your warning confirms my thoughts and I shall reinforce our security."

"I want to encourage you, Barak to continue to do good for humanity and this will multiply unto you the best in life. The good that you will do...will be written and remembered in the heavenly book of life...and when you are in dire straits, your Creator will come to your assistance," she explained as she turned away from him.

"Thank you Deborah, your words are very encouraging."

Deborah stood there with her back to Barak. She knew she could not tell him that she loved him. She knew that she could not let him kiss her nor embrace her because she was duty bound to the levirate law. She couldn't even let herself be obsessed with him because that would be a violation of the word of God.

Deborah turned slowly and faced Barak. As she opened her mouth to speak, her words weighted heavily on her lips. As she spoke, her lips quivered and tears ran down her cheeks. She said, "Take care of yourself Barak. I'll pray for you and for the safety of your soldiers, and keep me informed about the military situation. Go in peace and may God be with you."

Barak departed with a defeated look on his face—he lowered his head—then raised it, and said softly, "Peach be with you Deborah."

CHAPTER ELEVEN

In the fortress city of Harosheth-Hagoiim, the high officials of this Canaanite stronghold began to gather for a very important meeting summoned by King Jabin. After all of the officials of state had assembled, King Jabin marched toward his polish copper throne with his escort and soldiers.

The name Jabin was a title used by various kings of the city of Hazor. After Joshua, the successor of Moses burned the city of Hazor, some of its people escaped from Hazor in Upper Galilee and fled westward to southern area of the Carmel mountain range not far from the Kishon River.

It was here that the Canaanite expert builders constructed a city fortress in the forest and named it Harosheth-Hagoiim. The kings of Harosheth retained the title Jabin and retained the name Hazor, no doubt, for prestigious reasons because Hazor was the head or capitol of many Canaanite cities before Joshua destroyed it.

"Attention in the name of the King," proclaimed the crier. King Jabin sat down on his throne wearing a purple toga with a golden border draped around his shoulders. He was already past seventy years of age, and in good health. Then he turned to his ministers of state.

"Some of you are aware of why we are here today and some may not be. So at this time, I shall have my commander-in-chief of the army give you a complete report. To my left is General Sisera."

General Sisera stepped forward three cubits and began: "I shall set aside the introductions and get right to the point." The General was passed sixty-five years of age. Then he spoke. "We are here today to discuss the Hebrew problem. The situation has reached a new critical level," he said as he stroked his baldhead.

"Keep it short as you can," the King reminded him.

"Yes my Lord. The Hebrews are increasing in alarming numbers and they are pushing into the valleys. Our patrols are having more and more fights with the Hebrews. Recently, one of our spies reported that this...Barak; a mountain fighter, brought his soldiers into the Jezreel against the King's orders. Finally, Oh King, there are reports that a new leader is rising among the Hebrews," Sisera said reluctantly.

And what is his name?" the Vizier asked holding a map of Canaan in his hand.

The General was reluctant to mention the name because of fear that he would be ridiculed.

"What's wrong with you General? Speak up! Can't hear you," the King ordered as he sat upright on his throne.

"Deborah," he repeated louder.

"That's a woman's name!" the Vizier commented. "Are you sure?" he asked as the people laughed.

"I am as sure as Mount Carmel is outside," he answered.

The King said, "The name Deborah means bumblebee. Be careful less she lay her sting on you...and the Canaanite nations."

The Vizier took three steps to the right, and then returned. "Tell us, if you will, something about this...female!" he instructed as he struck the rolled-up map into his other hand.

"She is a judge...and a teacher of the laws and customs of her people," he pointed out slowly....

"Is there anything else?" he probed as he looked down at the stone marbled floor.

"There is...I hear that she is a prophetess." Sisera added.

"Prophets and prophetesses are dangerous folks. Have you heard anything concerning what she prophesizes?" asked the King.

"The only thing that I've heard is that she chastises her people and tells them to repent, to return to the laws of their God, to give to the poor, to help the widows, to help the fatherless, and to treat the strangers kindly. She teaches that our practice of marrying our daughters and sisters is an abomination before God. She says that the Canaanite gods, Baal and Ashtaroth, are idols and that the Hebrews should stop worshiping them."

"Blaspheme, blaspheme," yelled the High Priest who wore a large green mitre on his head. "We cannot let these Hebrews get away with this."

"That's right! That's right! That's right!" responded all the ministers of state at once as they looked at each other.

The King stood up quickly with his golden turban-like crown sparkling. "I see that we have complete agreement in the Grand Hall of the Canaanites," he said as he sat down pulling aside part of his toga behind him.

"General Sisera, are you finished?"

"No my Lord. I have one more thing to add..."

"Let's hear it."

"Our spies inform us that this woman, Deborah, tells her people that if they obey their God, He will send them a deliverer. This deliverer, she said, will crack the jaws of Jabin and his army."

"Did you hear that?" commented the King looking irritated. "Her words are pregnant with the seeds of insurrection...."

"I agree my Lord, the King."

"Thank you Sisera. I have heard your report and I have listened to you carefully. We must use cunning in dealing with the Hebrew problem that is growing larger and larger among us everyday. In view of this, this is what I propose. I want you to form yourselves into three groups and do a through study on the best way we can deal with the Hebrews. I don't care about what plan you come up with, just come up with one. My Vizier will head the first group, the High Priest the second and General Sisera, you will head the third. Are there any questions...If not, report back to me in three weeks."

***

Now, at this time, the season was moving towards middle winter and as usual, the winter manifested itself by plenty of rain in Israel. It had been raining for seven days without stop. As Deborah awoke on this particular day, she wondered whether or not it was still raining. She usually met three times a week with visitors to discuss their various problems and to hand down decisions in dispute. This morning was one of those days. Deborah got up and opened the window and saw that it was going to be a clear bright day. The people would be coming in so she quickly got dressed and finished all particulars. This morning was the tenth day of the Hebrew month of Shevat (equal to January 30th), and it was her fortieth birthday.

After she finished breakfast, she walked toward the study room and bumped into the side of the door.

"My Lady, you appear a little tired today," commented Sarah, her handmaid. "Maybe it would be better to have public meetings just twice a week instead of three times, and that would give you more time to rest."

"Thank you Sarah, but I'll be all right. It's a mental thing...you know...mind over matter. You see Sarah, when we came into this world, we came to learn our lessons in life, to grow spiritually and to help others. I am trying to do what I can."

"Well, you are surely doing just that I must say," Sarah admitted as she tightened her white apron around her waist.

"Sarah, before I go to prepare for this morning's meeting, I would like to make a point. When my soul leaves my body and pass over to my departed ancestors and finally, to God, then, my body that I leave here on earth will have plenty of time to rest."

"My Lady, you are as deep as a well of water," Sarah said as she walked away looking deep in thought.

Whenever Deborah had a meeting scheduled, she would place a piece of papyrus on the table so that when the people came in, they could write their names down. Then the attendees would be called on a first come and first serve basis. The only deviation from this procedure was when there was a very pressing mater that had to be dealt with right away.

After a while, the people started coming—men, women, some with their children, young adults and older ones. Deborah came in later with two of her handmaids, two male servants and one of them was Nachshon. These men helped keep order and they could handle themselves very well because they were trained in the army of Shamgar, the last judge.

When Deborah entered, she gave the general greeting of *shalom* (peace) and smiled. She completed her introductory remarks and Sarah called out the first name on the list. After Deborah had finished answering the questions of the first two names on the list, she went to the third.

"The next name on this list is Shemurah of the tribe of Judah," said Sarah, as she looked around the crowd for her to answer.

"I am Shemurah, excuse me my dear sister for not responding right away. First of all, I want to thank Sister Deborah for having these important hearings. These meetings permit us to get our questions answered by someone who knows our holy writings. I live near the city of Jebus where the Jebusites dwell and my son met a Canaanite girl he wants to marry. Since she is not Hebrew, can my son marry her?"

"Is that the young lady and your son sitting next to you? Deborah probed to get all the facts.

"Yes, this is my son Adam, and over here is his friend, Tamar." Tamar had smooth skin. She reflected the radiance of the full moon, and the purity of the springtime. Also, she had a tender loveliness that mesmerized.

"She is very beautiful and I get a very good feeling about her. Tell me...Tamar, where are your parents?"

"They are in the city of Jebus."

"Do they know that you are here?"

"No! My parents put me out two months ago and I now live with Mrs. Shemurah."

"In one sense," said Deborah, "You are fortunate; your father could have given you up to be sacrificed for a price," she pointed out softly... "I want you to forgive your father."

"That's hard," Mother Deborah..."but, I'll try."

"Why did they put you out, my dear?"

"My family is very poor, and there are thirteen brothers and sisters. My father said to me, many times, that he would put me out as soon as I reached child bearing age," she cried as tears ran down her dark brown cheeks.

Deborah paused a moment so that Tamar could get herself together. Tamar wore a beige color shawl over her head, which drooped, over her shoulders.

"Tamar, how did you meet Adam and Mrs. Shemurah?"

"I first met Adam in the market place where I went to buy food for my mother. Here we use to meet from time to time and talk. On the day that my father put me out, he said to me: 'You are a woman now, you can earn a living for yourself. I can not afford to take care of you any longer, but here is a few coins to help you get started.' As I left the house, my mother stood at the door and watched me leave without saying a word."

"I wondered around the market place until almost sunset and then, started down the road not knowing where I was going, but just going. That's when I met Mrs. Shemurah. She saw me crying and asked what was troubling me. I told her my situation and she invited me to stay with her," Tamar said as she wiped the tears from her eyes.

Deborah took a deep breath and sighed. Tamar's story was so touching that it struck at the core of her humanity. She knew that she had to answer Shemurah's question, could her Hebrew son marry a Canaanite girl? "There is an answer to the question, but it was not easy, she thought." The answer had to be given in a compassionate and prudent manner, if not, she would be heaping more hurt on the top of existing hurt.

She began, "We all are stricken with grief of the rejection that this poor young lady has suffered by the hands of her father, and we feel your pain. Will you please come up front?"

"Are you speaking to me," asked Tamar.

"Yes," Deborah said holding out her hand. When Tamar arrived up front Deborah took hold of her hand and drew her close. "Are you feeling better now?"

"Yes!" Tamar answered looking shy as she cast her head down.

"You see Tamar, every nation and people have their laws and customs and they are different from one another. Now, the Hebrew laws are very different from most nations." Deborah then took her hand and placed it around her shoulders. "Tamar, my dear, the Hebrew law is very clear on the point of marriage. It states that we shall not give our daughters to other nations to marry, nor shall we take their daughters for our sons," she said to her softly and gently as she pulled Tamar close to her.

With her head lowered, Tamar lifted her head and eyes slightly and said, "I love Adam! Is there something I can, at least...do?" Adam was a handsome, strong looking young man with a serious look on his face.

"Well...there is one thing...but you would have to make a sacrifice," Deborah assured her.

"Mother Deborah, what do you mean by that?" asked Tamar looking puzzled.

"You would have to give up something in order for a marriage to take place. By that, I mean you would have to study about our laws and customs for at least one year. Second, if you find that our God and laws are acceptable to you, at last, you would be asked to give up the graven images of Baal, Ashtaroth, and other gods with which you were raised."

"Would there be some kind of a ceremony after the one year training period?"

"You would have to stand before our priests and elders and they would ask you questions about our laws and customs. After that, you would be required to take an oath testifying to the fact that you believe in the invisible God of the universe and the law that He gave unto his servant Moses, the prophet. Finally, you would have to under go purification. This include the taking of a ritual bath and then rinsing or immersing the entire body under pure rain water collected in a pool. When all of this is completed, you will be accepted as one of us, just as Zipporah the Midianite, wife of Moses was accepted among us. Does this seem like something you... would want to do?"

"Yes!" Tamar answered without hesitation.

"Now, you don't have to make a quick decision today!" Deborah explained, "You can take your time...and think about it my child."

"Mrs. Deborah, I thank you, but in all due respects, I don't need to think about it because I have lived with Mrs. Shemurah for the last two months, and she lives a very righteous life. So, if it is all right with you and Mrs. Shemurah, I stand ready to begin my studies."

"All right...it is your decision my dear." At that climatic moment, Shemurah and her teenage son, Adam, ran up front and embraced Tamar and Deborah. Mrs. Shemurah and her son thanked her for all her help.

"Deborah, you were just wonderful. You handled yourself well," Shemurah said as her husband walked up.

He confirmed the words of his wife. "Now, I can understand why many people like you, and say good things about you. I had to see for myself and I am astonished at your knowledge, wisdom and the spirit of the Lord that abides in you."

Before Shemurah and her family departed, Deborah made arrangements for Tamar to meet with her once a month to review her studies. Moreover, Deborah informed Shemurah that if Tamar needed a job, she could come and work on her estate.

***

Not too far away in the city of Hebron, the elders and princes of the southern Hebrew tribes of Simeon, Benjamin, Dan and Judah held an important meeting. The subject of the meeting was to discuss the rising star of Deborah, which they considered a threat to their authority.

Prince Abihu of the tribe of Judah had just completed the welcoming ceremony for the meeting. "All of you have been informed of why we are here," said the thirty-five year old Prince, wearing a dark blue toga. "Now, feel free to voice your opinions."

"This woman...Deborah...as they call her...is taking away from us the loyalty of our people. Something should be done about it," stressed the Prince from the tribe of Dan.

"Yes, more and more of our people are ignoring us," shouted several others.

Then the Prince of the tribe of Simeon came forward.

"There are some people who call her a prophetess. Where is it written in our holy books that a woman can be a prophetess? This kind of behavior is insulting to us. Are we going to let a mere woman take the leadership of the tribes?"

"No! No!" they shouted.

"The leadership of the tribes belongs to the tribe of Judah. Is it not written that the '*scepter shall not depart from Judah...?*' " Prince Abihu asked them. Then he continued. "After the death of Joshua, the children of Israel asked the Lord saying '*who shall go up first against the Canaanites to fight against them? And the Lord said Judah shall go up.*' You see...the leadership belongs to the tribe of Judah and we cannot let a woman humiliate us."

Then the Prince of the tribe of Benjamin turned toward the crowd. "If we let her get away with this, we will loose control of our women and they will follow in her footsteps."

"Well, what can we do?" Another asked.

"I'll get to that in a moment," answered Prince Abihu. "Our spies have reported to us that Barak has been seen at least twice at Deborah's estate. They must have some kind of an alliance set up, or a romantic interest, or both."

"But, what can we do?" asked the twenty-five year old Prince from Benjamin.

Abihu then looked down; he thought and then, raised his head. "I can think of two things: One, we can send a letter to Deborah expressing our dissatisfaction with the way she is placing herself in a man's role. Two, we can send a letter to Barak asking him to come to me to answer certain questions. After that, we shall know whether or not we can support his war efforts."

"Yes...that sounds good to all of us," they all shouted in confirmation.

"Good!" Then Abihu said, " I'll have my scribe to write the letters **tonight**."

CHAPTER TWELVE

Three weeks later in the fortress city of Harosheth-Hagoiim, which was nicknamed Hazor, the high officials of King Jabin began to assemble for the second important meeting. It was three weeks earlier that King Jabin had appointed three groups to come up with the recommendations to deal with the Hebrew problem. Now, these groups were ready.

King Jabin was a hugh muscular man who sat on a throne made of polished copper. The throne was covered with animal skins dyed in purple and scarlet. On both sides of it, stood guards with spears and swords. The King had a dark brown complexion with bulging cheeks

The first order of business on this day was the receiving of the ambassador of Ethiopia. After this had been finished, the King summoned his advisors and the three groups to come in. Before he opened the meeting, he asked the High Priest to render a short prayer: "Oh Baal, our god, praise be thy great name. May thy might and power continue to possess the entire earth. And give us strength and wisdom to overcome our enemies, the Hebrews."

"We all know why we are here today so without further delay, we shall hear from my Vizier Mashchit.

"My Lord, the King, I recommend that we impose more taxes on the Hebrews, and if they don't pay, confiscate their property and put them into hard labor.

"Point number two: Let the King send out a decree that states that if any Hebrews bring any of their flocks into the Jezreel Valley, the flocks will be confiscated.

"Point number three: I recommend that the King offer one hundred talents of gold for information leading to the capture of Barak.

"Point number four: About this woman called Deborah, I recommend that we send out additional spies to keep a close watch on this queen bee. A queen bee like her could be dangerous to us, oh King."

"I'll give that some consideration," the King added. "Now, I want to hear from General Sisera."

The General stepped forward in full uniform with his sword on his side, saluted the King, and removed his gold helmet. "My Lord, I am in favor of a complete declaration of war against the Hebrews that are north of the Jezreel Valley."

"Why do you recommend war at this time?" inquired the King as he leaned forward.

"Because, now, it would be easier to destroy them while they are weak. Everyday that we delay, they will increase in numbers and skill."

"Why haven't Barak and his men been caught?"

"There are two reasons my Lord. For one thing, he is as fast as lightening, and that's what his name means. Two, he manages to avoid our larger units on level ground, where our chariots are most effective. Instead, he fights mostly in the mountains, hills, in gullies, and ravines where it is very difficult for us to use our horses and chariots against him."

"If that is the case, we must set a trap for him and lure him out into the opening." commented the King as he rested his head on his left hand sitting on his throne.

"Another thing my Lord, recently, my spies informed me that there has been contact between Deborah and Barak."

"Mmmm, interesting," the King muttered. "How was this contact made?"

"A horseman was seen receiving something from Barak and he went to the house of Deborah."

After listening to Sisera's words, the King commented, "Have your men to continue to watch these two rising leaders."

"It is done my Lord."

"Now, I want to hear from our High Priest, Eved-Baal, who is the servant of Baal, our god. He wore a green mitre on his head decked with silver and precious stone.

The entire hall of officials gave him a big applause as he walked in the direction of the King. "My priests and I have studied the records of the nations that had contact with these Hebrews. These nations are the Egyptians, the Midianites, the Moabites, and the Assyrians. We have checked their records to see how these nations dealt with the Israelites. Our search led us to a very interesting conclusion, oh King...."

"And what might that be?" inquired the King, as he leaned forward from his reclining posture.

"We found out that they can be conquered, easier, if we can get them to sin against their God."

"How do you know this?" the King asked.

"Well...we have learned this from one of the books of the Hebrews, called Deuteronomy. In this book, it is written that if the Hebrews didn't keep the commandments of their God, He will curse them."

"In which way would their God curse them?"

"With famine, with disease, with destruction of their cities, with oppression, with captivity, with slavery, with mental suffering and more."

"You mentioned that you had searched out the histories of such nations as the Midianites and the Moabites. Tell me, what did you find?" the King asked eagerly.

"After reading the histories of these nations, we read that Balak, the King of Moab, summoned the leader of the Midianites to discuss how they could deal with the Hebrews, because they were afraid of them. Finally, they decided to call Balaam of northern Mesopotamia to put a curse on the Hebrews. After Balaam arrived, he told Balak that he could not curse Israel because they were blessed."

"Why were they blessed?"

"They were blessed for the very reason that their God didn't find any iniquity among them nor had He seen any corruption in Israel. In other words, my Lord, they were living right and they could not be cursed. But, soon there after, everything changed. Finally, Balaam explained to the Midianites and Moabites how they could get Israel to sin...."

"Go on, High Priest."

"The Moabites did according to the words of Balaam," explained the High Priest. "They brought out the most beautiful seductive Moabite and Midianite women, and the Hebrew men gave into them. After that, these women called the Hebrew men to the service of their god and the Hebrews bowed down to them, and corrupted themselves in the eyesight of their God.

"According to the Hebrew and Midianite scrolls, the God of the Hebrews became angry and He sent out a plague that killed over twenty thousand Hebrews for their iniquities."

"Very interesting," said the King. "I want to thank you and your associates for the fine work you have done. Is there anything else?"

"Yes my Lord. These Hebrews came into our country over one hundred and fifty years ago under the leadership of a man called Joshua, and they have been taking our land ever since. They are like the ox that licks up the grass. They must be stopped or else they will take all the land of the Canaanites, destroy us, and destroy our culture including our gods."

"What do you suggest we do to get the Hebrews to commit iniquity?" asked the Vizier.

"We can put on festivals in various cities and invite the Hebrews to come. Then get our women to lure them into dancing, drinking, and you know what will follow next: The ladies will seduce them to drink and to eat creeping things." After that, the Hebrews will worship our gods."

"What else can we do to weaken, and destroy the Hebrews?" asked General Sisera.

"We can use an old plan called divide and conquer. We can sew the seeds of jealousy and hatred among the various princes and heads of the Hebrew tribes, by taxing one leader and not taxing another. By doing this, we can create discord and distrust among the tribes and families. This can be achieved by giving gifts to those families who worship our gods, Baal and Ashtaroth. This will make one family feel that it is better than another. In doing this, we will weaken the families and communities and produce more disunity."

"Excellent!" hollered the King.

"Ah...my Lord...one more thing. This...this woman Deborah, I think that something should be done about her."

"Are you afraid of a mere...woman?"

"Yes! Somewhat! I am fearful of what she can do to our nation, to our people, and to our gods. Her rapid growth in a man's world is a dangerous omen in itself," the High Priest said looking disturbed.

"Do you think that this mere...woman can rise to be a leader over the Hebrews?" asked the King."

"Yes...! We remember the rise of Queen Hapshesut in Egypt. She became the supreme ruler of the land because the gods favored her. It is very possible...that Deborah can rise also."

"I shall have my spies keep a close eye on her, if this will please you."

The King stood up on his feet. After that, he walked back and forward three times in front of his throne, looking down in deep thought with his hands behind his back. He stopped in front of his throne and faced toward his ministers and spoke. "Our plan will be to weaken and to destroy the Hebrews. We shall put into action various methods to get the Hebrews to sin against their God, and I will leave those methods up to you to implement. Are there any further comments or questions...? If there aren't, you are now free to proceed with the implementation of our plans."

After the meeting, the three groups went to work right away, discussing reviewing and putting the finishing touches on their plan to corrupt and destroy the Hebrews. According to the King, this was a matter of urgency and was to be put into action in a few days. First, they decided to carry out their plan against the Hebrew village near the city of Nahalol.

***

In the meantime, far in the Zebulun hills, Barak was relaxing in his tent. Then Barak heard the approach of a fast running horse. He quickly stood up and looked through the opening. There he could see a young man riding through his camp. The rider said. "I have a letter for General Barak. Where is he?"

"You are looking at him. Who sent the letter?"

"It is from my Lord, Prince Abihu," answered the young man as he dismounted his ebony colored horse.

"Oh yes, Prince Abihu...I've been waiting to hear from him. Finally, he has written to me."

Barak took the letter and began to read:

'To my fellow Prince Barak, Shalom lha (peach be unto you) I hope you are well these days. I shall not trouble thee with the small talk and get right to the heart of the matter. I have met with the elders and princes of the southern Hebrew tribes to consider your request for our soldiers. I would like for you to come to Hebron to meet with me so that I can be able to make a final decision. I do expect to see you soon. Signed, Abihu Ben Abinadab

After Barak finished reading the letter, he lowered the letter to his waist, raised his head and smiled. He thought—could it be that Prince Abihu was now going to supply Judean soldiers to help him fight the Canaanites. This was the moment he was waiting for and he was optimistic. He could not wait to return to the city of Hebron to meet with Abihu, the Prince of the largest tribe among the Hebrews.

CHAPTER THIRTEEN

The cool rainy winter passed and the warm bright spring came. It was the season of the first great festival that commemorated the liberation of 'the Hebrews from Egyptian slavery known as the Passover. Deborah was expected to be at this Passover to be held at the city of Shiloh and she had planed to give a speech. A month earlier, she had sent letters to all the tribes informing them that she had a special message for them.

Of course, the males didn't need an invitation to come to the Tabernacle on Passover, the Feast of Weeks, or on the Feast of Booths. God commanded all males to do so, but it was optional for females. This was one of the busiest festivals of the year. The roads were crowded with thousands of pilgrims going up to the Tabernacle. There were pack animals loaded down with food and drinks to last them for seven days. In addition, there were sheep and goats to be slaughtered at the Tabernacle, and its fat burned on the altar, the blood sprinkled at its base and each head of the household took the lamb or goat to his quarters and roasted it.

"Where is Deborah? Have anyone seen her?" the people asked. There was no positive answer, and many people shook their heads in disappointment, and much worry. "Deborah said that she would be here, but she is not," explained a middle-aged woman. Some people shook their heads again, then, went on with their regular business.

This was a great time for the celebration of freedom from oppression in Egypt. The priests and the Levites blessed and sang psalms of praises to the Lord and the people responded in the proper manner.

On the second day of Passover—also known as the Feast of Unleavened Bread, Deborah was expected to speak at the plaza outside of the Tabernacle. This feast would give an opportunity for Deborah and Barak to speak to many people from every tribe at once. Both of them knew that the Hebrew-Canannite crisis was getting worse. It was getting worse at a time when the Hebrews were celebrating their freedom from slavery in Egypt. It was just three weeks ago that King Jabin and his advisors devised a sinister plan to corrupt and destroy the Hebrews.

Finally, Deborah showed up with her bodyguard and handmaid, Sarah. As she walked through the crowd, going up front, the people greeted her with kind words and warm smiles. "We are so happy to see you Deborah; we were concerned about you," said a young lady.

"Thank you," she said. "I was in prayer and meditation."

After the priests had completed the morning service and sacrifices on the second day of Unleavened Bread, the people gathered in the plaza to listen to Deborah, Barak and the elders. A representative of the high priest spoke then Barak and a few elders. Deborah was the last person to speak. She felt a little nervous among all the men, but then she realized that she had to be strong like Sarah, Abraham's wife and Miriam, the sister of Moses. Also, she knew that the Lord was using her for a special purpose.

"Shalom Shalom alaychem. Peace, peace be unto you brothers and sisters of the various tribes. First of all, I want to give thanks and praise to the Lord our Creator for giving us life and strength. Moreover, it is pleasing in my heart to give thanks to all the priests, Levites and elders for their untiring service they have given for our people. I

would like to say that my uncle Yoetz, who sat on the Supreme Court of the seventy elders would have loved to have been here, but he is now pass one hundred and five years old and very weak."

"Yes, we know him," said several of the elders respectfully.

"As many of you know," she continued, "we are here to celebrate the feast of the Unleavened Bread. It was at this time several hundred years ago that the Lord our God brought out our ancestors from Egyptian oppression. However, our people today, especially the northern tribes, are suffering under a new oppression of Jabin, the king of the Canaanites. As of this month, it has been twenty years since Jabin and his General Sisera imposed their persecution upon us."

"Mm!" Many of the people sighed looking at one another.

"Within the last two weeks," she explained further with eloquence. "We have seen the worsening of the tension between the Canaanites and us. They have increased their patrols in the Hebrew territory. They have imposed higher taxes on top of existing taxes and those of us who cannot pay; they place in hard labor. Furthermore, they are doing everything that they can to get our people to convert to their pagan customs and to worship their idols.

"I want to encourage all of you to resist the efforts of the Canannites I have talked to the elders about this and we want you to fast, to pray fervently, cry out and pour out your souls in sincerity to God, and He will save us. I feel that war is coming and I want you to be prepared. I feel this very strongly. If we do this, our deliverance will come soon. I promise you this in the name of our Creator and in the name of our ancestors. In closing, I want all of you to pray everyday and I shall pray for you and all of our people. Remember...that the enemy from within is far greater than the one from without. This means that we are our own worse enemy."

As she finished her speech, the people gave a great applause and they shouted, *"hallelujah, hallelujah, hallelujah"* as she descended the platform. Her bodyguard, Nachshon and Sarah her handmaid were waiting for her as she stepped down. There were thousands of people in the plaza. Then Barak went over to her to congratulate her on her speech. She was most thankful for that and gave him a big smile. Many people crowded around her, greeted and began to ask questions. Also, one of the senior elders, Ariel, came over and stood by her. He was ninety years old. At that moment, the people began to ask questions.

"Deborah, may I ask you a question?" asked an old lady.

"I am here at your service," she answered.

" Will God send us a deliverer like Ehud and Othniel?" asked the old lady.

"Yes, I believe He will when our people become more spiritual."

Another lady rose up on her tiptoes, and asked. "We have been waiting for our deliverance for almost twenty years, and it has not come...Why?"

"We are not ready yet.... The sins of our people have caused God to hide His face from the tribes of Israel. The Lord wants sincerity of heart, not talk. What Benefit is there to be free from one bondage and then go into another! This is like being saved on one day, from the tiger...and on the next...day, you fall into the claws of the bear."

"What can we do Deborah?"

Deborah took a deep breath, and answered. "Put away your idols and serve the Lord. Speak, every man, the truth to his neighbor. Act with justice in all your dealings. Give to the widows, the fatherless, and the poor. Behave kindly to the strangers and walk humbly before God and your fellowman."

"These words, which you speak, I have been doing for many years," a middle-aged man pointed out. "Is there more for us to do? Is there more, Deborah?"

"Yes, much more. The Lord wants more of you to give more. I am talking about, not only material things, but nonmaterial things, such as: giving a smile, giving conversation, giving a listening ear, giving a helping hand, giving a kind word.... In short...with your willingness to give what you seek for yourself...you keep the abundance of the divine universe flowing in your lives, because the energies of the universe flow in powerful exchange.... This means, that you will be blessed."

"Talk on Deborah," yelled a woman from the rear of the crowd, "*hallelujah.*"

"When you give in these ways to humanity, you will be expressing true love to all of Adam's descendants, and goodness and success will come back to you. This is what the Lord meant when He said, 'Love thy neighbor as thyself.'"

A young lady about twenty cubits back in the crowd yelled. "Is this what our first great prophet taught?"

"Yes! Our prophet Moses taught that if you would keep all of the Lord's commandments and instructions, that all the blessings of the universe will come to you. Because, what goes around, comes back around whether it be for evil or good. If you put out evilness, evilness will return to you. If you put out goodness, goodness will return to you. This is the universal law of God."

As Barak looked over the crowd, he saw a man with a pot- belly pressing his way forward through the crowd. Because the man looked suspicious, Barak moved closer to Deborah to be of help if she needed it.

At that moment, the man shouted out a question. "Who are you? I never heard of you before."

Deborah took a deep breath and remained calm, then spoke. "I am Deborah Lapidoth, a woman of God, and a daughter of Israel."

"I know that...! But...

Barak interrupted him, "If you know that...why did you ask?"

Then the people roared out in laughter at the man. Finally, the crowd became quiet, and the fat belly man spoke up again. "Shouldn't you be at home cooking and washing dishes?"

Deborah knew that the man had insinuated that she was out of her place. Nevertheless, she remained confident, and spoke calmly. "At one time, I did these things as my everyday duties. But now, since the Lord has helped me, I have servants and workers to assist with these chores. Now, I can dedicate my life to helping others to attain higher spiritual heights."

The fat belly man looked defeated and spoke again. "One more question."

"Are you looking for trouble," Barak snapped.

"No...! I'm looking for an answer. I am here to have a good time. Isn't that what this festival is all about?" he asked looking around the crowd for support.

"You may speak," consented Deborah.

The fat belly man continued. "You said for us to give more. My wife and I give tithes to the priest. We have twenty sons and daughters to feed, and she gives to the poor. As it is, I don't get enough to eat. What shall I do?"

"Well, You don't look any thinner to me!" Barak snapped as the crowd roared again in laughter.

Deborah smiled at Barak's response then asked the man a question. "Do you have any sheep or goats?"

"Yes...I have one hundred fifty"

"Keep giving and next year you will have more than two hundred."

"What's going to happen next year?"

Deborah looked at him with surprise. "I thought you knew! There will be a mating of your sheep...and God will bless you."

Moments later, a young man raised his hand and remarked, "We are now in this land, we speak the Hebrew language, we have our princes and elders, and lastly, we have our customs, rituals, and our nationality. I feel that we have everything. What do you think?"

"There are more important things then just knowing your history, language, culture, and nationality. Our main purpose here on earth is to serve humanity and not just be religious, but above all, to be spiritual."

"Spiritual? What is the difference between being religious and being spiritual?" asked the young man.

Deborah took a deep breath and relaxed her shoulders. "A religious person is one who keeps the beliefs and practice the ceremonies of their religion in the home or the house of worship. But, a spiritual man or woman has a pure heart. They are in tune with God everyday, and they don't hold feelings of jealousy, anger, resentment, grudges, negativity, nor hatred in their heart against any person. The spiritual person loves mankind, in a pure way, without conditions. This is what the Lord meant when he said...to be a 'holy people.'"

"Mother Deborah, when I am nice to some people, they treat me evil in return. What shall I do?" the young man asked.

"Continue to love them...no matter how long it takes. Your good conduct will eventually break the cycle of hate...and win them over to your side."

"This seems so hard with hateful people."

"Well, sometimes the best things in life come with difficulty...and remember, that true love is caring and sharing. Furthermore, I want to remind all of you that our great prophet taught that you should strive to be a holy people, and love thy neighbor as thyself. Now, to express love in the true sense is to give something to another that is not for your immediate benefit, but it is for the immediate benefit of the other person."

At that moment, Elder Ariel turned to Deborah. "I am inviting Barak, you and your company to come to my house for lunch."

"Thank you Elder, but before I go, I want to say a few last words to the people."

"Indeed, go right ahead."

"People of the tribes of Israel," she said. "I am going to be leaving you soon. But, before I go, I want to encourage you to pour out your souls to God in prayer, meditation, and fasting. Remember everything I spoke to you today, if you take heed to these things, you will increase your spiritual vibrations and the Lord will hear your cry and the enemy will not be able to stand against you. May God be with you."

As Barak walked with Deborah to Ariel's house, he said to her, "you spoke very well today.... By the way, do you think...that young man back there will accept your advice?"

"I think he will...and he got it for free."

"Well, there is one thing about free advice...it's usually worth it."

She turned around and smiled at him. "Are you trying to be funny?" Then she hit at him in a playful way.

"Yes," he said, jumping out of her range.

As they walked towards Ariel's house, Deborah thought and remarked, "Oh Barak...I want to thank you for your support, back at the Tabernacle."

"I am glad I came...I wouldn't have missed that moment for all the gold in Ethiopia."

Finally, Deborah looked up at Barak with admiration, but her contenance changed when she realized that she was engaged to another man.

It was several days later at the city of Nahalol that the officials began to implement the diabolical plan of King Jabin, and Sisera. This plan was designed to corrupt and destroy the Hebrews, who lived in the village nearby. Then a Canaanite delegation came to the Hebrew village with their insidious scheme. The head nobleman named Nahash spoke to the Hebrew elders: "There has been harsh feelings between our people for many years...and we want to change this."

"Change this? How do you propose to make this change?" asked Elder Tamim.

The head nobleman pointed to five large baskets. "We have brought these victuals and gifts as a token of our sincerity and friendship," he said as he folded his arms in front of him."

"We do place value on your gifts," he said looking down and scratching his head. "But, with us, true friendship is determined by the actions of the heart, and not by valuables," the Elder stressed looking up.

"I agree, but we must start somewhere...and we have made the first start."

"Yes, you have," confirmed Elder Tamim.

The nobleman then, walked over to the Elder and touched him on the shoulder. "We have made the first move by coming to your village. We want you and your people to return the visit, by coming to a special festival at our city at noon two days from now.... This will give both of our people a chance to get to know one another and to build a better friendship."

Rolling his eyes and looking at his people, the Elder answered. "I'll have to think about this and talk it over with my people."

"Yes, we want you to talk it over, and we hope that your decision will be that you will come to the festival. We will see you then," said the noblemen as they bowed and departed.

After the noblemen left, the Hebrews discussed the invitation of the Canaanites. They discussed the issue for almost a half-day then they decided to go to the feast. Elder Tamim and those who dissented decided to go, reluctantly.

On the fourth day of the week, the small Hebrew community, of one hundred and fifty people came to the city of Nahalol. The Canaanites gave them a great welcome. After the mingling and chatting with the Canannites for a period of time, everyone began to eat and drink in the open plaza. There were all kinds of vegetables, fruit, nuts, meat and wine available. The wine was made from the finest red rapes grown in the rich Jezreel Valley.

Then Elder Nahash approached the pavilion and began to speak. "Citizens of our beloved city of Nahalol, our King is not able to be here today, but he has sent his greetings. He wants me to welcome you and our Hebrew neighbors to our city and feast. We hope that you will learn more about our custom, laws, and become a part of us in friendship. Now, everybody, fall in and have a merry time, and give the Hebrews plenty of wine that they can drink."

The music began to play in a louder and snappy tone. Then about twenty young ladies came out and started dancing in skimpy apparels. The ladies danced with intense, sexy gyrations and began to pull the Hebrew men into the dance.

"Come on handsome," said one lady.

Another said, "let's see what you can do." Then she grabbed a Hebrew by the hand. Before the Hebrews realized it, they were dancing before the idols of the Canannites, Baal and Ashtaroth.

After a while, the dancing stopped. At last, a trumpet blew to signal an announcement. The High Priest stepped forward to speak: "I welcome all of you here in the name of the King... Canaanites and Hebrews alike.... I

150

hope all of you have plenty of food and wine...and there is no end to our hospitality. At this time, I want to inform our Hebrew neighbors, that you can have anything...anything you want...for the satisfaction of your pleasures. Just feel free to indulge."

The head Hebrew, Elder Tamim, turned and spoke to his associate, "I am getting a chilly feeling about what I am hearing and seeing, and I don't like the looks of it."

"I agree," said one of the Elders."

" Spread the word around to our people to be on their guard," said Elder Tamim.

"Consider it done Elder."

As the people ate and drank, the High Priest continued to speak. "Now, while all of you have been standing here drinking and eating to the fullest, our god, Baal, has been neglected.... Is this right? Does not his hunger need satisfying?"

"Yes, yes," the crowd roared.

"Let the boys and girls be brought out and be sacrificed to our god, Baal." The statue of Baal stood on the summit of the highest place in the city. Baal sat on a large stone foundation. On his head, rested the helmet of a warrior with bull's horns projecting out on both sides. The attendees escorted the blindfolded boy and girl up the stone step to the god, Baal. As the boy and girl walked up the steps, they cried and screamed in fear: "I don't want to die." But, no one could hear them because of the loud sound of the drums and the flutes.

The Hebrews watched everything with disgust and contempt. Some said, "this is an abomination before God."

After the boy and the girl reached the top of the steps, the attendees laid the girl on a large flat stone to be slaughtered. The High Priest walked slowly to the flat stone, turned and took a sharp-pointed knife from the silver tray. The tray was covered by a red embroidered velvet cloth, which was carried by an assistant. He raised his left hand high above his head and proclaimed. "We dedicate these sacrifices to our god, Baal, and for the glory of the Canaanite people." Then he brought down the knife and stabbed the girl in the heart. She died instantly.

The facial expression of the Hebrews revealed that they could not stand to see the child killed and burned, as a result, they averted their eyes. Elder Tamim spoke to his associate again. "We are going to get out of here as soon as we can."

"This will not be easy.... We are surrounded by Canaanites and their ceremony is still in progress," said one of the elders. "If we leave now, they might consider it disrespectful." As the two Hebrews were talking in the crowd, the High Priest spoke to his assistant. "Take the girl to our god Baal." The god, Baal had a large opening in his stomach, with a hot fire burning from within. The assistant lifted up the girl and placed her in the fire and repeated the same process for the boy.

A few moments later, one of the noblemen shouted. "Let our neighbors, the Hebrews, bring forth a boy and a girl to be sacrificed!"

"Yes...yes...yes...let the Hebrews bring forth a sacrifice for our god, Baal," yelled the crowd.

The High Priest held up his hand for the crowd to be silent and looked down at the Hebrews. "Who among you will volunteer a son or daughter for a sacrifice to Baal?"

Elder Tamim stepped up and spoke. "We accepted the invitation to come here in order to bring friendship between us...not to bring about the death of our sons and daughters."

The High Priest leaned forward and pointed his finger with an outstretched arm.

"Do you think that you are better than us...that you can withhold your sons and your daughters from our god, Baal?"

152

"Tell me," asked Elder Tamim. "Is the flesh of the Canaanite children not good enough that you must, also, have the meat of the Hebrew children?"

"Our god, Baal, likes a change-up...every once in a while.... The Hebrew flesh...he would consider it a delicacy."

Elder Tamim took a deep breath and spoke: "Our God would consider it murder.... It is an abomination for us to worship another god and to sacrifice innocent children. We serve only the Lord, our God."

"Abomination?" asked the high priest. "Your god will not save you...Deborah and Barak will not save you...but our god will if...."

"Furthermore," interrupted Elder Tamim, "we have been tricked and allured into coming here. Now, it is time for us to leave."

"Wait...! We invited you here with good intentions. We opened the gates of our city for you...we showed you great hospitality...offered you everything that your souls could desire...and this is how you repay us?"

"I have stated my position...and I see, no need to repeat it...your Excellency. Now, if you will excuse us..." emphasized the Elder as he turned half way around.

"Wait! I'm not finished." The High Priest walked half way down the stone stairs and stopped. "Do you think that you can come here and show contempt for our god and our way of life...and get away with it...? Well, I had enough of you and your people. My patience is wearing out...Leave, leave! Go back to the woods from whence you came," he shouted with intense anger.

Elder Tamim starred at the High Priest with a serious face. Then turned around and departed with his people. As the Hebrews left, the Cananites gazed at them with anger and vengeance. Many Canaanites shook their fists at the Hebrews and others remarked, "You will regret this. You will regret this...! You will regret this!"

***

It was late at night when everyone was asleep that Sisera and his army marched into the Hebrew village near the city of Nahalol. The soldiers of Sisera approached the camp silently, then lit their torches. They began throwing their torches into the tents. When the Hebrews ran out of the tents frantically, the soldiers shot them with their spears and arrows.

"Burn! Burn everything...kill everybody," yelled Sisera, as he pranced his horse throughout the camp. "Leave no one alive. This is our revenge against the Hebrews for showing contempt for our gods."

A lady named Marah and her family was in a tent at the opposite end of the camp. "Quickly Marah, take the children and hide in the woods!" ordered her husband. At that moment, a spear struck him in his side.

"Oh my dear! You are hurt, I can't leave you."

"Go Marah! Leave me be; save the children."

As she was running into the bushes with the children, two arrows pierced the back of her son and daughter. When they fell down, she managed to pull them inside the bushes. She looked up and saw the entire camp in flames, clothing and blankets burning everywhere.

As she breathed in the air mixed with the heavy smoke that blew in her direction, she looked down at her children. They were failing fast. Then she murmured in anguish, "Oh Lord, my children are dying and there is nothing I can do." Then she heard a voice from one of the officers: "Is everyone dead?"

"I believe so lord Sisera."

CHAPTER FOURTEEN

It was in the spring of the year one week and a half after Passover, that Deborah awoke early just before dawn. She decided to say her prayers and do her meditation in the courtyard at the back of her house. On other occasions, she would do these metaphysical routines inside the house in a special room.

She sat down on a hamlet-like seat connected between two palm trees. As she breathed in the pure air of the morning mixed with the aroma of the palm and cypress trees; she had a wary feeling that this was going to be an unusual morning.

Then she began her prayers; but she didn't pray for herself—but for her people! She prayed that they would turn from their sins and she asked God to forgive them.

Now, it was time for her meditation. She closed her eyes and started inhaling and exhaling methodically with rhythm and pauses between breaths. She cleared her psyche of everything around her until her mind became blank. She sank deeper and deeper into a trance-like state. She felt light—like she had no physical body, but only an eternal soul. A soul tuned in with the eternal Father. The Lord spoke to her. "Deborah, Deborah, Deborah, I am the God of Adam, Noah, Abraham, and all the families of the earth. Send for Barak and tell him all the words I shall speak unto thee...."

After Deborah had heard all the words of the Lord, she came out of her trance-like state. She sat there for a moment and reflected on everything that the Lord told her.

Daybreak came and she could hear the chirruping of the birds. Her heart was heavy because of the words, which God had spoken to her and she knew that she had to carry out the command, which she received from God. Then she heard Sarah and Nachshon talking and she went over to them.

"*Shalom* Deborah, I see you are up early this morning."

"Yes. I was in the courtyard praying and...Oh Nachshon, make ready the fastest horse we have and send one of the workers to Kedesh of Naphtali and tell Barak, the son of Abinoam, that I want to see him at once"

"I'll do it right now," he said as he walked toward the gate.

"Uh...Nachshon, tell the rider not to take the open roads but use the round about way and watch out for the Canaanite patrols. Also, tell him to look for Barak at the Zebulun garrison."

The horse rider departed early that morning. Because he had sixty miles to travel to the garrison, it would likely take him an entire day. He would probably rest over night and get on the road with Barak the following morning, providing that Barak didn't have any pressing business to implement. This is what Deborah thought as she observed the rider glancing at the orange rising sun.

During the course of the day as Deborah was going about her business, she thought about Caleb the man she was duty bound to marry but didn't love. Then she thought about Barak the prince who liked her, also, she found him interesting. However, when he came around her, she tried not to encourage him, not even in the smallest way.

Now she was having internal conflict: The Lord had asked her to send for the very man she was trying to avoid. With him in her presence, he would only stir up internal emotions that she would rather keep suppressed.

Four or five months had passed since she had talked with Caleb and any day now, she was expecting to hear from him regarding their wedding plans.

All day and part of the night her mind reflected on and off about Caleb and Barak. She had to tell Barak what the Lord revealed to her and this would bring on a crisis for some of the northern Hebrew tribes. What she had to tell Barak, she wondered whether he'd accept it coming from a woman. Her whole life now was being inundated with the duty of her business, civic duties—and with the people coming to her with their problems. The situation of the marriage to a man she didn't love, and now what she had to tell Barak, all these things weighted heavily on her mind. The die had been cast, the Lord had spoken, and there was no turning back.

In the meantime, Seth, one of Deborah's workers, arrived at the Zebulun garrison. At that time, he told Barak that Deborah wanted to see him as soon as possible. He slept at the garrison during the night and the following morning they got up to travel south with a ten-man escort.

***

Barak had received a letter earlier from Prince Abihu of the tribe of Judah requesting the former to visit with him at his earliest convenience. In light of all of this, Barak decided that he would visit with Abihu first and then see Deborah later. When he arrived outside the city of Bethel, he instructed Seth to tell Deborah that he would come to see her on the following day.

He continued south to Bethlehem and slept there for the night. Little did he know that the future King David would be born here. He did not know that Bethlehem would be the birthplace of the future messiah of the Hebrew sects, of the Ebonites, Essenes, Nazarenes and the early Christians. He arrived on the outskirts of the city of

157

Hebron about twenty miles south of Jerusalem. Barak came here on the invitation of Prince Abihu because the latter wanted to discuss with him about supplying soldiers for Barak's army. Then, after these talks—Barak had planned, on his return trip—to stop by Bethel to see what Deborah wanted.

Now, Barak was at the northern entrance to the valley of Eshcol, which lead to the city of Hebron. Barak could see the city located on top of one of the mountains. As Barak rode southward, mixed feelings about Prince Abihu came upon him; yet, he rode onward, on this dreary and cloudy day.

It was now springtime and the entire valley was a beautiful site to behold with the mountains covered with green vegetation. Barak and his men rode pass the western slopes of the mountains first and drank water from the Brook of Eshcol. They could see that the northern entrance to the valley was very broad with many green vineyards, pomegranates, fig trees and olive gardens.

The shape of the valley ran from north to southeast. As Barak rode deeper into the valley going south, it became narrower and the peaks of the mountains got higher. Then one of Barak's'men asked, "general, can we visit the cave of Machpelah while we are here in Hebron?"

"Yes, I suppose so...I believe...it is on the east side of the valley," answered Barak hesitating. "Yes! my memory is coming back to me it is on the east side.

Suddenly, Barak remembered that the cave of Machpelah was the place where Abraham, Isaac, Jacob, Joseph and their wives were buried.

In later years, this cave became a holy shrine to Hebrews, Christians and Muslims alike.

When Barak and his men arrived at the eastern slope, they saw the cave.

"Beware," said one of the soldiers, "lest the ghost of Abraham, Isaac, and Jacob come out of the cave and haunt you." Because of those ironic words, several of the soldiers chuckled, and remarked, "don't be ridiculous." They dismounted their horses and bowed down to the ground and prayed. *"Ehoheynu elohey aboteynu, Elohey Abraham, Yishak, vi Yaakov..."*(Our God, the God of our fathers, the God of Abraham, Isaac and Jacob etc.) Everyone standing nearby could hear them praying. After the prayer and visit, they arose and rode over to the west side of the valley. On one of the slopes stood the mansion of Prince Abihu.

The house was made out of square stones and had a second story. Barak dismounted his horse and knocked on the front door leaving his men behind. A servant answered the knock. Barak said, "I came to see Prince Abihu."

"And who might you be?" asked the servant, looking at Barak from head to foot.

"Barak...Prince Barak!" he said with authority.

"My Master is busy at the moment, but you can wait for him."

The servant led Barak up the outside stairs that let to the second floor, and to the terrace.

As Barak stood on the terrace waiting for Prince Abihu, he overheard a conversation, coming from one of the adjacent rooms. The conversation was between Abihu and one of his tax officials, named Asa: "My Master, Prince Abihu, there are transgressors who commit robbery and murder in one town and flee to another. Something must be done about this."

"In what town did this take place?" asked Abihu.

"In the town of Arad, just south of here.... I recommend that you send soldiers to capture them."

Prince Abihu stroked his black beard slowly. "At the present time, I am busy dealing with the Philistine threat and trying to retaliate against these murderers."

"You always condemn the Philistines, who murder Hebrews,"Asa pointed out as he leaned forward gesturing, "but you say nothing when Hebrews murder one another. Why not my master? Why?"

Prince Abihu looked as if he was taken off guard; however, he managed to utter a few words: "The Philistines...are our old enemies...and even the warrior Shamgar had trouble with them...."

Abihu moved one step closer to Asa—and touched him on his upper right arm. "You must understand...my tax collector... that I must deal with the Philistine problem."

Asa turned away from him walking and talking. "No...I don't understand." Then Asa turned around and looked him in the eyes, "Is not the death of the Hebrews... murdered by other Hebrews...just as important as the death of the Hebrews murdered by the Philistines?"

"Yes! But..."

"Then why don't you do something to help stop the crime in our towns?"

"This should be the concern of the local elders," said Abihu.

"Local elders...? Elders...? I think that you should be concerned also.... These murderers flea from one city to another... this puts them out of the reach of the elders. You are the prince of our tribe, and you have the influence and jurisdiction over the whole tribe of Judah. If you act now, the people will follow you."

"Asa, I am taking action on behalf of the people.... I am saving them from the hands of the Philistines whenever I can," argued Abihu. Then he turned his back to Asa and faced the picture of a lion, which hung on the wall.

"That may be true..." said Asa, "but while you are saving us from the Philistines, who's going to save us from ourselves...?"

There was a pause, and Prince Abihu seemed stunned. At last he spoke softly. "I can't answer that."

" It seems that you don't have the will, nor the compassion to help save our people from themselves."

What makes you say that?"

"I have watched you. When a Hebrew is murdered by a Philistine, you go and visit the family of the slain, but when a Hebrew is murdered by another Hebrew, you pay no attention to the grieving family, even though the murder takes place right here in Hebron."

Prince Abihu turned around with intense anger. "You... offend me...and I have had enough of it. You may leave!"

Asa turned half way around to leave, but stopped. "I am not finished...just yet! I think I understand your motives.... Yes, it is becoming very clear to me.... You get most of your fame and money from our people by fighting a few Philistines. So catching Hebrew murderers have no interest to you. In the meantime, our cities sink in the mire of crime and hopelessness, while you fill your coffers with gold and silver. Isn't this the truth Abihu."

The Prince looked at him with disdain, "You may leave now!" he commanded.

"Why don't you be man enough to admit it.... I am waiting for an answer!"

"All right, you want an answer...? What prince wouldn't want fame and money?"

"That may be true, but I would hope that a leader would also want peace and brotherly love for his people. To me, this is the sign of a good leader."

Abihu stomped his foot on the floor like an earthquake, raised his fingers and pointed at Asa. "I don't need you to stand here and judge me. I've made you what you are...and I've paid you very well...and I will not tolerate any further insubordination from you...or anybody else. Now, leave before I...."

As Asa walked towards the door, he commented. "I hope you will change someday...before it is too late."

There was a silence, then Abihu spoke. "Wait!" Asa stopped then turned around slowly. "Why are you so hot

161

about a few dead Hebrews. You never questioned me before!"

"Because I was afraid that I would loose my position. But, I speak up now because one of the men who was murdered in the city of Arad was my brother. Another Hebrew murdered him. Now, his wife is a widow and his children are fatherless. As it stands now, I must support them, and do my best to be a father to his children," Asa said, as he left the room quickly.

After Asa departed, Prince Abihu sat on a stone bench with a soft cushion. He remained still and preoccupied. As Abihu sat in his room, his servant approached and spoke. "Prince Abihu, there is someone here to see you." Abihu remained silent and the servant spoke again. "My master, there is someone..."

"Oh...oh it's you.... I was in deep thought.... What is it?"

The servant bowed to the Prince and repeated. "There is someone here to see you, sire."

"He has a name doesn't he?" asked Abihu.

"Yes.... The man said that his name is Barak, and said that he is a prince."

After that, Abihu shouted with a loud voice as he raised his head suddenly. "Well...then respect him as one...and send him in!"

The servant stood there momentarily in a state of shock. After a moment he replied. "As you say my master." Then he bowed and departed.

When Abihu heard Barak approaching, he stood up. "Oh Barak, Barak...it has been months since I have seen you. How have you been?" he asked as he embraced Barak and patted him on the back. After the small talk and the smiles, Abihu led Barak back to the terrace. The floor of the terrace was made from granite stone. As Barak walked onto the terrace, he noticed the green plants and assorted purple and red lilies growing in the various large stone flower vessels.

Barak walked over to the stone banister and stood under the fronds of a palm tree that grew near the side of the terrace. Then he looked over the entire green valley. "Oh what beautiful country this is," he admired. Barak turned around and smiled at Abihu. "This is truly God's country," he commented.

"Yes! Barak...This country, which our ancestors inherited is indeed a land of milk and honey."

"And also a land of hills and valleys," Barak chuckled, "and dens and caves."

"You know Barak, this can be the beginning of a long friendship between us," Abihu said as he walked up and down with a smile on his face. But, Barak gave a frown, because he was not pleased with the conversation he overheard between Abihu and Asa.

Then Abihu clapped his hands giving a signal to one of his servants to bring in some refreshments. The servant brought in figs, dates, pomegranates, milk, curd, bread, wine, and honey. After they said the blessings, they dipped the bread in the honey. Next, they poured some wine in their silver vessels. Prince Ahihu held up his goblet in a toast fashion and commented: "To our long friendship."

At that moment, Barak responded with "Yes! And also to our success and happiness."

Abihu walked closer to Barak and said: "Barak, now...I think that we should get down to business and talk about why I sent for you. The last time you were here, you asked me to consider your request to supply soldiers for your army. This is pending on one condition." Abihu took Barak by the arm and guided him to the other side of the terrace. "You see Barak, I need your help!" Abihu pointed at Barak with his arm extended.

Barak looked confused, "My help? How can I...?"

"Well, you see...the situation is like this. Judah is the largest tribe and I believe that Judah should have the leadership over all the tribes...and I need you to help me to persuade the other northern Hebrew tribes to accept my leadership."

"Are you talking about kingship?" asked Barak.

"Yes...kingship! You see there is no king in Israel...and we need a king like the other nations."

"Why do you thing that Judah should have the leadership?"

"Because after the death of Joshua the children of Israel asked the Lord 'who shall go up first to fight against the Canaanites and the Lord said, Judah shall go up...' "

Barak hesitated and remained silent.

Now, If you can agree to my proposal, we stand ready to supply you with all the soldiers you will need."

"Why me? Can't you select somebody else for this task?"

"There is nobody else...Barak! You are the best man for the job! You are respected...and well-known...the people look up to you...as if you are some kind of...deliverer or savior as they looked up to Othniel, Ehud, and Joshua!"

Barak took one step forward, turned to one side and scratched his head. "You give a very persuasive argument. Suppose that I am not able to persuade them...then what?"

"Well then, I'll have to do a little arm twisting."

"Arm twisting? I see," said Barak softly looking at him suspiciously. "Are there any other conditions?"

"Yes, I am glad you asked that question. As a matter-of-fact there is. Do you know the woman Deborah?"

Barak raised his head slowly. He opened his eyes wider and answered softly. "Yes...I know her." Barak stood there and wondered what was on his mine.

"There is something you must understand. This woman, Deborah..."

"This woman!" Barak repeated loudly. "You speak of her with contempt...as if...she is some kind of low life." He retorted angrily.

"Well...you probably wouldn't use those words, but the point is that she is taking away the loyalty of the people from the elders and the princes. Furthermore, she is moving into a man's domain and your connection with her contributes to her rise in prestige. In view of all this, I must ask you to disassociate yourself from her."

"Disassociate myself? You have the...." Barak held back his anger momentarily and continued. "A little while ago, Abihu, I had asked you that suppose I could not get the elders to accept your leadership, and at that time, you said that you would 'do a little arm twisting.' What did you mean by that?"

"I simply meant...that if they give you any opposition to my leadership, let me know their names, and I'll have them eliminated."

"What? You are talking about tyranny and murder...and it would only lead to civil war among the tribes."

" You call it tyranny and murder. I call it an act of bringing order...and unity among the tribes" retorted Abihu gesturing with his right hand.

"The end does not justify the means," Barak emphasized. "I am disappointed with you Abihu, and you've wasted my time. You sent for me to tell me to disassociate myself from a respectful lady. Then you ask me to betray my own people so you could impose your selfish will on them. I shall not be a party to your diabolical scheme," Barak roared.

"I warn you Barak.... If you stand in my way..."

Barak gritted his teeth with boiling anger. "No...I warn you Prince Abihu! If you interfere in the affairs of the northern tribes, I'll fight you with everything I can muster," he shouted. "I had enough of this. I'm leaving."

Abihu watched Barak walk toward the stairs and said, "Shamgar and Jael did not complete the deliverance of Israel. What makes you think that you can...? Without my help, what are you going to do Barak?"

"I'll look to another source, snapped Barak as he turned and eyed Abihu.

"Without my help, Barak, Sisera will grind you into the dusk, like corn is ground in a millstone. Furthermore, if you set foot in Judah again, your life will be in great danger."

When Barak departed from the house of Abihu, it began to get cloudy. He had come to Hebron with great hope of getting help from Prince Abihu, instead, he got no help, but became an enemy of the man who he thought would help him. Moreover, this unpleasant experience weighted heavily on his heart.

Barak and his men rode away from Hebron with rapid speed because he wanted to leave that sour experience behind him as quickly as possible. As he rode north, he thought about Deborah and about what she wanted. He hoped that his visit with her would be better than the one he had with Abihu.

CHAPTER FIFTEEN

In the late afternoon of the same day, as Deborah was inspecting plants and flowers in her courtyard, Barak arrived. Seth, one of her young workers entered. "Mother Deborah, Barak has finally arrived with his men."

"Oh! Show him in. He must be tired," she said as she pulled the ends of her reddish purple shawl around her neck.

A few moments later Barak entered. He walked with an authoritative gait. "Peace Deborah. Is all well?" he asked as he gave her a pleasant smile.

She took a few steps toward him and wanted to embrace him, but she caught herself and just returned a smile, not wanting to give the wrong impression. "All is well. You must be tired after your long trip from Hebron."

"I'm just a little dusty from the long trip," he said, as he looked her up and down with admiration. "What happened to your pimple."

"I lost it."

"But, I liked it," he remarked smiling.

"Well...I'm sorry that I lost it." Seth, would you show Barak and his men to the guest quarters so that they may freshen up. Then we'll have supper and after that, I'll tell you Barak, why I sent for you."

"I'm eager to hear what this mountain-sized news is," he exaggerated smiling as he departed from her.

After that, Deborah went into her meditation room to review everything that the Lord had told her. At that moment, she heard someone calling. It was Sarah, her handmaid.

"Yes Sarah."

"A messenger just brought a letter for you. It is from Caleb's farm."

Deborah took the letter and put it in her pocket intending to read it later, thinking that it was about their wedding plans. She continued to reflect on what she was going to tell Barak because this was a more pressing matter.

After they had finished their supper, it was still daylight and they walked outside and sat under a palm tree.

"Barak, I heard that you went down to the city of Hebron."

"Yes, I went there to see Prince Abihu to see could I get him to supply soldiers to help me fight Sisera's army."

"And?"

"He placed conditions on his offer.... He said that Judah, his tribe, should be the ruling one over all the tribes. Furthermore, he wanted me to persuade the northern tribes to accept his leadership...and if they refused, he wanted me to turn over their names to him so that he could eliminate them."

"Everything has its place," said Deborah, "and every man has his time. This is your time to rise Barak, not Abihu's. Prince Abihu will not be king in his days."

"I hope not!" said Barak, "if he rose to power among us, he would not be a ruler, but a butcher."

"Nevertheless, Barak...after many years, great kings will spring forth from his tribe...and the messiah will arise out of Israel, and be a light and hope for many nations.... Did Abihu say any more?"

"Yes! Somehow, he found out that I had visited you on several occasions. He accused you of pulling away the loyalty of the people from the princes and the elders. Moreover, he..."

"You don't have to repeat anymore Barak. He sent me a detail letter stating his views. But, I would be interested in knowing what your reply was to him."

"I told him that he had wasted my time and that I would have no part of his diabolical scheme. Also, I told him that you were a good person and he had no right to talk about you in the way he did."

"I am so proud of you Barak, because you stood up to him the way you did."

She lifted her hands up to embrace him but she restrained herself thinking that it would be improper. Barak was ready to respond with his hands extended, but she sat down.

She sat quiet for a while looking down, then looked away, and finally, she looked at him. Barak's facial expression showed that he was getting anxious and he broke the silence.

"Did you send for me to talk about us?"

"No...! I sent for you to talk about the war. I was very open with you about my marriage to Caleb and as far as I know, nothing has changed," she said seriously. "Barak, have you ever thought about when all-out war will break occur, and what would be your geographical position and the position of your enemy?"

"I've thought about it, but war plans change according to the change of the situation. Tell me Deborah, I beseech thee. Why do you talk about war matters?"

"So that you can give deeper thought," she said, "to what I am going to tell you...."

"Go on," he said.

"The Lord appeared unto me, and these are His words: 'Send for Barak and tell him to go and draw to Mount Tabor, and take with thee ten thousand men of the children of Naphtali and of the children of Zebulun? And I will draw unto thee to the river Kishon, Sisera, the captain of Jabin's army with his chariots and his multitude; and I will deliver him into thy hand.' "

"Deborah, do I understand you to be saying that you want me to put ten thousand men into the field against Sisera's nine hundred chariots and the rest of his horsemen and his footmen?'

"I am not saying it; the Lord has said it! The Lord has said that 'before you were form in your mother's womb and before you came out of her stomach I appointed you to be the deliverer of the Hebrews."

"Listen Deborah, my forces are poorly armed. We do not have any chariots, not enough horses and camels, not even ten swords, and no shields. Sisera arrested all the blacksmiths years ago. How can my men stand up against his great multitude?" he wailed with a defeated look on his face.

"If you become more spiritual, you will be able to understand what the Lord has said. It is the Lord who will defeat Sisera. It is the Lord who will deliver Sisera into your hands."

"To ask me to go up against Sisera," he argued, "is like asking me to put a chicken in a den of hungry lions."

"Barak, it is written in our holy books that if you trust in the word of the Lord; 'five of you shall chase an hundred and a hundred of you shall put ten thousands to flight; and your enemies shall fall before you by the sword.'"

Barak listened carefully and stared at her with a long pause. "Sister Deborah...if...if thou will go with me...then, I will go," he propositioned as he gestured with his hands. "But, if thou will not go with me...then I will not go."

As Deborah sat there under the palm tree, she closed her eyes and she thought. "He probably has a secret reason for asking me to go with him." Then she was silent and still. At that moment, the spirit said to her, 'go with him Deborah...go!'"

"Well Deborah...I am waiting. Are you going to keep me waiting until the cock crows at dawn?"

"Oh Barak, I understand from your words that the authority that God has given to you...some of it, you have given to me... 'I will surely go with thee; notwithstanding the journey that thou takest shall not be for thine honor; for the Lord shall give Sisera into the hands of a woman.' "

"Into the hands of a woman?" he smiled with a doubting look on his face. "I understand," he declared. But, by the look on his face, the words went in one ear and came out the other.

"But do you agree?" she asked watching his facial expression.

"Yes, I agree to all the words that went forth out of your mouth," he uttered with a serious look on his face.

"Would it be all right if we leave out early in the morning?" she asked.

"The morning will be fine, and this will give me time to get a good night's rest. Finally...the time has come that we can confront Sisera and his army...I can't believe this is true and God has revealed it to you."

***

The next morning, they arose early and Deborah decided to take Nachshon and Sarah, her handmaid with her. Deborah gave final instructions to her overseer, Madreech and informed him that she would be gone for several weeks.

Nachshon prepared one horse for himself and a donkey for each of the women and a camel for a pack animal to carry food, water, clothing and other personal items.

As Deborah brought her heavy clothing sack, she said, "Barak, will you help me?"

"My pleasure," he commented as he lifted the sack up on the camel's back.

"Thank you," she said. "I have everything in it but the kitchen table"

"Well, at least you won't go hungry," he said smiling.

Finally, they took to the road. It was the usual north-south mountain road that ran from Jebus (Jerusalem) to Shechem and northward. Deborah rode in the front beside Barak and Sarah rode beside Nachshon about fifteen cubits in the rear. A rope connected the pack camel to Nachshon's horse; and the ten soldiers rode in the rear.

It was not too long before they passed through the center of the town of Bethel. Also, they passed over the east-west road that intersected the road that they were traveling. It was warm already and there was every indication that it was going to be warmer. Then Nachshon spoke up: "Deborah, do you think we should water the animals at one of the many springs in this area?"

"That's a very good idea...that way, we can save our own water," she remarked pleasantly.

They turned aside not too far from where Jacob had built his alter and called it Bethel, which means house of God.

Deborah then made a movement to get down off her donkey. "Let me help you, Barak commented as he extended his hand to her.

"That is so nice of you," she said as she felt the gentleness and strength of his hand and arms, then she moved quickly away from him.

After all the animals finished drinking water at the spring, they continued on the road again. Deborah thought about Caleb, but mostly about the impending war. She asked herself, "Did I partly agree to go with Barak so that I

172

would not be around if Caleb came. Another point, she hadn't even read the letter she received from Caleb's farm. She was clearly avoiding those matters. Then there was silence and Barak didn't say anything.

"You look deep in thought. What is heavy on your heart Barak?"

Deborah, I've just been thinking about my wife who died in child birth."

"What about her?" she asked.

"Well...there are several things about you that remind me of her, things like dedication, loyalty and compassion," he said as his horse stepped on a rock and jolted him for a moment. "I think a lot of you, Deborah."

"I am promised to Caleb and I believe there are many pretty and nice ladies who would like to have you...in the way that you are thinking, forget about me Barak."

"That is very difficult."

"Even if, I wasn't betrothed to Caleb, there are other stumbling blocks which stand in the way."

"There you go again Deborah, building a three hundred cubit wall between us. Now, what are the stumbling blocks?"

"They are: the responsibility that I have for my business, my commitment I have for my people to give them advice and help when they come seeking after it and my spiritual interest. These things can stand in the way of a good marriage," she said.

"I also have my business, a cattle farm, and I am committed to the liberation of our people. Nevertheless, I take time out to write and visit you."

Deborah stopped her donkey and turned to him and explained. "You are a good man Barak. You are a prince of your tribe and no doubt, you have a nice size farm. Furthermore, you are risking your life for our people. I admire these things in you...any woman would. But, there

173

is one thing that I need in my life that will make me happy and that is a man who will grow spiritually with me. With all your good points, Barak, you aren't at this level yet. Maybe you will get there two weeks from now, or a month from now, or six months."

"What can I say Deborah. I am only a soldier."

"Let me say this Barak, the things I tell you are in the great tradition of our ancestors. Our great forefathers were soldiers and spiritual men of God at the same time. Try to be more like Joshua, and if you try hard and pray, you will get there," she emphasized as they continued on their journey.

Finally, they arrived at the town of Shiloh where the Tabernacle stood. Deborah and Barak informed the seventy elders of the Supreme Court and the High Priest about the fact that the Lord told Deborah to call for Barak to go to war against Sisera.

Then the High Priest said, "You have our blessings and prayers; from what you have told us, it is evident that God has spoken to you."

"We know that your uncle Yoetz prepared and trained you well," Ariel, the Elder, reminded her. He sat on this court for many years...and we see that the spirit of knowledge, wisdom, humility, righteousness and, prophecy abide with you. May God be with you always," said Ariel as he waved good-by.

Continuing northward for twelve miles, they came to the city of Shechem. Shechem was an ancient city of the Canaanites forty-one miles north of Jerusalem in the pass between Mount Gerizim and Mount Ebal. This city controlled the important trade routes. They saw the beautiful gorges, and traveled through the mountain passes, and observed the lush green fertile valley with its yellow and purple wild flowers. It was just to the east that Jacob's sons shepherded their sheep. In this place, Schechem, the son of Hamor, violated Dinah, the daughter of Jacob.

Deborah and her party stopped in Shechem to get water and to eat, then they continued. As Barak rode along the road, he continued his conversation with Deborah. "When I first came to your house, I found you to be a likable person, and I didn't know you were obligated under the levirate law to marry Caleb." Then I came to your house the second time; I got the shock of my life. A ghost appeared and he was Caleb.

"Are you saying that I misled you?" she inquired as she looked at him with Mount Ebal in the background.

"No! I am just making a statement. It seems that I expected too much without knowing all the facts."

"Perhaps you are right...but don't blame yourself too much. You were only being a man. And I had not been sure what Caleb's final decision was going to be."

CHAPTER SIXTEEN

As they continued on the main road, they veered to the northeast and came to the town of Tirzah, which was about seven miles from Shechem. As they entered the town, they noticed the beautiful scenery of the mountains. It was here that they planned to sleep for the night.

After they registered for their quarters, they sat down to eat. There wasn't enough space at one table for all to sit together so they had to split up into two parties at the tables on opposite sides of the dinning room. Sarah and Nachshon at one table and Barak and Deborah sat together at another table. The ten soldiers slept outside in tents.

As Deborah and Barak ate supper, they discussed the details of how they were going to present to the leaders of the tribes what the Lord revealed to her. The discussion included the logistics of the army and they gave special attention to the areas of supplies, water, food, camping equipment and the mobilization of the troops.

"Well, I think that this covers most things for now—any additional matters, we can discuss them with the elders of the tribes," commented Barak.

"Yes, I agree."

After Deborah and Barak had finished eating supper a group of strangers came into the inn. The headman of the group fixed his eyes on Barak, and Barak returned the glance with a nod of his head. Then the strangers registered at the desk, and a servant took their personal items to their rooms.

The stranger looked at Barak again. As he walked by Barak's table to go to his room, Barak stood up and introduced himself. "Peace be to you sire, my name is Barak, Prince Barak of the Hebrew tribe of Naphtali. And yours?"

"Lysimacus, Demetrius Lysimacus." He was a man in his middle forties, and was dressed in a dark brown tunic.

"Are you from the region of the Caucasus Mountains?"

"No, I am from the Greek Islands."

"Oh...What brings you here to this part of the world?"

"I just completed my studies in Egypt, and I am returning home to set up my medical practice."

"Oh...I see.... Then you are a physician?" asked Barak with a thoughtful look on his face."

"Yesss," answered the Greek slowly.

"Sit down, have a seat sir! I would like to talk with you further," Barak urged him, smiling.

"Thank you. I would be glad to..."

"By the way, this is my associate Deborah."

Deborah smiled and nodded her head in recognition. At that time, Demetrius introduced his three associate doctors, his daughter, and his brown-skinned wife, Isis, who he married after his Greek wife died in childbirth. His twenty-year old daughter, Hapshepsut is the result of that childbirth. He kissed his wife Isis and daughter and told them that he would join them in their quarters shortly. Also, the medical associates went to their quarters.

At this time, Deborah spoke up: "Excuse me Barak, and Demetrius, I am going to my room, and this will give the two of you a chance to get to know one another. Call me when you have finished your conversation with Demetrius." Barak nodded his head in agreement.

Then the both of them sat down, at opposite ends of the table. "Oh Demetrius. Is your wife Egyptian or Ethiopian?"

"Egyptian. She is the daughter of the head of the medical college in the city of Memphis."

"In what area of medicine do you work?"

"My area is surgery."

"Ummm! Surgery? How wonderful," said Barak smiling.

Demetrius looked at him with wonderment. "You said that you are a prince, are you anything else?"

"Yes, why do you ask?"

"You dress somewhat like a soldier, and you have the air of an officer."

Barak smiled and looked him straight in the eyes. "Did you serve in the army?" asked Barak.

"Yes! I was the assistant to the chief surgeon in the army of Egypt, and I served in the Ethiopian war, on Egypt's southern border."

As Barak looked down, he raised the palm of his hands and covered his face and eyes. After a few moments, he lowered his hands to the table and turned to Demetrius. Then you have had a lot of experience treating the wounded, isn't that so?"

"Yes.... Barak, I want you to tell me the truth. You are a soldier, aren't you?"

Barak stared at him for a short while, shook his head up and down slowly, and smiled at him. Finally, Barak opened his mouth and spoke slowly "I am...the commander of the Hebrew army in the North."

Demetrius took a deep breath, then sat back erect. "Are you expecting war...commander?" asked Demetrius as he rubbed his brown beard.

Barak lifted his eyes slowly. "We are at war...and have been for the last twenty years. Now, we are approaching the final battle."

"Barak, are you thinking of having me to serve in your army to treat the wounded?"

"Oh Demetrius," Barak said softly and diplomatically. "I would be remiss and lacking as a commander, if I didn't seize this opportunity to request your expert knowledge and service. So I am...asking you to remain with us for two or three weeks. I will make it worth your while."

"But...I have other plans and objectives. I am supposed to be at the Aegean Sea in two or three weeks. I would not have been here tonight, if I hadn't missed my turn at the city of Shechem, which would have taken me westward to the Great Sea, and then northward."

"You see!" said Barak. "It was destiny that led you here."

"Destiny?"

"Yes, destiny!" said Barak. "Some unforeseen force guided your steps here."

"Why do you choose me? Someone that is so different from you and your people. There are other good doctors...like the Egyptians, the Lybians, and even the Ethiopians. I know.... I met them."

My dear brother, Demetrius, you are also a son of Adam...just as I am. When you crack open a brown egg or a white one...the eggs are all the same inside. When I am hungry, I'm not going to deprive myself of the good eating of an egg...just because its shell is white. In view of this, I'm asking you to remain with us."

"You are a very wise commander. By the way, who are you fighting?" asked Demetrius.

"Have you heard of Sisera, the Canaanite?"

"General Sissera? Yes, I have heard of him. He has almost a thousand chariots.... Do you have such a number?"

"No," Barak looked embarrassed and lowered his head."

"How many men do you have Barak?"

Barak hesitated for a moment, and then spoke, "Two...two thousand," mumbled Barak in a low tone.

"That's all?" Demetrius asked emphatically.

"We shall have another eight thousand soon."

Demetrius shook his head from side to side. "Only ten thousand men...against Sisera's chariots, and all his multitudes? This is suicide!" declared Demetrius raising his voice. "Only ten thousand men? And surely...you don't expect to win!"

"I do expect to win," he said staring at Demetrius. "The Canaanites are not unconquerable. It was King Thutmose III of Egypt who crushed the Syrians, and the Canaanites at Megiddo, not far from here, about three hundered fifty years ago."

"That is true...however, in all respects to you...you are not Thutmos III of Egypt," he said softly. And, do you know that Egypt was a powerful nation...a world empire, and the most advanced nation in the world," informed Demetrius.

"Yes, but there is something else I haven't told you. The lady Deborah, who you met earlier, is a prophetess, and she has said that we will win."

"Did she look into a crystal ball?

"Not exactly," answered Barak.

"Well, I'm not going to get involved in that. But, I did detect a spiritual quality in her eyes. Whatever she told you, that's between you...and her. I have said enough...as it is."

"Well, I'll just change the subject.... By the way, Demetrius, a few moments ago, I mentioned King Thutmos III of Egypt. He is a man that I admire greatly."

"This is understandable," concluded Demetrius, pulling his brown tunic up on his shoulder. "Thutmos III was a good king and a great military man. It is only natural that you would admire him."

Barak leaned forward and looked at Demetrius with inquisitive eyes. "Demetrius, tell me, what did he look like?"

"He was…tall and had a robust physique."

"Continue!" prompted Barak looking anxious.

"In addition, he was pure Hamite. He had thick lips and a broad nose with wooly hair, like the sheep that graze in the valley."

Barak asked again. "Was he very dark?"

"Of course," he said. "Darker than you…! Also, he had a bold and commanding appearance."

Barak looked contemplative. Finally, he spoke in gratitude: "Demetrius, I do thank you for your sincere advice, and concern. I do wish you would reconsider and stay over and take care of our wounded."

"If Sisera wins, you will not need my help. He will just slaughter everybody. Furthermore, it would just be too risky for my group to remain in a war zone. We would be just too conspicuous if your enemy wins."

"I understand. Well, I guess that's it."

"It's getting late." Demetrius stood up. I am sorry Barak! I like you, but I can't give you a yes answer at this time. If circumstances were different…I probably would," he said making a slight bow, and then began to depart.

"Oh Demetrius, if you should change your mind, you will be able to find us west of the Sea of Galilee. Just ask anybody and they will tell you."

Demetrius shook his head up and down with consent, and Barak watched him walk away to his quarters.

It was now a little after midnight, and Barak sent for Deborah to join him at the table in the dining room. Deborah came and listened attentively to Barak and to everything Barak told her about the Greek.

Deborah raised her head. "When Demetrius told you that he was a physician, I had the suspicion that you were going to ask him to remain and help take care of the wounded."

"You did?"

"Yes! But it is understandable that he would refuse you because of his prior duties, and your going up against Sisera with only ten thousand men."

"Do you think that he will change his mind?"

"I really don't know. We shall just have to let the Lord take care of that. But, there is one thing that you have in your favor..."

"What's that?"

"He likes you!" she said smiling.

After Deborah's last words, there was a silence, and her mind turned back to the letter she'd received from Caleb's farm. She had avoided reading it because she didn't want to face up to the reality of the marriage to a man she didn't love, nor trusted. However, as she sat there, she decided that she might as well read it, and free her mind, temporarily of the contents. In this way, she could concentrate more deeply on the impending war effort. She took out the pouch from her garment, opened it, and a bracelet fell out. At that moment, she unrolled the parchment and read. As she read the letter, she slowly opened her eyes and mouth wide in surprise. She took a deep breath and tears ran down her cheeks. "The Lord has answered my request," she said crying.

"Did you ask for a bracelet?" asked Barak.

"No Barak!" she said. "I asked to be freed from my pain," she remarked crying.

"What is the matter Deborah? What is it?"

"I.... received this letter from...Caleb's farm...."

"What did he say to hurt you?"

"It isn't what he said...it is what he can't say!"

"Explain that Deborah, don't keep me hanging by my neck" he demanded.

"This letter is from his sister." She said, 'He gave up the ghost on the ninth day of this month.' "

"What...How?" asked Barak in shock.

" He was found dead in his bed, and the cause of his death is unknown. Then Deborah wept.

"Why do you weep, Deborah? You admitted that you didn't love him, nor trusted him," asked Barak with roughness in his voice.

"I weep because his soul didn't use the chance it had on earth to correct itself, while it was in his body. And the other reason why I weep is because, if we pray, and wait on the Lord, He will always work out His purpose on earth, even though we may not understand it in the beginning. But, if we seek and wait for the Lord long enough, we shall understand many things in the future.

"Where is the soul of Caleb, at this moment?" asked Barak.

"In Heaven."

"Does the soul have any kind of physical form?"

"Not at all. Not in the sense that we are familiar. She looked up and leaned towards him. You must understand Barak, that when we go to heaven, we are neither tall nor short, pretty nor ugly, thin nor fat, Greek nor Hebrew, just you...an eternal soul buried in the eternity of time...learning and preparing itself for the next mission and journey."

"As I listen to you talk Deborah, it seems that you are on a different...or should I say higher level."

"Maybe you are trying to say spiritual level," commented Deborah as Barak shook his head up and down in consent.

Deborah continued to read the letter. Then she noticed that there was a document under the letter. Caleb's sister named Emeth, went out of her way to obtain a court document that stated:

" 'After a complete investigation, the court has determined that there are no surviving eligible males of the deceased Caleb Ben Lapidoth, to fulfill the duty of levirate marriage with Deborah Lapidoth. The court hereby grants Deborah the freedom and the right to marry anyone else if she so desire.' "

Three elders of the court of Gilgal signed the letter.

After reading this document, Deborah told Barak about the details. Then she commented, "Bless be the name of the Lord... and bless be those who wait on His...great mercy," she sobbed softly, with trembling in her voice.

"Deborah, the heavy burden has been lifted from your shoulders. Caleb may he rest in peace, is no more. Now, where do we stand Deborah?"

Deborah looked up at Barak with surprise: "Caleb's body is not even cold yet...and now you are asking me, where do we stand?"

"Yes, I am asking you Deborah, where do we stand?"

"We stand where we are? What does that mean?" he inquired, as he unfolded his hands in front of him.

"You have a duty. God has chosen you. Yet you seldom talk about God. I am not sure that you understand the spiritual importance of your mission," she reminded him bluntly.

"I've never dealt with spiritual things before, you have, and in that sense, you have the advantage."

"You can become more spiritual, if you let the Lord use you in this way. Then you and I will have more in common."

Barak had the look of deep thought on his face, and he looked away, and said," I see."

She continued, " The Lord chose you Barak…to lead Israel in battle, and He chose me to help His people, to comfort them, to guide them, to assure them, and to encourage you so that you will rise to a higher spiritual level. But don't reject it. If you reject the idea of trusting in God, then God will reject you at the very hour you need Him."

"What you are saying sound good Deborah, but it is hard. It is hard to change over to an idea that you are not use to," he remarked as he turned his head from side to side and took a deep breath.

"But you must try…and try again, and again, and again. Then you will be victorious. If you can do this, there is a greater chance that we can make it together," she assured him as she took hold of his hand and comforted him.

"You are a tough likable lady. Good…night Deborah," he said gently, "I'll see you at dawn."

Deborah really liked Barak. She wanted him, but she wanted him to grow spiritually, without coercion. She believed that he must see the light and truth from within himself, and not just because she said it.

She hoped in her heart that that moment would come. Until it came, she decided to hold herself back from him. She concluded that she would not even let him kiss her. They said good night to each other, and she went into her room.

Before Deborah went to sleep, she told Sarah all the details of the letter that she received from Celeb's farm and about his death. Moreover, she informed Sarah, that Ophrah, the servant of Caleb, had decided to remain with Emeth, since she inherited her brother's property. Under these conditions, Ophrah no longer feared any physical abuse, because Caleb had died.

CHAPTER SEVENTEEN

The night passed swiftly and Deborah and her retinue got up very early the next morning and went on their way. Before going to the tribes of Zebulun and Naphtali, Deborah and Barak decided that they would stop at one of the towns of the tribe of Issachar and speak with the elders and princes. This she thought would be proper in view of the fact that the Lord told Deborah to tell Barak to take the Hebrew army to Mount Tabor, which belongs to the tribe of Issachar.

As Deborah and Barak continued northwards, they came to Mount Gilboa. They stayed close to this mountain in case they encountered a Canaanite patrol; in this case, they would have a place to hide. While they rode around the west side of the mountain, they heard the prancing of the hooves of horses. Then Barak took Deborah and led her behind the ridges and boulders along the edge of the mountain.

"Nachshon, quickly take your horse and Sarah's donkey and hide behind that ridge over there, and keep the animals quiet!"

"Quickly Sarah go over there!" Nachshon urged her.

Barak and Deborah were pressed tight between a narrow passageway of the mountain. He stood facing her with his body pressed close to her looking occasionally to see when the horses would pass. She looked up at his handsome face and admired his well-trimmed black mustache and beard. He looked down at her and smiled with joy in his heart. She smiled shyly and thought how wonderful it was to be close to this handsome muscular man. They heard the hooves of the horses get louder and louder. Barak took his arms and put them around her shoulders in a protective manner. As he breathed hard in anticipation of the coming horsemen, his muscular chest rose up against her well-developed breast. She felt a sensation shoot through her, and she looked up at him. Then the horses passed. At that moment, he moved his lips slowly toward her and she wanted him to kiss her, but she turned away. She was not ready for that yet. Barak was not spiritual enough she thought, but a lot better than Caleb was. Moreover, there was a lot more to complete in preparation for the war.

"Why did you turn away from me?" he asked looking at her reactions.

"You were...you were hurting me."

"Hurting you?" he chuckled.

"Yes! You were squeezing me too tight."

Then Nachshon led the animals from behind the ridge. "I think it is safe to come out."

"I'll check," Barak said. At that moment, he went out from the ridge and looked to the left and right cautiously. All was clear and they came out and continued on their way. As they went on their journey, they passed by the many wild sweet-smelling blue flowers that carpeted the mountain area. The Iris flower is very popular in this region.

As they rode slowly through the Jezreel Valley, Barak began to speak. "We have known each other for about a year now, and I have been thinking about several difficulties that we have had in the past."

"Like what Barak?"

"I first got the thought that you were too independent, and that you didn't want to spend time with me."

"Oh...! And what are your thoughts now?"

"Now, my thoughts are that you were just taking charge of your life and taking care of the business that your husband left you. The people who came to you for guidance and legal advice, I believe, that you were performing a public service for them."

"I, also, had doubts about our relationship from the beginning. I didn't want to become seriously involved with you, because you were fighting the Canaanites, and my deceased husband was killed by the Canaanites. Worrying about the possibility of your death would have only caused me more emotional pain. But now, I have new insight into this problem, because the Lord has promised that He would deliver Sisera into your hands. You see, I don't have to worry about you being killed anymore."

"We both have suffered loss and pain in marriage. Many years ago, my wife died in childbirth. Therefore, when I first met you, I expressed doubt in ever getting married again, because I feared the same thing would happen to you."

"Well, what are your feelings now, Barak?"

"I have outgrown that fear...and have accepted the fact that my next wife doesn't have to die in childbirth."

"It is good that you have overcome that fear."

"Would you like to have children, Deborah?"

"Yes, a boy and a girl. How about you?" she asked.

"I would like ten sons."

"Not by me," she replied. I don't have that many child bearing years left."

As Deborah and Barak traveled on the road past Mount Moreh, they saw a group of people burying one of their dead. The group was standing about twenty cubits away from the main road. The body of a man was lying near the grave wrapped in a white shroud. Then the elder spoke his last words…"his spirit returns to God who gave it. May he rest in peace."

A woman kneeled down and leaned over the body. "Joseph, don't leave me," she cried aloud. "Please don't leave me…don't leave…"she said grabbing hold of his body. A few moments later, a few ladies came over and led the woman several cubits away from the body. Four men took hold of the ropes and lowered the corpse down into the grave.

While Deborah listened and watched what was happening, she knew that the soul-spirit of the dead man was hovering over the grave. She turned to Barak, "I can hear his voice," she mumbled.

"Voice…? Whose voice?" asked Barak.

"I can hear the spirit-voice of the dead man."

Barak looked at her as if she had lost her mind. "What is the voice saying?"

Deborah knew that he did not take her serious, but she continued to speak. "The voice said to his crying wife: 'My soul is hovering from above and looking down at you. The body that I once had is not my true self, my dear wife. It is nothing but disposable matter…made from fruits, vegetables, nuts, water and bread, which will rot…and the worms will eat.' " Again, Deborah said to Barak. "His wife didn't hear a word he was saying because she was in much emotional pain, and not tuned into his spirit."

"The words you just said are very deep Deborah, and have great meaning…. Are you going to tell…his wife what you heard?"

"No..." she answered looking like she was in a trance. "She is not ready to receive this...just yet."

"Not yet...my Lady?" Sarah probed.

"The widow is in no condition to listen. Perhaps...in the future when she is in a better state of mind. If she seeks, she will find when she has an open mind. Now, let's continue on our journey.

Finally, they came to the city of Darbareh, which is located on the northwest side of Mount Tabor. As they rode through the village and the town, the people asked one another, "Isn't that Deborah and Barak?" The news traveled fast and soon there was a crowd following them. Some of the ladies were singing and beating their tambourines. Then a chant began with cadence, "Deborah, Deborah, Barak, Barak." The people gathered on both sides of them. They could hardly get through.

Barak asked one of the men, "Where is the meeting-house of the elders and princes?"

"It is the pretty stone building on the right," said the man.

The crowd even got larger and some of the spectators began to circle Deborah and Barak singing, dancing and beating the tambourines. As the ladies sang, some of them gave Barak the flirting eye and big smiles.

"I see that you are well thought of," commented Deborah.

"Oh, a little bit," he replied modestly.

Finally, they came to the meetinghouse of the elders. Deborah and Barak turned around and faced the crowd. They thanked them for their reception and love.

"What news do you bring to us," shouted a man from the crowd.

"Yes! Tell us Barak...what brings you here?" asked a woman.

"We can't tell you now, but we will in due time. We must first consult with the elders and princes," Deborah assured them.

"The only thing that we can tell you now is that we are on an important mission." Barak informed them.

"Are you on a war mission Barak?" asked another man. "Because Deborah, the prophetess, came here with our top military officer, we think that you are here on war business. Tell us Barak, are you going to take our sons to war?"

"No comment," he said as he took Deborah by her arm and escorted her inside.

Deborah and Barak sat down with the local elders of the city of Dabareh. Dabareh was in the territory of the tribe of Issachar and this tribe gave the city of Dabareh to the Gershonite Levites. Deborah and Barak didn't have to introduce themselves, because the crowd had already announced their coming.

After Deborah and Barak ate a light snack, the elders asked them why they had come to Dabareh.

"The Lord God of our fathers revealed himself to Deborah and she has a message for you, and she will tell you the rest," Barak assured them.

"Oh ye honourable elders of this ancient city. It is true that our God appeared to me and commanded me to send for Barak. One part of his mission is to take ten thousand men to Mount Tabor. It is from this mountain that he and his men will wage war with Sisera," she informed them in a serious way.

Most of the elders had white beards, looked solemn, turned and looked at one another. Then one of them asked, "Is the battle set for a certain day?"

"No. But I'll know that when our army arrive at the place where we will begin the attack."

"I am sure you know what the outcome of the war will be?" inquired another elder.

191

"Yes...there is no doubt that we shall be victorious because God will intervene on our behalf," she said seriously.

At this point, Barak interrupted. "We don't have much time and we have a lot of miles to cover so I'm going to get right to the point. One, we would like all the elders, princes, and heads of the tribes of Naphtali, Issachar and Zebulun to meet together in the city of Kedesh of Naphtali in seven days to explain about the war and make preparations. Two, we would like you to help us in sending letters and messengers to the towns and cities in Zebulun and Issachar inviting the leaders to come to Kedesh of Naphtali. Three, we would like them to bring at least five thousand men with them including supplies, food, sheep, horses, donkeys, asses, camels, swords, spears, slingshots and tents. Also, we would be grateful if you could send a fast horse rider to Kedesh to inform the leaders that Deborah and I shall be arriving in Kedesh within three days, and tell them that six thousand men will be arriving within a week. Now, if there are any questions, we'll be glad to answer them for you."

"Yes, I have a question," said one of the elders. "How long will the war last?"

"Maybe the Prophetess Deborah can answer that question," replied Barak as he looked toward her.

"The main battle will last less than a day, but after that, there will be pursuits after the fleeing enemy," she assured them.

"Well, Deborah, you have been right in the past, I hope you are right now, because we don't have the means to fight a long war," commented an elder who hadn't spoken until now.

After consultation with the elders, Barak began to end the discussion. "I want to thank all of you for your time and cooperation on behalf of our people in these terrible times. In addition, I want to say that we would like our honourable elders to treat this matter top secret: especially, the place where our army will meet. Also, I want to thank you for giving up your precious time."

At that moment, the chief elder spoke up. "You are staying for the night aren't you?" he asked as he rolled his eyes back and forward looking at both of them.

At that moment, Deborah and Barak just smiled.

"Good," the elder said. "We'll prepare supper and quarters for all four of you."

"Did we say we were staying elder?" asked Barak as he stroked his beard.

"No! Not in words, but your smile spoke for you. Why did you ask? You don't like our company?"

"Your company is just great...elder," said Barak shaking his head up and then down.

When Barak, Deborah, and the elders had finished talking, they heard a commotion outside; there was a knock on the door. One of the elders opened the door, and a crowd of people stood outside. A middle-aged woman stood there crying and exhausted. She began to speak: "My family they...." She couldn't get all the words out because she was exhausted from running through Zebulun hills.

"Calm yourself down my dear! What happened to your family?" asked one of the elders.

"Sisera and his...soldiers, they came into our village during the night and killed everybody. All of my family is...dead," she sobbed bitterly dropping her head into her hands.

After that, Deborah and Barak approached her slowly. "What is your name madam? At what village did this slaughter take place?" asked Barak.

She raised her head slowly with tears running down her cheek. "My name is Marah.... Our village was located about five hundred cubits...east of the city of Nahalol in the Zebulun hills."

"Come...! Take a seat over here...will someone get her a container of water," requested one of the elders.

Deborah, then, brought over some water and comforted her. "We understand that you have been through a lot, and we are here to help you."

Barak came closer and sat next to Deborah. "Marah, I know that this is going to be hard for you, but we need to know...exactly what happened back there...everything!"

Marah looked at Barak with a long stare. "All right...I'll try." At that moment, she wiped the tears from her eyes with the sleeve of her beige dress. Marah began to tell them what happened about four days ago. She mentioned everything: including the coming of the noblemen pretending to want friendship, the Canaanite invitation for the Hebrews to visit their city, the Canaanite request for the Hebrews to sacrifice their children to Baal, and finally, she told them about the Canaanite threat to retaliate against the Hebrews for showing disdain for the Canaanite gods.

While Barak listened to her story, he dropped his head and he looked helpless. Next, he raised his head and looked at her. "Are you sure that the leader of the soldiers was Sisera?"

"Yes," she said softly. "I am sure," answered Marah looking him directly in the eyes.

"How can you be sure."

"Because after the massacre the leader asked one of his men...''is everyone dead?' The soldier replied, 'I believe so, lord Sisera.' "

"All right, those words convinced me.... Thank you Marah...you have been very helpful."

"When will we," asked Marah, "be delivered...from the heavy yoke of Sisera?"

"This is why we are here. The Lord has heard the cry of our people and He has sent Barak and I to rally together the army of Israel. For the Lord will destroy Sisera and his armies."

A man in the crowd shouted through the open door. "We heard that the Hebrews of Nahalol didn't bow down to the idol god, Baal, nor did they sacrifice their children...so why did they had to die?"

"The ways of the Lord are mysterious," she said as she turned and looked toward the crowd. "Your question is hard to answer...but if you be patient and seek the Lord in sincerity, He will reveal the secret things in His due time," she continued. "Sometimes the Lord causes us to endure bitter pain in order to improve our character. We must look within ourselves for the answer."

"Deborah, you said that our deliverance will come soon...but, it seems that we are suffering more now than what we were before. Why?" asked Marah.

Deborah thought a moment..."A new nation is soon to be born...can a woman give birth without pain...Our people cannot give birth to a new born freedom without suffering... From our grievous pain will come forth a deliverance and liberty which will echo throughout the centuries."

Marah spoke again with tears running down her cheek and in a crying voice. "Sisera killed my entire family even my son and daughter...I have nobody...and I am...am past childbearing age," she sobbed.

"I know how you feel Marah," said Barak compassionately, "Sisera murdered my mother, also."

"What can I do Deborah...? What?"

Deborah looked at her with compassion and a long stare. "Do you want the truth...?"

"Yes...! The truth," answered Marah wiping the tears from her eyes.

"Well then...here is the God-given truth: There are orphans among our people who don't have mothers or fathers. Adopt a son and a daughter...and be a mother to

195

them...raise them as your own...and give them joy and love. Then in return...they will give you love and joy."

"But, how can I raise children by myself, without a husband?"

Deborah took her by the hand. "The Lord and I shall help you until you are able to find a husband. Until then, you can stay with me."

"Thank you Deborah, I trust you."

"I shall help too," said the chief elder.

Another elder said, "I'll help also."

A third elder looked at the General—then Barak nodded his head in consent. "Yes...! We shall help you too."

At that moment, Deborah turned away from the elders and faced Marah. "You see, the Lord has already made a way for you."

Marah moved toward Deborah then kissed and embraced her. "You are truly a kind and spiritual lady...Thank you so much.

"Don't mention it," said Deborah.

"One main reason that we are here on earth is to learn to help one another...if we are not doing this, then we are contributing to the problems of mankind by our neglect and greed."

"Deborah...in light of what has happened to the village of Nahalol, and to Marah," Barak said, "I think that you should carry a sword."

"I thank you Barak for being concerned about me; however, if there is any danger, the Lord will send his angels."

"Well...I would feel a little better if you would carry it anyway...just in case the angels be a little late."

CHAPTER EIGHTEEN

After enjoying the great hospitality from the elders of the city of Dabareh, the next morning Deborah and Barak set out for the city of Kedesh. This is where Barak grew up. Kedesh was a special city from all other cities in the province of Naphtali. First of all, it was a special city because it was a fortified one. In addition to that, it was a Levite city and a city of refuge. Before Moses and Joshua died, they had designated six cities in the land of Canaan as cities of refuge where the manslayer could flee when anyone would kill someone accidentally. At these cities, the manslayer could live without fear of the avenger of blood until his trial came up.

The city of Kedesh was located in upper Galilee, northwest of Lake Merom (now called Lake Huleh), not far from the Jordan River.

As Deborah and Barak traveled from the city of Dabareh to Kedesh, Barak picked up two hundred and fifty soldiers from the Zebulun-Naphtali garrison to accompany him. A few miles, just before they entered the city, they stopped at a spring and set up a tent so that they could freshen up and change clothes. They arrived at the city of Kedesh in the hills of Napthali on the third day. Along the side of the road were many people waiting for the arrival of Deborah and Barak. They clapped their hands, made a yodel like sound and chanted Barak, Barak, Deborah, Deborah, Barak, Barak, Deborah, Deborah. This chant was repeated over and over and over again. The people were dressed in their best colorful garments, because they came to see Deborah and Barak.

The people came out in large crowds because they wanted to see their Prince. He was their General who was fighting their enemies, the Canaanites. In addition to this, their Prince was coming with the famous Prophetess, Deborah.

"I didn't expect to get a reception like this," said Deborah looking at his medium blue tunic in admiration.

"This is how we do things here in Naphtali," he said bragging.

The men, women, and children continued to wave at Deborah and Barak as they passed. While they rode on their horses and donkeys, they returned the waves with eager smiles. As they rode along the main road, Deborah was overwhelmed by the joy of her people. Towards the background of the people were the fresh green grass of the springtime and the stately mountains of Naphtali laden with tall evergreen trees. To the right side of the road, they saw the green grass in the valley that led down to the Jordan River.

"Do you see the large house over against the mountain," asked Barak.

"Do you mean the white one to the left?"

"Yes...that is where I live."

"It is beautiful Barak. I like the courtyard that surrounds it, and the side stairs that go up to the roof and terrace."

"Thank you," he said. "If I had more time, I would show you around my property."

"That is so thoughtful of you Barak...but there will be another time." Looking over into the distance, Deborah asked, "To whom belongs those sheep and goats over there?"

"They belong to me."

"Barak... how many do you have?"

"At the last count, there were 1,655 sheep, 945 goats, twenty camel, fifteen asses, and twenty-five yokes of oxen."

"You must have a lot of servants?" she asked.

"Twenty-three, all total," he said as he passed by the crowd waving.

Because it was a bright warm day, that helped to bring out many people. As they approached closer to the city, the crowd grew larger and the sound of the trumpets became louder.

"Is your father going to be in the city?" Deborah asked hoping that she looked presentable enough.

"I think he will be there. He usually attends these kinds of functions.

"Well, being head of his tribe, I would think that he'd have to attend," she remarked as they passed through the main gate. By the way, do you think he'll like me?"

"Like you? He will love and adore you!" Barak assured her emphatically as he looked into her eyes smiling.

"Oh..." she remarked expressing surprise as she continued to wave at the crowd.

Then they came out to the open plaza where thousands of people were waiting. While the drummers continued to beat, they passed by many white stone buildings until they arrived at the Great Hall of the elders and judges. The elders and judges were lined up and standing on the stone steps in front of the Hall waiting for the arrival of Deborah and Barak.

As Barak came within ten cubits of the stone steps, he dismounted and went over to Deborah and helped her off the donkey.

"Walk with me over to the lower steps and wait there. Then I shall ascend the steps to greet my father and the elders. Afterwards, I shall return to get you," he whispered. Deborah stood there in her dark green dress with gold fringes on the borders, and on her head was a light green mantilla.

Barak walked up the steps. "Shalom my father," he greeted, bowing at him and then to the rest of the elders and judges. Then he stepped closer to his father, embraced him and kissed him on each cheek.

"How have you been father, you are looking well?"

"Fine, fine my son. I see that the God of our ancestors has been taking care of you," he replied as he looked him over to see if he had any disfigured bones. "Is she the famous lady, Deborah?"

"Yes, she is," Barak answered as he shook his head up and down.

"Well! Bring her up! We would like to meet her."

Barak went down the steps, which were lined with pretty green tropical plants and returned with Deborah.

"This is my father, Abinoam."

"Peace be unto you," she greeted bowing to him slightly.

"Peace be to you my daughter. Barak, she is so beautiful, and graceful. It is so nice meeting you. I have heard so much about you."

"Good things, I hope," she replied gently.

"Mostly good, but every person has some opposition, and that is to be expected."

"Now I can agree to that father."

After their meeting and greeting, Barak and his father introduced Deborah to the rest of the elders, then went and had an afternoon meal. The people prepared roasted lamb, goat, and roasted beef. Deborah and Barak could smell the aroma in the spring air. They had ground corn called mush, beans cooked in onions and garlic; fresh green vegetables, olives, dates, figs, raisins, wheat bread, apples, cheese, curds butter, fish from the sea of Galilee, and pomegranates. The entire Hebrew community of

Kedesh contributed to the food, and there was plenty for everyone.

After Deborah and Barak had finished the afternoon meal, they went to a special chamber in the Hall of the Elders. They briefed the elders concerning what the Lord told Deborah and they were willing to supply ten thousand men for the war against Jabin and Sisera. The elders agreed that they had enough of Sisera and that he had become more and more brutal and intolerable. They said that they wanted to do something and this was their opportunity. Now, they received the endorsement of a Prophetess of the Lord and He chose their tribal son, Barak, to lead the campaign. The elders of the people agreed to supply all the necessary food, horses, cattle, flocks, donkeys, camels, mules, tents, and slingshots.

It was about two hours after midday when Deborah and Barak came out of the meeting with the elders. The white stone plaza was still full with people. Some were still eating some were talking, and others were singing spiritual songs. As soon as the people saw Deborah, Barak, and his father approaching to the top of the steps, they began to yell for Deborah to speak.

"They want you to speak Deborah. Do you feel up to it?" Elder Abinoam inquired.

The people yelled again, "Deborah, Deborah, Deborah."

"All right," she said knowing that she couldn't disappoint them. "First of all, let me make a few remarks, then I'll introduce you," he whispered.

The crowd was still shouting for Deborah when Elder Abinoam took two steps forward to speak. He raised his left hand for the crowd to stop. Once they became silent, he began to talk. *"Baruch Elohey*.... Bless be the God of our ancestors who is merciful and just. I want to take this time to give my thanks to all the elders and judges who made the sacrifice to come here to our city on a moment's notice. Moreover, I want to welcome and thank all the soldiers and ordinary citizens for putting forth your great effort.

"Many of you have heard of why we are assembled here today. We've suffered under the yoke of the Canaanites for many years. Now, the opportunity has arrived for us to be free. I am not going to talk long because Deborah will be speaking after me. The elders and I have heard what the Lord revealed to her and our discussion confirms that she is a true prophetess. The Lord has declared all out war with Jabin, and his commander Sisera, and He has appointed Barak, my son, as commander of the Hebrew army. Furthermore, the elders of the tribes of Naphtali and Zebulun have given their unselfish support for the war effort, *emanuel* (may God be with us). In closing, I want to thank the elders of the tribe of Issachar who brought a company of men to help take care of the wounded. Moreover, we are grateful to have the Princes of Issachar with us. The Princes are known for their special knowledge: These men have the understanding of the times...and know what Israel ought to do. They will consult with Deborah and Barak on all-important matters. Now, at this time, I present to you Mother Deborah."

The crowd went wild shouting Deborah's name and giving the yodel praise-like sound with their tongue. As Deborah stepped forward, the crowd the crowd continued to shout her name. She raised her right hand for them to stop but they continued for another two minutes to applause her. She attempted to speak twice but the cheers were too loud for her to speak. Then, at last, the voices died down.

"Blessings and prosperity to all my brothers and sisters. In addition, may we continue to give praises and glory to our eternal God, the God of Abraham, Isaac, and Jacob. I ask our Lord to give peace and good health to all our great elders who made this long journey to come to this city in such a time as this."

Deborah spoke for an hour and a half, revealing what God had told her, reminding them to keep all of God's commandments, and to deal righteously with one another without hatred. Her speech was interrupted four times by cheers and great applause. Then she began to bring her speech to a close and her final remarks were as follows:

"Many of our ancestors didn't drive out the Canaanites. Therefore, many of us live among them. It is written in our holy books that God places temptation among us to see if we shall keep His commandments or not. Even though you live among the Canaanites, don't be tempted to copy after them. For they worship idol gods, commit incest, cohabitate with animals, sacrifice and burn their sons and daughters in the fire to their gods. We must resist temptation and not become like them. Because they did these things, our God dispossessed them from this land.

"Now, a few words about Sisera. Even though Sisera oppressed us, remember that God raised him up to punish us for our disobedience. We shouldn't blame Sisera because the fault lies in ourselves. Now, we can correct this by doing what is right.

"At this season, God has heard our prayers and He has decided that twenty years of punishment is enough. In order to redeem you, God chose Barak and I to be your leaders. As I close, I want to remind you that when we go to war against Sisera and defeat him, the victory belongs to God. So let us give Him the glory, *hallelujah*."

"*Hallelujah! Hallelujah! Hallelujah!*" repeated the crowd.

When Deborah finished her speech, the crowd went into frenzy and began to cheer her enthusiastically. Finally, the crowd went automatically into groups of folk-like dances. They sang as they danced praising God for answering their prayer, and for sending them Deborah and Barak. Not being able to resist the gaiety, Deborah and Barak joined in with a circle of dancers. They went around

203

in a circle. They took steps back and forwards and they danced to the rhythm of the drums as they clapped. They looked at one another with joy in their hearts, smiling and teasing each other with seductive gyrations and looks. It had been years since either of them had enjoyed themselves with such intensity.

They stopped dancing and walked together away from the crowd. "Oh, it was so wonderful," she remarked looking up at him and panting out of breath.

"Yes, it has been years since I've danced like this. I believe it was at one of the Sukkoth festivals."

"You know Barak, I've enjoyed myself ever since we arrived at the city of Dabareh, and since we arrived here. The countryside has been beautiful. Your people have been so warm, friendly and receptive. Even your father is sensitive and kind," she said patting him on his chest softly with the palm of her hand.

"Well...thank you, Deborah,"

"And you...you've made me feel like I am fifteen years younger, she said. "You have made me feel alive again."

"Well...you know it doesn't have to end.

Then Barak looked over the crowd and both of them remained silent for a moment. Finally, he looked down at her; took her by the hand and said softly, "I love you Deborah. I want you to be my wife Deborah...will you?"

"Oh Barak, you are a good man...you came from a good family, but it is too early to think about marriage," she said as she turned to the right.

"You were going to marry Caleb...now, he is gone! Now, what is there to stand in our way?" he asked as he looked into her eyes.

"That was different.... Now, the war will be starting soon and there are a few things that remain uncertain."

"In regards to my question Deborah, is that a yes or no?" he inquired.

"It isn't a yes or a no. It is a go slow…we don't have to make any definite promised right now, do we?"

"No…but I think we should be able to make a decision soon after the war."

"Now, I can agree to that."

Deborah was glad that Barak asked her to marry him. It proved his good intentions, she thought, and her journey to his hometown showed a more positive side of his life that she liked. However, there was one thing that held her back from committing herself; she felt that his spiritual faith was questionable. In view of this, she wanted to give herself more time to see how that played itself out.

The following day Barak met with his regiment commanders. They made preparations and drew up plans for the journey. Then Barak sent an advance detachment of 500 men to take control of Mount Tabor. After the priests, elders and soldiers were ready, Barak shouted, "We march tonight!" Moreover, the Princes of the tribe of Issachar were with Deborah and Barak when they arrived at Mount Tabor three days later.

CHAPTER NINETEEN

On the next day after Barak departed from the city of Kedash, Sisera called an urgent meeting with King Jabin, and his courtiers. When the King sent word to Sisera that he was ready to see him, he marched into the Grand Hall of the Canaanites at rapid pace. Sisera was in full battle dress with chest protection, a sword on his side, and a brass helmet on his head with a purple plume on its peak. He strutted in like a rooster with its red plume on its head.

"This better be urgent...for you to interrupt my meeting with the ambassadors," said the King looking serious.

Bowing to the King, Sisera remarked. "Yes, it is my Lord! Our spies have reported to me that Barak and this...this woman, Deborah, have taken control of Mount Tabor."

"How many men are you talking about?" inquired the King as he changed positions on his copper throne.

"Between ten and fifteen thousand."

"As my commander-in-chief of the Canaanite army, what do you make of this troop movement?"

"It is simply an act of war...my Lord. It appears that Barak and Deborah want us to declare war!"

"Go on...explain!" the King ordered as he placed his elbow on the armrest of the throne.

"When Barak and Deborah took Mount Tabor, this meant that they intended to attack our forces in the Jezreel Valley and try to put an end to our control of the valley," said Sisera.

It was twenty years earlier that Sisera conquered the Jezreel Valley. As a result, many Hebrews fled to the mountains and hills where they lived in the dens and caves. This easy conquest by his iron chariots, enabled Sisera to divide the Hebrews north of the Jezreel from those south of it. In effect, his military operation helped contribute to the disunity and separation between the Hebrew tribes.

"Why do you think that Deborah and Barak took control of this particular mountain?" asked the Vizier.

"There are at least two reasons.... Tabor is a good place to assemble soldiers because it is a flat top mountain. Two, it is the highest mountain that overlooks the Jezreel Valley and from there, they can watch all our troop movements."

"What?" the King switched positions on his throne and remarked. "It seems like Deborah and Barak are not so foolish after all; furthermore, it appears that the rabbit has outfoxed the leopard," he said leaning forward with his head facing toward Sisera. If this mountain is such an important piece of property and a good lookout post, why in the hell didn't you take control of it before Barak?"

Sisera stood there dumbfounded with a sheepish look on his face. "I never thought..."

"You never thought what...? Speak...! Speak up General!" ordered the King.

"Well, they were just mountain and cave dwellers...and I never thought that they would have the sense to organize an army of more than five hundred men."

The King sat back slowly. "I see.... In the future...I would suggest that you remember that even a jackass has a brain," said the King looking down at him in disappointment.

"Our spies," said Sisera, "saw the Hebrew soldiers marching north and they stopped at the city of Kedesh...."

"Go on," prompted the King.

"Night fell and the spies went to sleep. By the next morning, the spies learned that the Hebrews departed during the night, and marched to Tabor, my Lord the King."

The King stood up and placed both hands on his hips and spoke: "We have the most powerful army in Canaan, and have experts in every field of knowledge. Inspite of this, we have been outmaneuvered by this so-called mountain boy and his consort Deborah.... Now, they can watch us like hawks watch their prey, waiting for the first chance to dive down on their victims. We...the mighty ancient Canaanite people, will become the laughing stock of the civilized world."

Sisera made a gesture with his hand and attempted to speak. "My Lord the..."

But the King interrupted him and continued. "Barak, and his woman have the best position they could want. Barak and his army are protected on the north by the hills of Zebulun, and the people of Naphtali. We have been made to look like fools...! like fools...! Isn't this true Sisera?" the King asked.

Sisera hesitated to answer the question, but he knew that he dared not displease the King. At that moment, he lowered his head slowly, and answered cautiously, "Yes...my Lord the King."

Dressed in his purple tunic, which extended from his shoulders to his feet, the King turned around sharply in a stately fashion and sat down gracefully. "There is one thing that troubles me." The King rubbed his chin and closed his eyes for a moment. "Why would the Hebrews want to go to war with such a small number and without chariots?" he asked raising his head slowly with piercing eyes looking in Sisera's direction.

Sisera looked surprised—he squirmed and struggled to speak. His head moved in several directions at once. "I...I don't exactly know.... Perhaps they have armies hidden in the mountains north and south of the Jezreel and intend to surprise us."

"You know Sisera...that I hate surprises! Barak will most likely attack us from the north; however, we shall need additional soldiers to protect our rear in case the Hebrews attack us from the south."

"I agree my Lord."

At that moment, the High Priest stroked his chin and appeared deep in thought. "If it pleases the King... may thy servant, the High Priest, say a word or two?"

"You have my ear, oh servant of Baal."

"When I researched the history of the Hebrews, I discovered that one of their leaders, Moses, took a census of the men from twenty years of age who were able to go to war. At that time, there were more than 110,000 men from the tribes of Zebulun and Naphtali alone, and this was 150 years ago...."

"What is your point?" asked the King, showing a little impatience.

"My point is that, I am sure that their number has increased. Therefore, isn't it good sense to conclude that they are able to muster far more than ten or fifteen thousand men?" explained the High Priest as he extended his arm.

"Yes," said the King. "That makes sense. They must have reserve forces hidden away somewhere."

The King then turned toward his advisor, Kenaz, an expert on Egyptian and Nubian affairs. "Do you think that we should send to Egypt for help?"

Kenaz threw his dark green tunic over one shoulder and spoke. "Not at this time...my Lord."

"And why not?" asked the King raising up suddenly.

"These are very unstable times in Egypt: From the reign of Rameses IX and after, Libyan marauders have threatened the Theban Capitol. Civil war has been rampant. Moreover, because the silver and the gold had been cut off, the economically distressed people robbed the tombs of the kings and nobles. In view of this, the government at Thebes had to call in Nubian troops to restore order. As you can understand my Lord...Egypt, and our Hametic brothers are in no position to send us help."

"Who can we turn to then...? I don't want to be surprised by these Hebrews. There must be at least a token force that Egypt can send."

The grand Vizier stepped three paces toward the King. "There is no need my Lord to send to Egypt for help...when we have friends nearby..."

"Nearby? Continue!"

"We can summon help from the nations of the East, from Ammon, from Amalek, from Moab, and Syria."

"What makes you think that they will send help?" asked the King.

Pointing toward the East, the Vizier explained: "These nations are the old enemies of Israel...they will be glad to get revenge because of their humiliating defeat over eighty years ago."

"Who was the Hebrew leader at that time?"

"Ehud, Ehud Ben Gera...oh King, I think that we need to do three things immediately: One, call up the kings of the East. Two, call up all the Canaanite nations from Zidon down to the city of Dor. Three, call up all the Canaanite city-states from Megiddo, and Taanach to Beth Shean. Then we can confront and defeat Barak and Deborah across the Jezreel ...near the city of Megiddo.

"Umm." The King sat back on his throne and placed his fingers on his chin. "This sounds like a splendid idea. Yesss, we shall go with the Vizier's recommendation. From this day, I hearby appoint you responsible for the assembly of all the said mentioned Canaanite nations."

"I'll start to work right away my Lord," the Vizier promised and departed.

The King commanded, "Approach the throne, General Sisera." Sisera came near, stopped at the bottom step, did a slight bow, and saluted the King by bringing up his right fist briskly to his chest. Then he released his arm, and stood at attention. "At your service my Lord the King."

"General Sisera, many years ago, my father appointed you as commander-in-chief of his army, because he saw competence in you. However, within recent years, there has been several events that have made me wonder about you...the lost of over five hundred soldiers at the Japhia Pass, and now this spy debacle."

"My Lord, but I was not present at the Japhia Pass!"

"I know that...! But as commander-in-chief of my army, I hold you responsible for the conduct of your officers and soldiers. It is your duty to instruct your soldiers on how to behave in every situation. Is that understood?"

"Yes, my Lord."

The King then asked Sisera to come closer to the throne, because he had something to say to him in private. The King whispered: "Deborah and Barak outsmarted our spies, and made us look like fools. Now, after the war is over...make sure you don't have to return in disgrace. Can I depend on you General?"

"Yes, my Lord," said Sisera humbly, as he bowed.

Finally, the King gestured to him to return to his former place. "Oh, there is one last thing. Sisera, do you think that we should attack Mount Tabor?" inquired the King.

"No! My Lord. Absolutely not."

"And why not?"

"Our losses would be too great...Barak, the mountain boy...has the advantage because he controls the high ground. This gives him the opportunity to roll down on us large boulders and to rain down on us rocks and stones like hail from heaven."

"Then what do you suggest?" asked the King.

"We move our army into the Jezreel Valley and wait for him to attack. When they do, we can use our charioteers and horsemen against them, and crush them like ants. This way, we can annihilate the forces of Deborah and Barak in one central location."

"Ohhh! Your words are pleasing in my ears...you have my permission to take up your positions as soon as possible, and keep me informed of everything," ordered the King.

"Yes my Lord."

"Furthermore, when you defeat the Hebrew army, I want you to bring Deborah and Barak to me...alive...I want them to stand before me...in chains...in chains. Is this clear General?"

"Yes, my Lord...in chains," Sisera repeated, and snapped to attention.

"'There is one last thing. Deborah and Barak outsmarted our spies, and made us look like fools. Now, make sure...that you don't return in disgrace with a defeatist look on your face! Now go."

As Sisera stood before the King, it irked him to entertain the thought that Barak, the mountaineer and his female consort, could defeat him. He asked himself what kind of a man was this that needed to hide behind the skirt of a woman. He dubbed Barak, the mountain boy, that dashed over rocks and cliffs, and who was scared to come out and fight.

When the King finished speaking the High Priest, Eved-Baal, said: "Oh King, for the success of the war, I think it is only befitting to offer special sacrifice to our god, Baal, who needs to be pacified."

"Yes, I agree. When would you like to have the ceremony?"

"The sooner the better...in an hour would be good my Lord." Then a priest blew the trumpets to announce that a ceremony for a sacrifice would take place in an hour. For these ceremonies, the people would usually gather in the area of the temple of Baal and next to the temple was a large head of him. Before the bringing of the sacrifice, the High Priest rendered his prayer: "Oh Baal, our god, Lord of the world, we beseech thee to grant us victory in battle over the Hebrews and their leaders Barak and Deborah."

The priests heated a large fire in the stomach of Baal. They brought in four persons to be sacrificed: two Canaanite boys, and two Hebrew captives: one male and one female.

"Bring forth the two Hebrews," ordered the High Priest.

They brought the Hebrew male and female blind-folded with their hands tied behind their backs. The Priest placed his hand on the head of the female and recited. "This sacrifice is offer to thee oh lord Baal to grant us victory over the woman known as Deborah.

The face of Baal was about ten cubits wide and about twelve cubits high. He had thick lips and a broad nose. His stomach was open so that he could receive the human sacrifices. They marched the Hebrew girl over to the large idol where the hot flame was, and cast her inside.

The same thing they did to the Hebrew boy. The only thing that was difference was that his sacrifice symbolized the victory over Barak.

Finally, they sacrificed two Canaanite boys so that their idol god, Baal, could be appeased enough to grant them victory over the Hebrew army. All of these persons were cast into the fire and consumed by the god, Baal.

When the High Priest finished the sacrifice ceremony, the King, Sisera, the Vizier, and the rest of the courtiers returned to the palace. Sisera gathered up his essentials such as: war instruments, charts, maps and rode off with a detachment of soldiers to where his army was in bivouac.

Sisera had a surprise for Deborah and Barak. He was not about to let his soldiers be trapped between two Hebrew armies on both sides of the Jezreel. He didn't want it to be said that a woman and a mountain boy defeated Sisera.

CHAPTER TWENTY

The army of the Hebrews now occupied Mount Tabor, a flat top mountain excellent for the mustering of troops and high enough to observe much of Sisera's troop movements. Tabor is located on the northeast side of the Jezreel Valley not far from the southwest shore of the Sea of Chinneret, which is now called the Sea of Galilee. From Mount Tabor, Deborah and Barak looked due south in the direction of Mount Gilboa.

Deborah and Barak walked around the mountain to check the physical figures. At the foot of the mountain on the northwest side, they noticed the spring of water that drained into the Kishon River to the southwest. The most common ascent to Tabor is on the northwest side. This is the route that Barak's army took when they climbed to the summit. They ascended in a serpentine course and passed by beautiful varieties of grass, oak trees, and green bushes. Tabor has lower peaks on the northwest side leading to the hills of Zebulun and the city of Nazareth. However, the city of Nazareth was not in existence in the time of Deborah and Barak.

It was the second day that the Israelite army was encamped on Mount Tabor. The Israelites gathered rocks and stones to hurl at the enemy. They didn't have many spears and swords, and were forced to use slingshots as weapons, because the Canaanites had taken away their blacksmiths.

Just yesterday, Barak sent out more spies to keep a careful watch on all the activities and movements of the Canaanites. Barak read books on warfare used by other Hebrew generals and warriors so that he could be better prepared for the big battle to come. Everything was on a high war footing. Sisera increased his military presence in the Jezreel particularly on the main artery of the Kishon River, northeast of the city of Megiddo. The Israelites saw hundreds of chariots moving bristly up and down the Valley, along with thousands of horsemen and tens of thousands of infantrymen. The Hebrews knew that it would be only a matter of days before all hell would break loose.

As Barak sat in his tent reviewing military matters, one of his guards entered. "General, a lieutenant is here to see you."

"Send him in," ordered Barak.

The lieutenant walked in and snapped to attention. "Our patrols have captured a group of people, General."

"How many are there?"

"Five. And I believe they are spies, General," commented the lieutenant.

"Oh? You do huh...? That's up to me to decide what they are."

"They have the appearance of the heavenly moon."

"Now, what makes you thing that they are spies?" Barak asked gently tilting his head to one side.

The lieutenant extended his hand in gesturing. "Because their kind are not from around here."

"Oh...? I see...And if you visited their country, your kind would not be from around where they live...Would that make you a spy?"

"I...I ...I... guess...not," he stuttered.

"Did you get their names?"asked Barak.

"The head man of the group said that...his name...I think, he pronounced it Demetrus."

"Do you mean Demetrius?"

"Yes, that's it. Do you know him?" he asked with surprise.

"Yes! A little better than you...! Did you tie them up?"

"Yes, General!"

"Untie them...and bring them to me!" Barak ordered forcefully.

A short while later, the lieutenant and a few of his soldiers escorted the Greeks to Barak's tent. As soon as Barak heard them coming, he stepped out from his tent with a big smile. "Peace be with you Demetrius. You have returned. You have returned to us." Then they embraced like old friends.

"Peace Barak...you look good in your uniform."

"Thank you, is everyone well?"

"Yes, here they are: my three medical assistants, my wife, Isis, and my daughter, Hepshepsut, who I named after the queen of King Thutmose III, of Egypt."

Everyone looked pleased and smiled at Barak for his warm greeting. After that, Barak excused the lieutenant.

"I want to apologize for any discomfort that my soldiers may have caused you to endure," said Barak.

"Come!" invited Barak. "Come into my tent! I have water and food for you to satisfy your hunger and thirst."

After his guest partook of the victuals, Barak asked the important question. "Oh Demetrius, did you return to us to help with our wounded?"

"Yes, that is true."

"May I ask what made you change your mind?"

"Well, it was the dream that I had on the night that we slept in the Canaanite city of Tyre. In my dream, the wolves attached my neighbor's sheep and I did not help them. Then I ran away and I felt very sad. After discussing this dream with my wife, my daughter, and my medical assistants, I decided to return to help you, General."

"I am very happy that you decided to return," commented Barak.

"My wife always tells me that there is deep meaning in our dreams, if we think about them and apply them to our everyday lives. I have listened to her advice in the past and it has been very helpful to me."

"You are fortunate to have such a valuable wife." Her wisdom has not only benefited you...but it will also benefit my people," said Barak as he glanced at her. Barak paused, lowered his head and thought for a moment. "Now, I think, that I should introduce you to my people," said Barak, as he looked directly at Demetrius.

"Whatever you think is best is all right with us," commented Demetrius turning his head toward his family and friends for approval. On their faces was the look of consent.

Then Barak called out aloud, "Guard!" The guard came in and snapped to attention. "Blow the ram's horn and assemble the people."

"Yes, General."

A short while later, Barak and his guests went out of the tent and they stood on an elevated part of the mountain for everyone to see them. The news had spread like a windstorm that unusual visitors were in the camp. As a result, the people were eager to assemble in order to learn what Barak had to say. The people were very quiet and pensive—not one soul moved. A few moments later, Deborah and the Princes of Isashchar came up. Finally, Barak began to speak:

"Our sages, elders, priests, princes, Prophetess Deborah, officers, soldiers and people of the Hebrew tribes. I greet you all with great love. Many of you know why I summoned you here today. For those of you who may not know, it is only befitting for me to inform you that earlier today, visitors came into our camp of their own free will.

They came from Greece, a distant country northwest of Asia, Minor.

"For the last twenty years, they have been studying in Egypt and Nubia. Now that their studies are complete, they were returning to Greece. Deborah and I, first, met them in the city of Tirzah more than a week ago. Their knowledge and learning is of a high quality and because of this, I felt that their service would be very useful to us. In view of this, I asked them to remain with us for a fortnight.

"The soldiers of the tribes of Zebulun and Naphtali are encamped on this mountain because we are expecting war any day now. Like any war, there will be injuries to our soldiers and they deserve the best medical care that can be given. To my right, are Demetrius Lysimachus and his staff. They have been trained as expert doctors in the land of Egypt. The most advanced nation in the world. His Egyptian wife, and his daughter, from a previous marriage, are both trained nurses. As of this moment...I have placed Demetrius as head over the hospital and I want you to give him and his staff your greatest respect and cooperation. Anyone found faltering, would be dealt with by me and the court of the elders. However, I know that you will conduct yourself in the proper manner. If anyone has any questions or complaints, this is the time to utter them...."

Barak remained silent for a short while. Then when no one spoke up, he continued. "There maybe some children here who are old enough to remember Moses...when he stood on Mount Sinai," smiled Barak. "At that time, Moses advised us with these words: *Thou shall neither vex a stranger, nor oppress him: for ye were strangers in the land of Egypt.*' " The crowd went wild, clapped their hands, shouted and greeted the visitors with smiles and words of joy. Moments later, the elders, priests, princes and officers lined up and passed by the visitors saluting them and expressing words of welcome, and gratitude.

Then Barak summoned a war council meeting of his staff officers, and other officials. This group included the princesses, elders' priests, and Deborah. The meeting was scheduled to take place in the large headquarters' tent at sunset.

After the reception for Demetrius had been completed, Deborah returned to her tent. She and her handmaid shared a tent together, and Nachshon had his own tent nearby. "Sarah, would you mind going down to the watershed to get some water?" asked Deborah.

"Surely, my Lady...right away."

"And take Nachshon with you!"

As Deborah sat in her tent alone, she reflected on the impending war. She knew that it had to come but once it was over, she knew things would be normal again.

Then she thought about Barak, how they first met, and his warm smile. He was like sunshine she thought. Afterward, Caleb came to her mind—how she was duty bound to marry him, a man she didn't love, but the law of her people required it. She thought of the times in the past when she was fond of Barak—but couldn't show it, nor dwell on it unless—she be guilty of sin. She remembered how hurt Barak was when he found out that she was betrothed to someone else. Later, she thought about the letters that they sent and received from one another. Moments passed and she reflected on how the months came and passed so quickly. Finally, she sent and called for Barak and told him what the Lord wanted him to do. At that time, he asked her to go with him on his mission, which she agreed.

On the road to Zebulun and Naphtali, she recalled when she opened the letter and found out that Caleb had died. At that time, she shed tears because the Lord worked out his purpose beyond the understanding of mankind. She thought about the fact that after the reading of the letter at the city of Tirzah, how Barak and her were beginning to become closer and closer. Also, she reflected on that little intimate moment at Mount Gilboa when they hid among the cliffs and boulders of the mountain to hide from the Canaanite patrol. Next, she thought of how Barak embraced her tenderly and wanted to kiss her, but she turned her head, preventing him from doing so. These moments she cherished dearly.

After that, her mind became full with great emotions because of those wonderful moments she experienced at the cities of Dabareh and Kedesh. She recalled how the people cheered and applauded both of them as if they were a king and a queen. Then she thought about her meeting with Barak's father, how nice he was and the wonderful reception she received from the elders, and people of the city of Kedesh. At that moment, she thought about the great joy she had dancing a folkdance with Barak. A moment she cherished, and hadn't experienced in years. Finally, the time came that she remembered when he asked her to marry him. This meant a lot to her because it indicated that he didn't just want her to be his woman, but to be his wife.

These final days just before the war brought her great happiness. She felt herself drawing emotionally closer to Barak. She knew that he was not perfect and lacked spiritual knowledge; however, he had many other good qualities such as honesty, truthfulness, integrity, and maturity. She felt emotionally good around him. His father accepted her. Barak made her feel important, wanted and loved. She hadn't felt this way around any other man, not even Caleb. She became saturated with optimism in her relationship with Barak and she wanted to help him grow.

At that moment, Deborah stood up in her tent and looked through the opening and saw Barak talking to one of his officers. She wanted to go to him and embrace him because she felt deep down that he had almost everything she wanted in a man. Deborah was beginning to think of

Barak as her man. "After all, didn't the Lord ask me to send for him? And didn't the Lord remove Caleb from the scene? There must be some special meaning in that," she thought.

At last, Sarah and Nachshon returned with the water. "We were able to get three skin containers full, my Lady," said Sarah.

"That's great. Oh Sarah, I have to go to a staff meeting with the officers, the elders and with Barak. Would you like to walk over with me?"

"Sure my Lady," said Sarah smiling.

When Deborah arrived at the large tent of the military headquarters, she greeted all the elders, princes, staff officers and Barak. They smiled at one another and Deborah was pleased. Barak was waiting for two more people and after they arrived, he opened the meeting. The head priest of the city of Kedesh opened the meeting with prayer and ended with the priestly three-fold blessing: "... *'May the Lord bless thee and keep thee...'* "

When the priest finished his prayer, Barak spoke after him. "We are here today to discuss plans for the war; and it is just a matter of a few days before the war will breakout. By the way, my staff estimates that the enemy has us outnumbered ten to one. Now, I would like to hear the report from Captain Maher."

"All the food and water supplies are ready General, including all bandages and medicines for the wounded."

"Good...! I want you to hand over all those medical supplies to Dr. Demetrius. Now, Captain Enoch! Give us your report."

"The weapons, slingshots, spears, and rocks are ready; and we have strengthened the ramparts that surround the top of this mount."

"What about the training of the men?" inquired Barak with concern.

"We trained them in all the body movements, riding horses, and how to take the enemy's spears. And, we taught them how to use them," explained Captain Enoch confidently.

"Captain Enoch, have you heard anything from our spies yet?"

"No General, but I am expecting a report any time now."

Barak remained quiet for a moment and appeared to be in deep thought. Then he asked: "Do any of you priests or elders have anything to say?"

"Yes," answered one of the elders. "Just before the battle, the priest must blow the trumpets; and recite the conditions that exclude some soldiers from war duty."

"Thank you elder, are there any questions?"

"Oh General Barak," said a senior priest. "We understand from your own words, that our forces are outnumbered ten to one. Now, what is this rumor that we hear that you refused help from Prince Abihu? Is this true?"

"Yes! But, it is also true...that I refused his help because his offer was based on harsh conditions. He wanted me to pursuade the northern tribe to accept his leadership; and if they refused, he wanted to have them murdered. As a result, I refused to be a party to his scheme...."

"Don't you think it would have been better to have had his soldiers so that they could help us get rid of Jabin and Sisera?" asked the priest.

"No! I do not. We must not trade one cruel master for another, just to say that we have a Hebrew king.... The end does not justify the means. The scheme proposed by Abihu would have plunged the Hebrew tribes into civil war, and that's too risky. If civil war came, more people would be killed by us, than by the swords of Sisera. I can take some cruelty from Sissera...but I shall not take...the persecution...and dictatorship of Prince Abihu," he said shaking his head from side to side in opposition.

At that moment, a young officer raised his hand and received recognition to speak. "Some of our elders tell us that we have enough men from the tribes of Zebulun and Naphtali to put in the field more than two hundred thousand soldiers. If this is true... why are we calling up only ten thousand men?"

"Deborah, would you like to answer that question?" asked Barak.

"I'll be glad to answer.... The Lord asked for only ten thousand and no more."

At that instant, one of the guards outside of the tent handed Barak a letter from Sisera. Barak read the letter then read it to the counsels.

> " 'In the name of Jabin, King of the Canaanites. I General Sisera order you Barak and Deborah to surrender to me by noon tomorrow. If you do this, your soldiers will be allowed to go free. If not—our gods, Baal, Ashtaroth, and Mot will deliver you into our hands. Then, some of you will be sold into slavery and the rest of you will be sacrificed in the fire to our gods. Furthermore, don't think that your God will save you out of our hands. He hasn't delivered you during the last twenty years, and He will not save you now. This is the only letter you will receive.' " Signed General Sisera

"You have heard the letter, shall we send him an answer?"

Everyone remained silent. At last, Elder Ram spoke: "If no one has anything to say, I do..." he said looking to one side of the tent, and then to the other. "General Sisera has the gall...to ask Barak and Deborah to surrender to him.... Then he insults our intelligence further by telling us that our soldiers will go free.... His words are only lies...lies...lies.... Let's not honor him... by giving him an answer," he said looking around the tent. "But let him wait...! And sweat...! Until the water runs down into his breaches," he said, as the people laughed in agreement.

"Does anyone have anything to add?" asked Barak.

Then a young officer raised his hand. "When will we attack?"

"I...don't really know. I guess, Prophetess Deborah...will give us that information," Barak answered slowly and cautiously.

"When do we start taking instructions from a woman?" asked a young officer.

"Listen young man! If I don't question her, don't..."

"Thank you Barak," Deborah interrupted. "I would like to speak for myself." She spoke softly and calmly: "I would like to remind my brother that you received your first instructions from a woman and she, no doubt, was your mother or a another woman. Also, you probably have heard that some say that I am a prophetess; but I am not the first one. Miriam, the sister of Moses, was a prophetess, and that is not all my young brother," she said calmly as she spoke to him the way she would speak to her own son. "Have you not heard that Abraham, our father, listened to his wife Sarah in the matters of Ishmael; and the Lord agreed that she was right. Furthermore, have you not heard from the elders that the Lord revealed himself to Rebecca, the wife of Isaac, and told her that twins were within her? Now, the Lord has revealed to me, my brother, what we must do to defeat Sisera...and if you have a problem in accepting this; then, you are not rejecting me, but the Lord."

"Very well put, Deborah," said one elder.

Another remarked, "You handled yourself very well."

After Deborah finished speaking, Barak gave her a compliment. "The manner in which you presented yourself was great and I hope my officers have learned something from you," he commented as he looked over at the young officer.

Deborah was proud of Barak because he wanted to speak up on her behalf. But, she wanted to keep the respect of the officers, princes, and elders based on her own wits and merits and not just on what Barak could say for her.

For many years, Deborah fervently hoped that the Lord would put an end to the Canaanite oppression. For this purpose, she prayed day after day, month after month, and year after year encouraging her people to do the same. Now, her hopes were coming closer to being fulfilled.

The Lord had revealed Himself to Deborah and told her what to do. There were three major phases to the command of the Lord. The first one was to call Barak and this she did. The second phase was to tell him that the Lord commanded him to take ten thousand men from the tribes of Zebulun and Naphtali and bring them to Mount Tabor. And this they accomplished. There remained one final phase yet to be achieved, and that was the victory over the enemy in battle. Deborah had come to that final moment; and she was very hopeful that her people would be free at last.

She admired Barak more and more and she prayed to the Lord that He would help Barak to increase his spirituality and trust in Him. Deborah concluded once he had arrived at that spiritual level; she would be ready to accept his marriage proposal without hesitation. She knew that he would have to go through more trials and tests before he would be ready to accept a higher spirituality. He was almost there but not quite, she thought. Nevertheless,

226

she was optimistic. Because she wanted him, she was beginning to feel that he belonged to her.

Returning to the war agenda Barak said, "I have something to add. Our army will be divided into two parts. Each part will contain five thousand men. I shall lead the frontal attack, and Captain Enoch will head the second part. But, Captain Enoch you will remain about five hundred cubits behind me. Your men will act as a reserve unit to protect my rear against any surprise attack.

"Deborah, and the elders will remain here on Mount Tabor, and if they have any information to relay to us, they can do it by flag signals or by horse messengers."

As Barak finished explaining his point, Deborah spoke: " If we have completed the most important matters of this meeting, I would like to be excused to leave."

Everyone nodded their head in consent, and Deborah departed.

CHAPTER TWENTY-ONE

A few minutes later, a man approached one of the guards at the rear of the tent and whispered in the ears of the guard. The guard then waived to General Barak who was talking in the back of the tent.

"Captain Enoch, will you see what that man wants who is standing next to the guard."

"Yes General!"

As the Captain went out the opening of the tent, he could see that the man was the chief of his spy network. The man whispered something in the ear of the Captain.

"Are you sure?" asked the Captain. "Did you check your information?"

"Yes! I got the same report from all four of my spy units," he said confidently.

"Thanks chief," commented the Captain. "The General will want to know this."

The Captain walked back into the tent. He stood at the front but to the side of the tent as Barak was talking. After Barak had finished explaining a point, he turned to the Captain.

"Yes Captain Enoch?"

The Captain walked over to General Barak and whispered in his ear. Barak opened his eyes wider and had a very serious look on his face. Then the Captain returned to his place.

"Alas!" sighed Barak as he took a deep breath.

All the officers, princes, and elders in the tent were tense and silent. You could tell by the glances on their faces that they were wondering what was happening.

"People of the Hebrew nation, I have...evil tidings." Barak said with a slow deep bass voice. "There has been a great change in the number of men, horsemen and chariots in Sisera's army. Two weeks ago...we knew that he had about nine hundred chariots, ten thousand horsemen and thirty thousand footmen. At that time, he had us outnumbered eleven to one. Now, everything has changed. The chief of our spy network has reported to me that Sisera now has three thousand chariots, thirty thousand horsemen, and 300,000 footmen. These new numbers give Sisera a total of 333,000 men arrayed against our little ten thousand. This situation is compared to a fight between the lion and the mouse, and we are the mouse."

"Alas!"

"Alas!"'

"Alas!" said the various elders, as they looked at one another and shook their heads with grief and disbelief.

Then Barak continued. "It was bad enough when they had us outnumbered eleven to one; now, they have us outnumbered thirty...thirty-three to one" he pointed out as he gestured with his hand.

"General, are you sure that the numbers in Sisera's army are correct?" asked one of the priests.

"Yes, I do. They are very close estimations. The report that we have is that more than fourteen kings have joined up with Sisera. Even if our numbers are off as much as one hundred and thirty three thousand...and I don't think they are, the fact remains that Sisera would still have two hundred thousand soldiers...and that is a lot...of men," he emphasized looking around the tent at the solemn faces.

"General Barak, from whence came these great numbers?" asked Captain Maher.

"Two large armies came from across the Jordan from the nations of Ammon and Moab. Moreover, our spies have sighted a third army moving south from Tyre and Sidon. Finally, a fourth army marched down from Syria," said Barak pointing at a map.

"General, what do you make of the large hordes that Sisera arrays against us?" asked Captain Enoch.

"I am not sure...but it could be that he thinks that we are going to array against him all the twelve providences of Israel."

"What do you think that we should do General?" inquired one of the elders.

"You want the truth?"

"Yes...! The truth!"

"To be honest about it! I think that we should call off the attack," said Barak looking stern as he stared at the elder.

There was complete silence in the tent and many of the officers, princes and elders seem confused.

"Call off the attack?" asked another elder, as he stood up. "Our people have been waiting in great anticipation for this moment."

"Waiting in anticipation of victory..." asked Barak, "or waiting in anticipation of defeat? I...am not willing to sacrifice the lives of our twenty-year old young men against Sisera's overwhelming odds. If we go into a war with Sisera and lose, all of our young men who aren't killed in action will be captured and sacrificed in the fire to the Canaanite god, Baal. I cannot...support a war wherein the enemy has the advantage of thirty-three to one.... It is as though all the surrounding nations have risen up against us." After Barak's words, the elder sat down.

Elder Ram raised his hand and began to speak. "General Barak, priests, officers, princes and elders," he said as he struggled to his feet slowly needing the support of the man next to him. As he arose, his dark blue dashiki-like garment became more visible. It was embroidered on the neckline and sleeves with gold and silver thread. "My father was a young man when Joshua was alive," he reminded them as he leaned on his stick and stroked his long white beard. "My father use to tell me stories how Joshua was out numbered by the Amorites...and other nations; yet, he was victorious. I remembered when the deliverer, Ehud, fought the Moabites and they outnumbered us. But for now...I say lets take a poll count and see how many are for war, and how many are not."

Barak and the entire body agreed that they should take the poll. They took the poll and it was deadlocked, five for, and five against.

"Barak is the General, why don't we let him decide," suggested a younger elder.

One of the Princes of Issachar made a counter proposal. "Lets not be hasty my brothers," he said, as he adjusted the white turban on his head.... "It is getting late...and I think we need to do two things. One, close out this meeting right now.... Two, continue this meeting tomorrow morning when Deborah can be here..." he said as he turned around slowly and looked in their faces.

"Yes, yes, yes..." Everyone stood up in agreement.

At that instance, Captain Enoch approached General Barak. "General, we have to check the fortification on the northwest lower spurs before it gets too dark."

"Oh that's right...let...let me have a word with the Princes of Issachar, then, I'll be ready to go."

Barak walked over to the Princes "Peace be unto you my brothers."

"Peace, Brother Barak."

"If it isn't too much trouble, I would like to ask a favor of you. I have to check the fortifications before it gets too dark. Would you be so kind as to inform sister Deborah about everything that was discussed at this meeting?"

"We shall be glad to do this for you Barak. May God be with you until we see you in the morning."

After everybody had departed, the Princes of Issachar sent for Deborah to meet with them in the headquarters' tent. Deborah came with her handmaid, Sarah and her bodyguard, Nachshon.

When Deborah arrived, the Princes of Issachar explained to her everything that she had missed. They told her about the spies who brought the bad news, and about the fourteen kings that had joined up with Sisera. This gave him overwhelming odds of thirty-three to one. Furthermore, they told her that Barak said that he would not take his men into battle to be slaughtered by Sisera's all-powerful force. Also, they informed her that the meeting would continue tomorrow morning.

After Deborah heard this depressing news, the Princes departed and Deborah hung her head in grief. She sat there for a short while and reflected on the bad news. Then,Barak came. He saw her sitting in the tent with her head lowered in grief and he asked.

"Why has thy continence fallen Deborah?"

She raised her grief-stricken head slowly. "What is this...I hear that you have called off the attack?"

"I did it because I felt that it would be suicide to go up against Sisera's overwhelming numbers," he replied as he walked towards her.

"Where is your spirituality? Where is your trust in God? Where is your belief in me? Where is it Barak?" she demanded.

He stood there silently starring at her. Then he labored to speak. "I...am responsible for the lives of my men."

"When you came to my house that last time, you said to me, '*if thou will go with me, then I will go: but if thou will not go with me, then I will not go.*' Is this not true Barak?" she inquired with trembling in her voice.

"Yes...It is true," snapped Barak with a little anger.

"At that time, I agreed to go with you and I kept my word. Now, you...are refusing to go into battle! Doesn't your word mean anything?"

"Of course! But, the situation has changed."

"Changed...? But the Lord has not changed," she retorted, as tears ran down her cheeks. "Barak I've had enough. You have rejected the Lord and disappointed me. There will be no marriage...I cannot live with a man, who has no trust in God to deliver his people from Sisera," she reminded him frantically as she marched out of his presence broken-hearted.

Barak stood there and watched her leave. Finally, he walked to the opening of the tent, and yelled to her: "A man must do what he has to. You are just like a woman. You blow off steam, just like a hot-water pot."

Deborah went to her tent. It had gotten dark, so Sarah her handmaid lit a small lamp. Then Deborah sank her head into the palms of her hands as she sat down. Soon thereafter, Sarah asked, "Is there something that I can do for my Lady?"

"No thank you Sarah...I just want to be alone with my thoughts."

Deborah reflected on how she came with Barak to Mount Tabor with great hope. A hope about how their relationship developed from one stage to another, from the first time they met until now. She thought about those warm romantic moments at the city of Kedesh, when he danced with her and made her feel alive again. There he asked for her hand in marriage.

When she agreed to go with Barak to Mount Tabor with the Hebrew army, she had great hope that he would put his trust in the Lord. Now, the man whom she was growing to love had refused to lead the Hebrew army and refused to trust in the Lord or even to believe in her. In essence, he dashed all her hopes and she felt empty in her stomach. She tried to forget him, but the pain gnawed in her stomach.

Then she prepared to go to sleep and Sarah put out the oil lamp. But sleep would not come. She thought about when she departed from the outskirts of Bethel and went to Tirzah, Dabareh, Kedesh, and now to Tabor. She had come a long way, met a lot of people, and raised their hope. Now, it seemed that all was in vain. As the moment, minutes, and hours passed, she sank into deep despair and her future with Barak seemed very uncertain. As a spiritual woman, she knew that she could never have any harmony with any man that didn't trust in the Lord. It was now several hours after midnight and still no sleep. Barak's actions weighted heavily upon her, interrupting her rest. She couldn't even discuss it with her handmaid, Sarah, because it was too disturbing. During the night, she tossed and turned and got only about an hour and a half of sleep. She seemed to be fearful to think of what the next morning would bring. The only conciliation she got was when she prayed to her Lord. Finally, she resigned herself to the fact that at sunrise the moment of truth would come.

CHAPTER TWENTY-TWO

The next morning not long after sunrise, the officers, princes, priest and elders continued their meeting in the large headquarters' tent. The atmosphere was solemn, tense, and uncertain. When the officials came in, they moved slowly and had serious looks on their faces. Everyone was present except Deborah.

"Can we start the discussion?" asked one elder.

The senior, Elder Ram said, "Let's give Deborah a little more time to get here."

In a short while, Deborah arrived. Finally, they reviewed all of the issues that they had discussed in the previous meeting, including Sisera's overwhelming numbers.

"General Barak, have you changed your thinking?" asked Elder Ram.

"I am not sure what my position is at the present time. I have mixed feelings," he confessed. "I need more discussion."

One of the young officers raised his hand to speak. "Yesterday, I asked Prophetess Deborah why we recruited only ten thousand men when we are capable of putting into the field over 200,000. Would you be so kind to explain this more in detail?"

"Yes, I shall be glad to explain. If the Lord had told us to choose out more than 200,000 men, for war, and we became victorious, then our people would say that it was because of our might that got us this victory. However, instead of this number, the Lord chose ten thousand men. Because, when we win, we can't say that we gain this victory by our strength and by our great numbers. But, we will surely say only by the help of God did we win this battle," she said as she noticed the smiles of approval on the faces of the men.

"Are there any more questions or comments?" asked Elder Ram.

Deborah realized that if she was going to win over the elders and princes, she had to take the initiative and keep it. Then she raised her hand.

"Deborah, you may speak,"

"Elders, priests and officer of the Hebrew nation. There is no need to fear the great numbers of our enemy. All we need to do is to keep God's word, be righteous and trust in Him. I want to remind you that Moses wrote: '*When thou goes out to battle against thine enemies and seest horses and chariots, and a people more than thou—be not afraid of them—for the Lord thy God is with thee....*' This...I swear in the name of the Eternal One and in the spirit of our ancestors. For after tomorrow, Sisera will not breath another breath,' " she assured them, as she held out her hand in gesturing.

"I hope you are right my sister, because...if you are not," emphasized Elder Ram, "some of the people will want to bring charges against you for being a false prophetess."

"My dear Elder Ram, on the words that the Lord had spoken to me, I stake my honor, reputation, and my life."

At that moment, Deborah stepped forward three feet. She closed her eyelids and she remained still momentarily. During this moment of silence—she received a revelation. Her face shined radiantly and the power of her aura permeated throughout the entire tent. She opened her eyes and turned toward the General. "I have a message from the Lord for you Barak: '*Up...for this is the day in which the Lord has delivered Sisera into thine hands: is not the Lord gone out before thee?*'" she asked with tears in her eyes.

Everyone present, including Deborah fixed her eyes on Barak. No one spoke a word. They waited patiently to see what his reactions would be. It was obvious from the look on his face that he was under much emotional pressure.

"All right, we shall put all battle plans into action and let's meet on the lower northwest spur."

Suddenly, Barak grabbed a spear from the corner of the tent and held it high above his head. "Oh ye officers of the Hebrew nation...follow me!" he shouted as he marched bristly out of the tent.

The priests blew the ram's horn to assemble all the soldiers, priests, elders and princes. They met on the northwest ridge of Mount Tabor. This ridge is the lowest section of the mountain and the easiest to ascend and descend. As the Hebrews assembled, they could see the army of Sisera doing their maneuvers off into the distance.

When everybody had arrived and all plans were prepared, Elder Ram stepped forward and spoke: "We shall have the recitation of the words of encouragement."

One of the priests began to recite from the sacred laws of the Hebrews: "*Hear Oh Israel, ye approach this day unto battle against your enemies: let not your hearts faint, fear not and do not tremble, neither be ye terrified because of them; for the Lord our God is He that goeth with you, to fight for you against your enemies, to save you.*"

After the priest finished, Elder Ram turned to Deborah and asked? "Are there any more formalities Prophetess Deborah?"

Deborah lowered her head and touched her nose on both sides with her index finger and thumb in deep thought. "Oh yes! Now, we must have the reciting of the exemptions for the soldiers," she reminded him raising her head.

"Thank you Prophetess Deborah, I knew that you wouldn't forget anything."

Next, Elder Ram called for one of the military officers to recite the exemption rights to their men. "Now, hear this...oh ye host of Israel: *'What man is there that hath built a new house, and has not dedicated it? Let him go and return to his house, lest he dies in battle, and another man dedicates it. And what man is he that hath planted a vineyard, and hath not yet eaten of it? Let him also go and return unto his house, lest he dies in battle, and another eats of it. And what man is there that hath betrothed a wife, and hath not taken her? Let him go and return unto his house, lest he die in battle and another man take her.'* "

Furthermore, another officer recited the psychological conditions to the men, *"What man is there that is fearful and faint-hearted? Let him go and return unto his house, lest his brethren's heart faint as well as his* heart and may God be with you."

Elder Ram spoke up once more. "With the authority given to me by the princes of the tribe of Issachar, the priests, and the elders, I confirm Barak to be the general of the Hebrew army as spoken by the Lord through the Prophetess Deborah. Moreover, we grant Barak the authority to designate his deputy and his staff officers. All this, I do even though we are like mice who go up against the crocodiles."

After all of the introductory formalities were completed, Barak divided his army into two parts, each under the head of a captain with five thousand men each. Then, he appointed Captain Enoch to be his first captain of the army and his next in command to succeed him.

"Captain Enoch, I want you to organize the soldiers into battle formation," Barak said. "Line up all of the men facing the southwest in the direction of Sisera's army and stand by for further orders."

"Yes General."

They brought up the standards of the tribes of Naphtali and Zebulun, which had the images of a deer, and a ship embroidered on them, respectively. Afterwards, the priest came up with the ram's horn and the drummers. The horns blew and the drummers beat the drums.

"Boom! Boom! Boom!" This sound became the beat for the marching army and it was repeated over and over and over. Barak bade farewell to the princes, elders, and to Deborah.

"God be with you," Deborah said.

Finally, he turned his horse away and waived.

"Take care of yourself Deborah, I shall return."

Deborah smiled frostily, understanding in his words his intention to pursue her. She knew in her heart that his decision to go into battle was based only on her encouragement and on the indirect pressure of the elders. In view of this, she knew that Barak didn't have any deep faith in God. Therefore, Deborah resigned herself to the fact that Barak would not be an appropriate mate; even though, he was a man of high social standing, and temptingly handsome.

The army marched off to the beat of the drums. Barak could see the armies of Sisera across the Jezreel Valley. The army camp of Sisera was about twelve miles southwest of Mount Tabor. This camp was between the city of Megiddo and the Kishon River. The Kishon River flowed northwest and the calm water of the surrounding mountains fed it.

***

Just outside the city of Megiddo, stood Sisera, the General of the Army of Jabin, King of Canaan. He welcomed and addressed the allied kings, and soldiers who came to support him in the war effort against the Hebrews.

Sisera stood on a six-feet bolder and saluted the kings as they drove by in their metal chariots. He said, "Thank you oh kings of Taanach, Dor, Megiddo, Ibleam, Beth-Shean, Kitron, Nahalol, Acre, Sidon, Ahlab, Aphik, Ammon, Moab, Syria, Beth-Shemesh, and Beth-Anath." Sisera continued: "As you know, the Hebrews came into our land over a hundred and fifty years ago, under the leadership of that notorious Joshua, the son of Nun. Since they have been here, they have destroyed our gods, and altars. Furthermore, these Hebrews have become a danger to our way of life. We came here today to unite against them. There is no doubt that we can win. Our numbers far exceed theirs, and we control the Jezreel Valley with over three thousand metal chariots. We have divided the Hebrew nation by our control of the Jezreel.

"Furthermore, Barak and that...that...woman associate of his...made their worse mistake when they took their army up to Mount Tabor. Because of their action, this gives us the opportunity to destroy them in one central location."

The soldiers then hit their swords against their shields to express applause. Clang! Clang! Clang!

Then Sisera called up the High Priest, Eved-Baal. "It is with great pleasure that I take this opportunity to come before all of you kings of majesty, princes, and soldiers of the Canaanite nations. We thank you for your cooperation and unity. Let us pray: "Oh beloved Baal, our sun-god, giver of light and life, god of fire and summer heat, we ask thee to be with us in our fight to destroy our enemies, the Hebrews..."

The High Priest spoke for fifteen minutes and he concluded by saying that Baal can be appeased only with human sacrifice by fire. Then he called the custodians to bring forth one young male and a female to be sacrificed. After the sacrifices, the parade began.

Every army of each nation passed in review. They passed onward by hundreds, and by thousands marching in cadence with the trumpets blowing, and the drums beating.

"General Sisera, our soldiers look just magnificent...in their new uniforms," said General Kara. "Their red shirts, and kilts were made by our best weavers."

"Yess...and they look very neat in their army uniforms with their brass leggings, and coats of mail. Their brass helmets glow in the bright sunshine. That alone... is enough to terrify the enemy, emphasized Sisera."

The armies put on a great show of pomp and pageantry changing into right and left flanks, to the rear march, companies combining with others to form one unit, and then separating again. It was a great show of well-trained disciplined troops with horses and camels prancing and soldiers waving their spears, swords and flags.

Finally, Sisera received the news, which he eagerly waited for. One of his staff officers, Kara, reported. "General, the enemy has been sighted approaching from the north."

"How many would you say there are?"

"Between ten and fifteen thousand, General."

"What fools they are to come against our mighty force," commented Sisera as he gave a wicked smile. "This will be an easy... victory!"

"General, do you think that they have more soldiers hidden in the mountains of Zebulun?"

"I don't believe so...if they do, they better not come down into the Jezreel," he concluded. "Prepare the soldiers for battle and pass the word down that I want Deborah and Barak brought to me alive...that's an order!"

"Yes, my Lord Sisera, and what units shall we use for the first attack," asked Kara.

"We'll use five thousand horsemen, and fifty-five thousand footmen...all new recruits. This will give the new recruits a taste of battle on an easy prey," said Sisera as he stepped down the latter that was placed against the bolder.

When General Kara came down the ladder, he asked Sisera, "Are you going to use any of our chariots against the enemy?"

"Nooo...that will not be necessary, but we will hold our charioteers in reserve."

It was a bright and shinny day. After Barak and his army marched for four miles, they stopped to rest and they could see the Canaanite army.

***

Across the other side of the Jezreel Valley, eight miles away, Barak continued to lead his army toward Sisera. Because it was a bright day, Barak and Captain Enoch could see the army of Sisera moving into formation.

"What do you think of the situation?" asked Captain Enoch.

The General leaned forward over the long white mane of his horse and gazed into the distance. "It seems that the bulk of Sisera's charioteers are in the center, the horsemen are on both sides of the charioteers, and the foot soldiers are out in front," commented Barak, as he drew back and sat erect.

"I would agree, General," Enoch added. "If Sisera attacks us with his charioteers first, we shall suffer rapid, and very heavy losses, but if he uses his footmen first, we shall have a better chance...but, that chance would only be temporary."

"Yes, that seems logical," said Barak.

"General, look at Sisera's forces," Captain Enoch pointed out. They are line up like tidal waves, ready to overflow their banks."

"Yes, I see Captain."

At that moment, Captain Maher came up from the rear to talk to Barak. "General Barak, there are about ten horsemen approaching from our rear. Furthermore, the men are getting restless because of Sisera's large numbers and there is talk of some of them turning back."

"Thank you Captain for the report."

"Shall I return to my unit?"

"No! Wait here until the horsemen arrive."

As Barak and his officers waited for the horsemen to arrive, they saw dark clouds coming out of the north from the rear of their soldiers. At the same time, they could hear Sisera's band blowing their trumpets and beating their drums. There was no stop to the drummers. They continued on and on.

Finally, the horsemen arrived. It was Deborah with the three Princes of Issachar, her handmaid, Sarah, and her bodyguard, Nachshon. "Barak, we came because we felt that the soldiers needed our moral support," said Deborah.

"Only a prophetess or spiritual men would know that. I am glad that you came. It was thoughtful of you."

"If it is pleasing in your eyes, on the way back, we would like to ride between the ranks of the soldiers and encourage them," she said as she looked over his shoulder, and refused him direct eye contact."

"This is all right with me." Then he turned to Captain Maher. "You can go with Deborah as you return to your unit, Captain."

"Yes General," he said as he nudged his horse forward.

At last, Deborah and the Princes of Issachar began to speak. "Hear oh warriors of Israel; be not afraid of the numbers of our enemies for God is with you to fight your battle. Direct your heart, soul, and mind unto the Lord and He will save you."

When Deborah spoke these words in the ears of the soldiers, the soldiers and Barak were grateful for those words. Then they finally departed.

CHAPTER TWENTY-THREE

The Hebrew army continued to march southward toward the Kishon River. At this time, small drops of rain began to fall. The Kishon was just a small stream, but during very hot spells it became like a dried-up creek or wadi. However, during the rainy season, it overflowed its banks and became a mighty torrent being fed by the water running down from the nearby mountains.

"Boom! Boom! Boom! As Sisera's drummers continued to beat, dark clouds overcast the entire Valley. Then the drummers stopped beating. Also, the Hebrew army came to a halt. There was complete silence in the dark cloudy valley. "Oh God help us," said Barak.

At that quiet, tense, eerie moment, there came a powerful sudden crack of thunder and lightening that seemed to shake the foundation of the whole valley. In an instant, as if by divine inspiration, Barak shouted. "Charge! Attack!"

Barak dashed forward with the Hebrew army with him. He reacted as though the thunder and lightening was his signal from God to begin the attack.

When Sisera saw the Hebrews advancing, they charged toward the Kishon River, footmen in front, and horsemen behind.

"I cannot understand," said Barak, "why Sisera is putting his footmen into action first."

As Barak's army came within three hundred cubits of the Kishon, hail began to fall: thunder and lightening in repeated succession flashed forth; and harsher rain and

245

wind continued. The rain and wind was at the backs of the Hebrews but it blew in the faces of the Canaanites and blinded them. In light of this, the Canaanites were not able to use their arrows, spears, or swords.

The Canaanite army reached the Kishon first. By this time, the entire central valley north of the city of Megiddo became a marshland and very muddy. Horses ran into each other and slipped and fell, because the hail and rain blinded them.

"Use your slings men," yelled Barak as he approached within fifty cubits of the enemy. The slings were very useful to the Hebrews. The rocks remained airborne longer because the wind was behind them pushing the rocks forward. Barak then ordered his soldiers to take up defensive positions along the Kishon. The Hebrews then seized the spears and swords of the dead and wounded Canaanites.

An hour passed and it was still raining. Finally, Sisera put his charioteers into action. The horses and chariots were slipping and sliding in the muddy water. Many horses and chariots ran over dead horses and turned over. Many charioteers ran over their own footmen because they could not see for the rain and hail that beat down in their faces. Many Canaanite soldiers fell in the Kishon River and the torrent swept them away.

***

Meanwhile, back at Mount Tabor, Deborah prayed in her tent. She knew that her people would get the victory; in view of this, she prayed that the Lord would keep the causalities low. After she finished her prayer, she went outside to join the rest of the people, and the elders, as they watched the battle.

It was raining a little on Mount Tabor as they watched. The day turned into semi-darkness.

"Did you see that lightening bolt?" said Demetrius. "It struck down into the heart of the Canaanite army."

"Yes…" said Deborah, "The heavens are fighting for us."

The bolts of lightening struck one after another, in repeated succession, creating havoc and destruction on the Canaanite army. The lightening lit up the sky like fireworks. It was only during the time when the lightening flashed, that Deborah and the elders could get a good glimpse of what was happening out there—in the valley.

"Deborah, you were so right when you said that the Lord would fight our battle. You are truly a servant of the Lord."

"Thank you, Elder Ram."

As Deborah and the elders watched the battle, they began to sing praises to the Lord, because they were greatly inspired.

***

Back at the front lines, the army of Sisera became very confused and began to scatter. Then Captain Enoch looked to the right and saw a man dressed in a very majestic uniform riding in his chariot. At that moment, one of the Israelite soldiers threw a spear at the man in that chariot and missed. Instead, the spear struck the horse just below the neck. The horse fell down to its knees and didn't move.

"General Barak! Look at that fancy chariot over to your left," said Captain Enoch.

"Yes, I see, that could be General Sisera.

"He is dismounting from his chariot and running away. Do you want me to pursue him General?"

"No, I need you here. I'll get that crocodile sooner or later. Right now, the destruction of his crocodile army is more important."

"Yes General."

"Captain Enoch, I am going to pursue after the rest of Sisera's army. It seems like they are headed toward the city of Harosheth-Hagoiim near Mount Carmel. Can you and your men hold this line?"

"We'll hold General...at the risk of our lives," said the Captain confidently.

"If the enemy takes off and run, you have my permission to pursue them to the gates of hell."

Barak and his men then pursued after the chariots and the remainder of Sisera's army fighting and pursuing them all the way up to the gates of the city of Harosheth, which was located on the east side of Mount Carmel. As Barak led his men, he remembered the words of Deborah; "The *Lord hath delivered Sisera into thy hands: is not the Lord gone out before thee?*" Barak then became more encouraged and shouted, "*hallelujah*."

The city of Harosheth soon fell quickly before the onslaught of Barak. Then, his soldiers gathered up the spoils of the city and liberated the Hebrews who were working at hard labor in the Canaanite stone quarries.

After Barak finished his war operations at Harosheth, he returned to Captain Enoch at the front line. When Barak arrived, he learned that fresh troops from the tribe of Issachar had joined up with the Captain. The Captain pursued the Canaanites all along the Kishon River from Megiddo to the city of Taanach.

"Captain Enoch, congratulations! You've done a splendid job here! I see that the Lord has been with you."

"That is true General Barak, and lot of the credit must be given to our soldiers who fought with valor."

"I see that you have things under control here so I'm going to take fifty men with me and go after Sisera before I lose his trail entirely.

"Do you have any idea of his where-about?"

"Not exactly, but I think he is headed for the city of Damascus. I had heard some time ago that he was born not far from there." The rain stopped and Barak rode off into the twilight. That night they camped not far from the city Beth-Shean to rest for the night. But, before Barak could retire, he received a message from his nephew, Joel.

***

As Barak pursued Sisera toward the Sea of Galilee, his nephew, Joel was brought into the hospital tent on Mount Tabor in severe pain. He was found alive, lying under two dead Canaanites with a broken leg and an arrow wedged below his right shoulder. Joel sent for Barak after they had taken him from the battlefield. Lying on a table-like object, he was writhing in pain and hollering for his uncle. Mud and blood covered his entire body. The doctors wanted to give him a sleeping potion but he refused all care until his uncle, Barak, would come.

Then Demetrius, the head doctor, came into the operation tent. He lifted the cover from Joel's legs and his facial appearance changed with shock. "We can not delay," he uttered. The boy made an attempt to resist and they restrained him, "If you continue to move, you could rupture a blood vessel or puncture your lung," warned Demetrius.

Joel yelled: "No! No! Not right now! I must see him first."

Demetrius looked at his leg again. Then he leaned over his chest and spoke; "We can not delay forever, Joel...." Everyone looked down at him and remained silent.

As they held Joel down, he turned his head from side to side in defiance and shouted. "I sent for my uncle, Barak. I know he will be here. He will come! He will come!"

Demetrius looked at his leg once more and pleaded, "If you want us to save your leg, we have to work on you right away. Do you understand?"

"I must talk to him first!" he emphasized strongly.

As his head was facing the tent opening, he saw his uncle standing there. "He has come!" Joel informed him.

Everyone stopped what they were doing, turned around, and looked at General Barak with awe. "Congratulations General Barak," said Demetrius, "on your victory."

"Thank you." Barak walked slowly toward the mutilated body of his nephew, and looked down at him with tears in his eyes. He raised his head with a grimace on his face and then lowered it again in emotional agony. "I promised your mother...that I would take care of you and it seems that I have failed..." said Barak as he held Joel's hand with tenderness and love.

"I know...." He struggled to speak with labor, and the sound of pain was in his voice. "She...told me...that you would. I'm glad that you came. Oh Uncle, are they going...to cut off my leg?" he asked gritting his teeth in pain.

Barak glanced at his leg. Then he looked at the doctor. "What do you think Dr. Demetrius?"

"Well, the arrow is not that close to his vital organs, and it did not penetrate very deep; so it shouldn't be any problem in that area. However, we are concerned about his leg. The tibia bone is fractured and will have to be reset in place," he said seriously, leaning his head to one side.

"Dr. Demetrius, what could prevent him from having a complete recovery?"

"Well...there are a number of things: poor blood supply, infection, and leg movement. We will have to stabilize the leg to prevent it from moving. Any movement will hamper the fractured bone from binding together. To help prevent infection, we need to go to work right away!" he urged.

"I shall not keep you much longer. How long will it take for him to walk again?"

"It can take anywhere from four to eight months. But, before we can start to work on him, he needs to cooperate with us and take the sleeping potion. Without it, he will not...be able to endure the pain.

Barak then turned to Joel. "I want you to cooperate with the doctors and take the potion."

"But..."

"No buts in it," Barak interrupted. "Do it for your mother! Do it for me; and above all, do it for yourself!" explained Barak as he leaned over him and held his hand tightly.

"Yes...Uncle Barak," he said softly. "I wanted you to be here, so that I would know...that I am in good hands."

Barak lowered his head. "You are in good hands...." Then he let go of Joel's hand. "I'll pray for you," he promised.

Finally, one of the doctors gave Joel the sleeping potion and within a short while, the herb-like drug put him into a state of deep unconsciousness. As the doctors began to work on Joel, Demetrius turned his head toward Barak. "I'll contact you and let you know how he is progressing." Then he continued with his work.

"I am not leaving...just yet."

"Not leaving...? Huh....?" Demetrius paused and turned towards Barak again. "I can understand how you feel about your nephew General; however, did not you appoint me as head over this hospital?"

"Yes...that is true!"

"Well, by your authority...and as head...I must ask you to give us the privacy to do our work. We are perfectly capable of taking care of your nephew, and saving his leg...." They both looked at each other. "If Deborah was here, I am sure she would tell you the same thing."

Barak looked at him and smiled. After that, the Hebrew medical assistants looked at Barak and nodded their heads in agreement. Barak began to walk away slowly. Finally, he stopped and turned around. "I can see that they trained you well in Egypt, and I know that you will do your best. Peace be with you."

"Peace," said Demetrius. "Your nephew is young and strong. He should recover without any problems."

The operation lasted for a couple of hours. Afterwards, Demetrius had the look of satisfaction on his face. As he washed and dried his hands, he gave instructions to his assistants. "When he wakes up, give him some of that herb tea called, Genseng, which I bought from the men coming from China. It will help in the healing process."

After Barak departed from Mount Tabor, he joined up with his men near the Sea of Galillee, to continue the search for Sisera.

***

The next morning, Barak and his men got up early and prepared for the arguous search. He sent out three men in an advance party to inquire if anyone has seen Sisera, and, if not, to be on the lookout for him. They went to towns, villages and searched in fields, woods, hills and caves—hour after hour—from sunrise to sunset, and found no Sisera.

On the second day, Barak and his men arrived at Lake Merom about eleven miles north of the Sea of

252

Galilee. As Barak was searching for Sisera, a fast riding horseman rode up and said: "I have a letter for General Barak."

"I am Barak! Who sent the letter? "

"It is from the Prophetess, Deborah."

"Oh! It is?" asked Barak with surprise. Barak took the leather pouch and opened it eagerly. He wondered what she wanted, in light of their last breakup on Mount Tabor. He read:

> "*Shalom giborei Israel...peace ye warriors of Israel. Hallelujah. Praise the Lord for the great victory that He gave to us this day.*
>
> "*To General Barak, your officers and gallant soldiers who jeopardized your lives unto death in the high places and fields of the valleys. We invite you to a victory celebration of praise to the Lord. This celebration will take place at the city of Dabareh beginning seven days from today. We look forward to your appearance; from Deborah and the elders.*"

After Barak read the letter, he informed his men of the contents, and they were jubilant to hear the good news.

"Are ladies going to be there?" asked one soldier.

"Yes, many ladies," answered Barak.

"Hurrah, hurrah, hurrah," expressed the soldiers with cheer and excitement.

"All right men, it is time for us to continue our search for Sisera." They began to search the area west of Lake Merom, and came to a place of the great oak tree of Zaanannim not far from Kedesh. As Barak and his men advanced toward a tent which belonged to a woman named Jael, she came out to meet Barak and said unto him: "Peace be with you General Barak *'Come! and I will show thee the man whom thou seekest.'* "

At that moment, Barak drew out his sword, entered the tent cautiously, and behold Sisera lay dead with a tent nail in his temple.

"Did you do all of this?" he asked looking astonished as he scratched his head."

"I did!" she answered softly. "Now, I got my revenge."

"Revenge? Why did you kill him?"

"Because he killed my sons. My sons had lived not far from here, and when they were not able to pay their taxes, Sisera carried them off, and had them sacrificed to Baal, his god."

Then Barak walked slowly around the tent inspecting everything. He picked up a jawbone of an ass, and an ox goad and inspected them. "This jawbone has had a lot of use," he said looking at Jael. "It has cracked a many a skulls, and this goad has pierced the bodies of mighty warriors. To whom do they belong?"

"They belonged to Shamgar, the warrior, who slew six hundred Philistines, and some Canaanites."

"You knew him?" asked Barak.

"Yes General! After my first husband Heber died, I married Shamgar. We fought the Canaanites and the Philistines, a long time, before you came on the scene.... Barak, you finished the great work that we didn't complete."

"I thought King Jabin, and your previous husband, Heber, had a treaty?"

"My husband had a treaty with King Jabin, not I...!"

"Oh how I wanted the glory of capturing this man...and I forgot that Sisera was supposed to be given into a woman's hands."

"A woman's hands?" asked Jael.

"Yes. When Deborah called me to undertake this mission, I said to her, *'if thou will go with me, then I will go: but if thou will not go with me, then I will not go.'*

"And she said, *'I will surely go with thee: not withstanding the journey that thou takest shall not be for thine honour; for the Lord shall give Sisera into the hands of a woman.' "*

Then Jael asked, "So that which I did, was a result of a prophecy?"

"Yes! Oh Deborah, oh Deborah, I cannot escape thee, your prophecy is fulfilled before my eyes. Thanks Jael for helping us to capture Sisera."

"May I keep the sword of Sisera?" asked Jael.

"Yes! It is your victory! It is your sword!"

Barak looked down once more at the corpse, and tears ran down his cheeks. "Why do you shed tears for Sisera, General?" asked a soldier.

"I am not shedding tears for him, but only for my dear mother, whom he murdered," he said as he wiped the teardrops from his eyes. Barak turned to walk out of the tent then he stopped. "Bury him!" he commanded his soldiers and walked out of the tent with a feeling of accomplishment.

When Barak left the tent of Jael, he wasn't far from his family estate. He stopped by to check with his overseer about personal affairs and to take care of the needs of his soldiers. Also, his overseer gave him a letter, which he opened and read:

"To Barak, Deborah, and the elders: the nobles of the tribe of Judah, and I want to congratulate all of you on account of your great victory. There is no doubt, in our minds, that the Lord fought for you on such an occasion as this.

"Furthermore, I want to take this time to inform you that Prince Abihu has been removed from office and is now in exile. As of this month, I, Jonathan Ben Judah, am the chief prince of my tribe. I wish you and Deborah well, and we are looking forward to a cordial relationship with you." Signed Jonathan Ben Judah.

After two days rest, he set out for the city of Dabareth to attend the victory celebration.

CHAPTER TWENTY-FOUR

The next day came and it was the day of the victory celebration. Barak rode into the city of Dabareth with his soldiers. It was a little passed midday. The city was crowded with men, women, children and soldiers. Soldiers, who fought bravely and listened to the encouragement of Deborah, came to thank the Almighty and to celebrate their victory.

Captain Enoch and Captain Maher marched behind Barak with their troops banishing their latest weapons captured from the enemy. They blew the ram's horn, the trumpets and struck the drums. The people rejoiced in their victory and yelled *hallelujah.* You could see smiles on the faces of everyone.

Barak and Captain Enoch stopped in front of the receiving stand and saluted the elders, priests, princes and other dignitaries. He caught the eye of Deborah and they gazed at one another as if they wanted to talk but it wasn't the right time.

Then there was a yell from the crowd: "Where is Sisera?" Barak turned and looked at the man.

Before Barak could answer, another man shouted: "Yes Barak, we want to know.... What happened to Sisera?"

"He was taken away by a woman," commented Barak as he turned toward the man.

Another man asked, "Barak, are you saying...that you didn't capture Sisera?"

"That is right. I didn't capture Sisera. A woman named Yael killed Sisera in her tent. She took a tent nail and drove it through his temple with a hammer."

Men and women turned to those standing near by and asked: "Did you hear that?" "Sisera killed by a woman?"

"Yes, Sisera killed by a woman," said another man.

"Can you believe it?" repeated an old lady, "the mighty Sisera killed by a woman!"

The news spread like wildfire throughout the city. Then the women began to chant: "Sisera stood tall before his fall: the Lord delivered Sisera into the hands of a woman...." Everyone began to dance in the streets and in the open places. They danced to the music of the flute, tambourines, and drums praising the Almighty for their victory.

As the ladies moved to the rhythm of the music, they pulled Barak into the dance. "Come...come...Barak! Let's see if you are as good a dancer as you are a soldier," said a pretty lady to him seductively as she smiled. The ladies danced with him in circles; and they all grabbed him by the arm as they danced.

Barak became caught up in the joy of the moment and it was difficult for him to break loose. As he danced, he looked up and caught Deborah's eyes and he wanted to go to her; but the ladies continued to pull him around the circle. One lady said to him, "come on and enjoy yourself.... You act like you are in a daydream."

Finally, Barak broke loose from the ladies and approached the platform. As he approached, the soldiers snapped to attention, and raised their right fist to their chest. On all sides of the platform, stood the soldiers with their weapons captured from the Canaanites. A few moments later, Elder Ram whispered to Barak. "It is your time to speak next.... I've spoken already and Deborah will speak after you. I'll introduce you."

When Elder Ram walked to the center of the platform, the large crowd was still dancing and singing. He raised his hands high over his head to indicate to the crowd to stop dancing and singing. The music stopped. The people slowly became quiet and the crowd gave attention. "Oh people of Israel, I stand here before you again not to give a speech, but to introduce to you a man who has dedicated twenty years of his life fighting for you.... The Prophetess Deborah told us that the Lord had chosen him for this work...and without further delay, I bring to you, Barak Ben Abinoam, the deliverer."

Barak went to the center of the platform to speak. As he walked, his eyes fell upon Deborah standing at the opposite side with Demetrius and his family.

The multitude went wild with applause chanting his name, clapping their hands, and making the yodel sound with their tongues. The applause lasted for a long time, then finally stopped when he raised his hands.

"Hebrew citizens...!" shouted Barak with a loud base voice, looking over the entire crowd. The crowd went wild again with applause, but the voices soon subsided. "Hebrew citizens...! I welcome you...to this victory celebration in the name of our God...and in the name of our elders, and in the name of Deborah, the Prophetess," explained Barak as he looked over the crowd to the right and then to the left. Today...we dedicate this great victory...to the glory of God...and to the glory of Israel...which we are all a part...! Let us honor our brave soldiers...who sacrificed their lives unto death for the freedom of our people...! When our soldiers captured the city of Harosheth-Hagoiim, they killed King Jabin and liberated thousands of our people who were held in hard labor. They have now returned home to their wives and children...."

Again, the crowd gave him a great applause and chanted his name: "Barak, Barak, be our judge; Barak, Barak be our judge."

Barak quieted down the crowd again with his upraised hands and continued. "This celebration would not be complete without special recognition given to our friends who came from a far land.... These visitors have been with us for more than a week. As you know, by now, Demetrius and his associates were trained in Egypt as physicians. They have rendered their services unselfishly for the healing of our soldiers. As a result, they have saved many lives!"

"At this time, I'm going to ask Dr. Demetrius, and his family, with his associates to come up front." After they came up, Barak said, "Dr. Demetrius, we salute you...!" Then the drums and trumpets sounded and the soldiers snapped to attention. After the salute, Barak presented Dr. Demetrius with a golden medallion, which Barak placed around his neck. Also, Barak instructed two of his soldiers to bring up a chest of gold coins.

Demetrius' eyes lit up and he smiled. "This is so nice of you General Barak...but...I cannot...accept this," he said flustering.

"Yes...But, we want you to have this...because of your great generosity and untiring service," explained Barak as he shoved the chest closer to him.

"We know how you, your family and associates spent many sleepless nights caring for the wounded."

"Well...if you insist.... We shall use the money to help build a hospital and a medical school back home. This is truly a blessing," he said. Demetrius then looked at the gift again in amazement.

Barak once more raised his eyes up at Demetrius. "You have nothing more to say...? We want to honor you by allowing you to speak to us for a short while," explained Barak as he smiled.

"Oh...! Yes, yes, surely," he uttered as he squirmed to gain his composure. "But, I'll need more time...because I want to praise you and your God!"

"Well, in that case...then take all the time you need."

Demetrius turned around slowly and the crowd remained very quitet. "This is truly a surprise. It is with great honor that I stand here before you today.... I want to thank you General Barak...Deborah...the princes...the priests...the elders...and all of you good people for your hospitality and kindness," he said with emotion as he wiped the tears from his eye. "I get much pleasure to share with you these few moments of your great victory.... It was more than two weeks ago that I first met your commander at the city of Tirzah. At that time, he informed me that he was going up against Sisera with only...ten...thousand soldiers. I told him, at that time, 'that it was suicide...and surely you don't expect to win.' However, little did I know, that the stars and the God of heaven would fight for you.... For the windows of heaven opened up...thunder and lightening terrified the enemy and a fierce storm broke out with a heavy rain and hail that blinded the eyes of the enemy. Now, it is befitting, at this time, for me to relate to you a true story.

"The great king of Egypt, Thutmose III led seventeen military campaigns into Asia and he won by his strategy, his numbers, and his great war machine. But, you Israel...you didn't have these luxuries.... You won by the spirit of right and not by might! The sages of the pyramids and temples of Egypt taught that there was nothing more powerful than the idea of freedom...when its time has arrived. Oh Israel, your time has arrived..." he emphasized pointing his outstretched hand toward the sky. "And this is evident by your great victory. In closing, I want to thank Barak and Deborah for asking me to remain here to attend to the wounded.... Their request gave me the rare opportunity to experience a victory unique in the annals of military science. For, I saw...with my own eyes...the manifestation and intervention of God on behalf of a weak people....

"Now...my work here is almost complete...and I will be returning home in a few days to join my people. Peace be with you."

After that momentous and timely speech, the crowd went into a frenzy and roared with applause. To hear those words coming from a Greek was very inspiring to the people. When Demetrius turned around and faced Barak, the General spoke. "Well done Dr. Demetrius! I couldn't have done better myself." Finally, Barak embraced him and patted him on the back. Also, at that moment, his wife and daughters wiped the tears from their eyes because they were overcome with great emotion.

After Demetrius finished his speech, Elder Ram beckoned to Deborah for her to come forward. When she came to center stage, the multitude gave her an exceptionally prolonged ovation. She attempted to speak several times, but could not. "Oh people of Israel... O people of Israel..." But the crowd continued to applause her. Finally, she continued to speak and the ovation subsided. "Oh people of Israel... the previous speakers have spoken very well and what I would add, on the most part, would be repetition. So, I am going to be brief. I am asking you to love one another, and if you do this, you will make me very happy. Will you do this?"

"Yes! Yes!" answered the crowd.

"Will you do this?" she repeated.

"Yes! Yes!" Again the crowd answered much louder.

Then Deborah and Barak began to sing a song:

"Praise ye the Lord for the
avenging of Israel, when

*the people willingly offered
themselves.*

*"Hear, O ye kings; give ear,
O ye princes; I even I,
Will sing unto the Lord"
I will sing praises to the
Lord God of Israel.*

....

*"Blessed above women shall
Jael the wife of Heber the
Kenite be, blessed shall
she be above women in
the tent."*

....

Then Deborah turned around and called for the wife and daughter of Demetrius to come forward. The wife and daughter looked at each other with surprise then walked up to her. Deborah then began to speak. "In appreciation of your devoted service to our wounded soldiers, I present to both of you these valuable necklaces." Deborah then placed the necklaces around their necks and kissed both of them on their cheeks. The ladies were very touched by the gifts and by Deborah's warm smile.

Isis, the wife of Demetrius, stood there in her pink silk dress. "This is truly a surprise," she commented. "We didn't expect this. However, we do thank you so much."

At last, Hapshepsut, the daughter of Demetrius stepped forward. "Deborah, we shall never forget your kindness." After she finished speaking, Hapshepsut hugged Deborah warmly, and kissed her on the cheek.

As Deborah returned to the back of the platform with the ladies, she noticed a woman placing a chaplet of flowers around Barak's neck.

Barak conversed with the various dignitaries on the platform for quite a while. After that, he looked around casually for Deborah, but she was nowhere in sight.

Later, he saw his first officer. "Have you seen Deborah, Captain Enoch."

"Not recently. She was standing with the dignitaries," he said as he looked toward the viewing stand.

"I know that Captain, tell me something I don't know!" he snapped harshly looking around for her.

The Captain looked startled momentarily with disbelief and then gazed around the crowd.

"Excuse me Captain for being snappy. Would you have some soldiers look for her."

At that moment, Captain Maher approached Barak. "The elders want to see you, General."

At last, Barak returned to the platform, and saluted the elders. Elder Ram approached Barak smiling and said: "The people and the elders want you and Deborah to be our judges. Do you accept?"

"Well, this is…a surprise."

"Do you accept Barak?"

"Well…Yes! Yes…" Indeed."

"Where is Deborah?" asked the Elder.

"I don't know," answered Barak looking worried. "She just…just disappeared," he remarked shaking his head.

"Disappeared!" repeated the Elder with disbelief on his face. "Well, come with me! It is time for me to swear you in as ruler of the people."

"I'll be right behind you Elder."

When the both of them reached the center of the platform, Barak stood at attention, with his eyes fixed directly on Elder Ram. Then Elder Ram recited the oath of office:

"Do you Barak swear to uphold the commandments of the Lord and to protect and defend the Israelite tribes from all their enemies whether they be foreign or home born?"

"Yes! I do swear," answered Barak with a stern look on his face.

"I now pronounce you judge and ruler."

At that moment all the people cheered and shouted with great joy.

Finally, Elder Ram informed the people that the formalities were finished and he encouraged them to enjoy themselves by eating, dancing and singing praises to the Lord.

Not long after, Barak turned around toward the crowd and shouted, "Hebrew citizens...! Let the celebrations begin!"

As Barak walked to the other side of the platform, he noticed Elder Ariel, the Chief Elder of the council of the seventy elders. The Elder looked up at Barak, and said, "Congratulations on your appointment as ruler of the people."

"Thank you Elder. I am glad you were able to come to the celebrations...."

"Oh Barak...I have some advise for you: When you become ruler of the people...remember...that thou art mortal," said the ninety year old elder, as he stroke his long white beard. "Walk humbly before God...and before your fellow man in righteousness and in justice.... At that moment, he looked around the platform. "By the way, where is Deborah?"

"I don't know.... She just disappeared," answered Barak throwing his hands in the air.

Elder Ariel starred at Barak, and repeated, "You don't know...? Go...find her...! Find Deborah and join up with her.... She will help you...and together, the both of you...will rule the people of Israel."

"Yes Elder, I'll go.... I'll go find her."

The soldiers looked around the city, checked the roads, and asked about Deborah, but they were not able to locate her. After Barak finished meeting with the elders, he returned to Captain Enoch.

"Have your men located Deborah Captain?"

"No General! She just vanished like a young doe among the brown bushes," he said shaking his head. "Have you had any harsh words with her lately?"

"Yes, but that was the night before the battle. She was very angry with me because I suggested to the council of the elders that we should call off the war. She said that I had no trust in God, and no belief in her. She ended the conversation by saying that there will be no marriage and stormed away with tears in her eyes."

"Marriage? You asked her to marry you?"

"I did.... And what's wrong with that?"

"Nothing General. It's just...just the first time I've heard of this. When did you ask her...and what was her answer?"

"She didn't give me an answer, she left it open. I can't understand it. She sent me an invitation to attend the victory celebration. Then she just disappeared like a gazelle in the wheat field."

"I think she is interested in you General. I could tell the way she looked at you."

"I think so too, but then she got so angry at me and we haven't had any kind words or gestures since."

There was a silence and after a few moments Barak spoke. "Well...I think I'll go down next week, and visit her and see where I stand."

***

It was on a late cloudy dreary morning one week later that Barak arrived at the estate of Deborah. Nachshon, the gatekeeper, escorted him to the back courtyard where Deborah sat under her palm tree.

"Peace be with you," said Barak.

"Well, this is a surprise Barak. What seeketh thou?" she asked with her back to him denying him the privilege of face to face contact.

"I seek thee!"

"Of all the women in Galilee, why thou seeketh after me?"

"I'll get right to the heart of the matter," he said standing five cubits behind her. "When you were at the city of Dabareth, I wanted to see you."

"You did see me," she said looking over her shoulder.

"I meant...I meant I wanted to talk with you."

"Why didn't you Barak...? I was there."

"I was busy celebrating our victory with the people of the town."

"I understand," she said. "You were very busy with the ladies."

"Yes, and when I looked around again, you disappeared." Barak then raised both of his hands and leaned forward and asked. "What happened Deborah? Why did you disappear?" he asked, throwing his hands in the air.

"I left because I didn't want to interfere with your happiness...."

"But, you...are my happiness," he interrupted.

"And the second reason I left was because I had completed my work there. Therefore, I felt no need to linger."

"I see...my dear."

"Now, since you know why I left the city of Dabareth, what is the real reason why you came down here?"

"I've made war...and that is over, now I want to make peace with you."

"To make peace? First, I need you to answer a few questions," she said as she turned around.

"This is pleasing in my eyesight."

"When you were at the war council meeting on Mount Tabor, you told the elders that the attack should be called off. What made you change your mind?"

"After thinking about the situation for several hours that night, I finally had to admit the truth, that our people would not be better off without the war, because Sisera was making our lives more bitter. I could be a good mountain fighter leading a few hundred men. But, I realized that if I didn't take advantage of the moment, it would be even harder in the future to gain the support of the masses. In addition, you did make a strong appeal for me to take action on the next day."

"Barak, I want you to know that on that very night on Mount Tabor...you put me through a lot of pain. I promised my people that they would be free, and you almost make a liar out of me."

"I didn't mean to. I get no pleasure out of hurting you or anyone else. I thought that I was doing the right thing for my men and my nephews."

"You had nephews in the war?"

"Yes, two."

"Did they survive?"

"Yes...but not without injury."

"I'm so sorry to hear that," she said with deep concern lowering her head.

Barak continued to speak. "If they had not survived, I don't know how I would have revealed the bad news to their mother. In addition to thinking that I was doing the right thing for my men, I didn't realize the truth until after the war?"

"What truth?"

"It was after the war that I decided that the Divine Creator could have chosen another man instead of me. After the battle, I realized that I was wrong about you, wrong about God, and wrong about spiritual things...."

"Go on."

"The war became a revelation to me. I must confess...that when I first marched into battle, I didn't believe that we could win against those great odds. I guess I didn't believe..." he scratched his eyebrow as he spoke slowly, "because I didn't know how we could win...."

"I didn't know either," commented Deborah. "Excuse me for interrupting, would you please go on."

"But when I saw the heavy rain beat down into the eyes of the enemy and blinded them, then I became connected with God and convinced that the Almighty was fighting our battle. When I heard the thundering and saw the lightening, I instinctively gave the command to my men to charge forward. It was as though God, the lightening and I became one at the same moment."

"I can assure you Barak that you were born for this task and as you know, your name means **lightening one**," she explained. "Are you finished Barak?"

"No. After God fought our battle and after the victory; then I realized the importance of all the spiritual things you had been telling me all along."

"This is wonderful Barak," she said turning around smiling. "Even though war has many horrible consequences, I am glad that it had; at least, a spiritual awakening for you..."

It had been a dreary cloudy morning when Barak first arrived. As he continued to converse with Deborah, he gazed up into the heavens. The thick dark clouds started to break up and the bright warm sun began to shine through bringing hope and promise of a better day.

"Deborah, everything seems to have come full circle."

"Full Circle? What do you mean?" she inquired with a puzzled face.

"Well." Barak took one step to the side and look down. Then he looked up at her as he walked. "I mean...our first meaningful conversation began here. We went to many places together, now that the war is over; here is where I return."

At that moment, Barak turned around faced the courtwall raised his hand to his mouth and eyes, as if he was preoccupied with deep thoughts. Then he turned to her and spoke. "We came through peacetime, war time, and now peacetime again.... Where do we stand Deborah...?"

"We?"

"Yes! You and I?"

Deborah lowered her head smiling then she looked up. "I am waiting for the right man."

"Well! I believe that you have found him. I am the right man!"

"Oh...! You think so...? What makes you so sure?" she inquired sensing a little arrogance.

"I think that the Lord meant for us to be together... from the beginning..." Barak paused. "If this wasn't so...your deceased brother-in-law, Caleb, would be standing right here...where I am standing, my dear sister."

Deborah smiled slightly and momentarily couldn't speak. Then she mustered enough energy. "Since you've been here today, I haven't heard how you fee...."

"How I feel about you...?" asked Barak, finishing her unspoken word.

"Yes! How do you feel?" she asked vigorously as she stared into his dark brown eyes.

"My feelings are very strong for you Deborah. They haven't changed since the dance and our conversation at the city of Kedesh."

He moved closer to her and took hold of both of her hands. He said to her softly. "I love you...Deborah and I want you to be my wife."

She wanted to shout *hallelujah* but she retained her composure. Then she smiled and looked away. "Are you sure it's love ... or is it passion?"

"Oh Deborah...! I am sure. When I say love, I don't mean passion. I mean love...from the dept of my heart...and from the dept of my spiritual inner soul. I could have had plenty of passion. I ran away from passion to find you...."

"You have really changed Barak," she commented.

"How so?"

"I remember the times when you were reluctant to say the Divine name or to talk about spiritual matters."

"I know. The war changed all of that. It was just no way we could have won without the heavens fighting for us."

Barak looked into her dreamy eyes and drew her up closer to him, placing his arms around her shoulders. His strong chest pressed gently against her well-developed breast.

She began to feel wanted, loved and alive. "I haven't felt this way in over four years." she thought.

Then Barak lowered his head and kissed her on her cheek. "Will you be my wife Deborah?" he asked in a whisper.

She lifted her small soft right hand to his face and stroked the side of his cheek affectionately as she looked into his eyes. She choked for the words, Yes...! Yes...Yes...! she said in a whisper. "I'll be your wife Barak. I'll be yo...."

He interrupted her last word and kissed her gently on the lips and then on both sides of her face.

She lowered her head. Then he placed his finger under her chin and lifted it up kissing her simultaneously on the lips. She opened her lips and he explored the depths of her mouth, probing in and out, and probing again and again until she pulled away.

"What's wrong Deborah? Why did you pull away?" he asked with the feeling of the loss of pleasure.

"It's a woman's...way," she said turning her back to him. Barak, do you have any idea when you want to get married?"

"As soon as possible my dear, Deborah."

"Good, because if you want to be around me, I suggest we start making plans right away."

"That's fine with me. You want to begin right now?"

"Yes.... We can start right now because we are going to have a lot of preparations to make."

They decided to have the wedding in three months at Deborah's estate. After the preparations were complete, hundreds of people came to the ceremony from all parts of the Hebrew nation, including priests, princes, elders, and businessmen with their families.

Finally, the wedding came to an end and Deborah and Barak settled down to as much of a normal life that public servants could expect. They decided to spend their lives together partly in the city of Kedesh and partly at Deborah's estate outside of Bethel.

Many people continued to come to her to seek advice and judgment. She became a mother in Israel. Moreover, Deborah and Barak judged and ruled Israel for forty years and the land rested in peace.

Windsor Golden Series Shopping Page

P.O. Box 310393 – Atlanta, GA 31131-0393 770-939-2293

To order these videos and cassette tapes, please use this form

Qty.   Title   Cost

Qty.	Title	Cost
	Videos Tapes	
	Lost Identity	$20.00
	Whoever You Thought You Were...You're A Jew	$15.00
	Ethiopian Jews	$15.00
	Audio Cassette Tapes	
	The Historical Background of Jesus	$10.00
	The New Testament Analyzed	$10.00
	Paganism in the Ancient World	$ 7.00
	The One God Concept	$ 7.00
	The Bible an African Book: The Resurrection of the Dry Bones.	$ 7.00
	Prophecies of the Nations Coming to Jerusalem	$ 7.00
	The Agreement/Why We Are Here on Earth	$10.00

Name: _____

Address: _____

City: _____ State ___ Zip Code: _____

Credit Cards Welcome:
__Visa __Discover __Master Card   Exp. Date: __/__
Credit Card No:
Signature: _____

Shipping cost: $4.50 (UPS) $.50 for each additional item.
Allow 1-2 weeks. For faster service send money order.

DEBORAH AND BARAK

THE AUTHOR OF:
FROM BABYLON TO TIMBUKTU

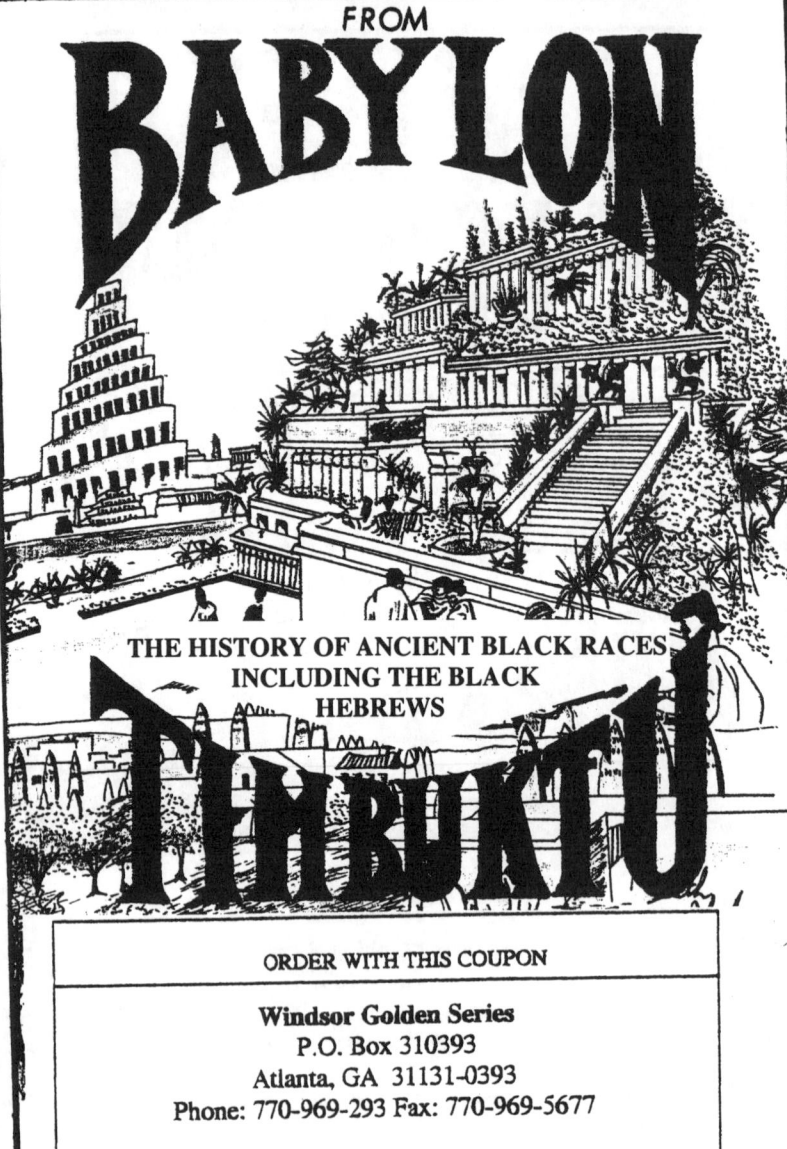

FROM

BABYLON

THE HISTORY OF ANCIENT BLACK RACES INCLUDING THE BLACK HEBREWS

TIMBUKTU

ORDER WITH THIS COUPON

Windsor Golden Series
P.O. Box 310393
Atlanta, GA 31131-0393
Phone: 770-969-293 Fax: 770-969-5677

Please send me ___ copies of : **From Babylon to Timbuktu $11.95**

Name: _____

Address: _____

City: _____ State: _____ Zip _____

Phone: ___ - ___

__Visa __Discover __Amer Exp. Exp. Date: __/__

Credit Card Number:

Signature _____

For faster service, send money order

Shipping cost: $4.50 UPS $1.75 USPO $.50 for each additional order.

When Is the Next War?

Nostradamus:

Biblical and Psychical Prophecies For Our Time
The Middle East, Russia and America in Prophecy

REIKI

(Rei: God's Wisdom or the Higher Power)
(Ki: Life Force Engergy)

What is Reiki?

Spiritually guided life force energy

An ancient Japanese technique for stress reduction and realization that also promotes healing. It is administered by "laying on hands" and is based on the idea that an unseen "life force energy" flows through us and is what causes us to be alive. If one's "life force energy" is low, then we are more likely to get sick or feel stress, and if it is high, we are more capable of being happy and healthy.

A treatment feels like a wonderful glowing radiance that flows through and around you. Reiki treats the whole person including body; emotions, mind and spirit creating many beneficial effects that include relaxation and feeling of peace, security and well being.

The Essential Body offers Reiki sessions

For information or appointments, please call or write to:

Rev. Mary L Windsor
6555 Newborn Drive
College Park, GA 30349
770-969-2293

Rev. Rudolph R. Windsor was born in Long Branch, New Jersey. After living in a number of Jersey communities, his family settled in Philadelphia. He has four sons and a daughter. He attended Community College, studying Psychology and Political Science; Gratz College, where he majored in Hebrew/Aramaic Studies; and Temple University, where he majored in Middle Eastern Studies. In addition, he says of this book, "My motive in writing it was to give spiritual insights to mankind, so that all of us can develop to a higher level of humanity. In serving mankind, he has been a member and president of several organizations. He was a delegate to the Civil Rights Conference of 1968 and was designated a delegate on behalf of the Ethiopians, to meet with Mr. Makonen, an official of the Ethiopian Mission to the United Nations in the early 1970's.

Moreover, Rev. Windsor is the author of five books. After a change in publishing arrangements with several publishers, Rudolph Windsor established his own company in 1986.

Again, Rev. Windsor, over the years, has appeared on radio and TV shows. He has lectured at organizations, and universities. In addition, he has preached at various religious denominations. Also, he has traveled to Europe, the Middle East and Africa.

Rev. Mary L. (Robinson) Windsor was born in Waterbury, CT. She moved to Indianapolis, IN in 1977. In 1978, she attended Indian University and majored in Business. She received her Bachelor of Science Degree in Business Administration in 1986. In 1989, she received her Masters Degree in Business Administration from Indiana Wesleyan Univ. She has taken several courses in pursuant of her Ph. D. Degree in Family Mediation and Counseling from LaSalle University. She continues her formal education, in addition to her social involvement, helping people to understand the dynamics of Corporate America, and life in general.

What inspired her to co-author this book with her husband, is her passionate desire to share with mankind the true essence of spirituality—religion and and spirituality are not the same.' From early childhood, she said that she was taught religion, and now she is interested in spirituality. Her quest for a higher level and understanding of spirituality was the catalyst for her to become a certified Reiki practitioner, a channel for spiritual healing, and an ordained minister.

She is married to Rev. Rudolph R. Windsor and has a son.